Praise for
ONE FOOT in the BLACK

"Kurt Kamm has been there with the firefighters, step by step, and you will feel in the pages of this book that you are right there in the middle of a firestorm as well."

—Dennis Smith, author of *Report From Engine Co. 82* and *A Decade of Hope*.

"With *One Foot in the Black,* Kurt Kamm has used the tools of popular fiction to shine a light on the inner workings of the wildland fire service. The tortured main character, who tries to pull a brutalized life together by joining Cal Fire, the Golden State's fire protection agency, takes us on a journey from training ground to fire ground that vividly captures the sense of family, of pulling together, of physical challenge and mortal danger that go with this increasingly vital occupation. "

—John N. Maclean, author of *Fire on the Mountain* and other fire books.

INTRODUCTION
TO THE
SECOND EDITION

WHEN I COMPLETED *One Foot in the Black* in 2008, my character Greg Kowalski had just turned 21. Although Greg is a fictional character, his surroundings are real. Greg trains at Los Angeles County Fire Camp 8 in the hills of Malibu, a wildland helitack facility built on a former Nike missile base. He also visits the female inmate Fire Suppression Camp 13 which is located in Malibu. By the end of the book, Greg has learned some tough lessons as a wildland firefighter. He survives a burnover in a massive fictional fire on the Central Coast of California resulting in the death of his mentor, the superintendent and captain of Camp 8. Today Greg would be 25 and a hardened veteran of some of the biggest wildland fires in the history of the United States. According to the National Interagency Fire Center, more than 82,000 wildfires burned across 10 million acres in the United States in 2011.

In a case of fiction and reality coming together, the 2009 Station Fire in Los Angeles County is eerily similar to the fictional Pozo Fire that Greg battles. On August 26, 2009, an arsonist ignited a fire not far from the Angeles Crest Ranger Station. The first report came in at 3:20 p.m., and within 11 minutes Forest Service personnel noted that the fire had already ballooned to "three acres and running." This conflagration, called the Station Fire, raged through the Angeles National Forest for more than a month, consumed more than 160,000 acres and was the largest fire in Los Angeles County history. For much of the time, pyrocumulus clouds billowed thousands of feet into the sky over the City of Los Angeles.

The fictional Pozo Fire in the Los Padres National Forest burned 149,000 acres. While the superintendent of Camp 8 is killed in the Pozo Fire, there were two real fatalities in the Station Fire. On the morning of August 30, the fire ran in the direction of LACoFD's Camp 16, a fire-fighting training facility with more than 100 male inmates. As they attempted to set a backfire to protect the camp, the superintendent of Camp 16, Captain Tedmund Hall, and Arnie Quinones, the foreman of Crew 16-3, were trapped by the fast-moving flames, thick smoke and blistering heat. They tried to drive to safety, but veered over a berm and plunged to their deaths in a burning canyon. Their deaths were deemed homicides because the fire was started by arson. Camp 16 was overrun by flames and destroyed, but miraculously, no other lives were lost.

Like Camp 8, Camp 16 was originally a Nike missile base. Camp 16 sits atop a rocky ridge in brutally rough country deep inside the Angeles National Forest. The slopes fall away at 70- to 90-degree angles and at the time of the fire, the surrounding canyons, ridgelines and mountainsides were covered with fuel loads of pine, oak, chaparral, manzanita and other vegetation which were tinder dry. Portions of the Angeles National Forest, especially around Camp 16, had not burned since 1919.

This edition of *One Foot in the Black* is dedicated to Tedmund Hall, whom I had the pleasure of meeting, and Arnie Quinones, both of whom risked their own lives to save others. They were dedicated and brave men.

Kurt Kamm,
Malibu, CA, 2012

One Foot in the Black: A position on the fireline that is next to an area already burned ("the black"). It is at once the most dangerous place—right at the edge of the flames—but also a safe zone for immediate escape.

This book includes a glossary of technical terms used in wildland firefighting, the **10 Standard Firefighting Orders** and the **18 Watch Out Situations** known by all wildland firefighters.

PROLOGUE

A YEAR AGO, I WATCHED A MAN go up in flames. Our helitack crew was fighting the Pozo Fire in the Los Padres National Forest in Central California. That morning, we dropped onto a remote ridge on Black Mountain. Our job was to cut a control line along the flank of the fire burning in the valley below. We struggled to clear a 3-foot wide break through thick brush on the side of the mountain. Without warning, the wind changed direction and a firestorm with a 90-foot wall of flames roared up the canyon at us. In a heartbeat, the oxygen was gone, hot smoke and ash filled the air and we couldn't breathe. Our entire crew was caught off-guard.

It was every firefighter's nightmare. The heat was staggering. The brush was an inferno. Trees weren't burning, they were exploding. Trapped on rugged, steep terrain, we had no time to deploy our fire shelters. Our only escape was to climb back up to our safe zone. We shouted warnings, dropped our tools and daypacks and clawed our way up the side of the canyon.

We had 60 seconds to escape the firestorm raging behind us. I felt the radiant heat on my neck and wrists and I knew I would die from breathing superheated air before I burned to death. I looked back and saw TB, our captain, for a few seconds before he disappeared behind the wall of fire. If he cried out, I couldn't hear him. The roar of the blaze was deafening. Jake, Luis and everyone else in the crew made it to the safe zone. TB was trapped and perished.

In a state of shock and anguish, we were pulled off the fireline and airlifted back to the incident command post. We received medical treatment and were sent back to Los Angeles. Our physical injuries were minor, but each of us struggled to cope with the death of our captain. It hit me hardest because TB was my mentor and my substitute father. We went out on stress leave and the

Los Angeles County Fire Department sent us to see their psychiatrist for a Critical Incident Stress Debriefing.

Fighting a wildland fire is dangerous business and entrapment is always possible. At least once in every firefighter's life he fights for survival and thinks the unthinkable. The Pozo Fire, one for the record books, started July 23, 2000 and burned 149,000 acres. It occurred the year after I came to California to escape a lifetime of abuse and neglect from my real father. My struggle to survive his mistreatment continued long after I recovered from the events on Black Mountain.

ONE
Malibu, California

L UIS AND I are in our yellows, sitting on the manicured lawn at Pepperdine University. A flock of sleek black crows ignores us and scratches for insects while conversing in gravel-voiced calls. Pepperdine has acres of grass and an irrigation pond designated "Helispot 88-Alpha." In case of a fire around Malibu, it is used to fill the water tanks of fire helicopters. Jake and the rest of the crew from the Bird are checking the condition of the pond.

I've known Luis Zambrano since I joined the Los Angeles County Fire Department 18 months ago. We went through the Camp 8 Fire Academy together and endured several months as the rookies on the crew. I can't think of anyone I'd rather have next to me on a fireline. Luis is solid and reliable—he'll give you everything he's got.

"In the evening," Luis says, "deer come out of the hills and graze on the lawn."

"There are deer all over Michigan, " I tell him. "They shoot them to thin the herds."

"This is different. Families bring their kids. The kids run around and watch the deer. The parents love it."

Luis has a wife and son, which is where we part company. Three years ago he got his girlfriend pregnant and decided to marry her. Who needs a wife and a kid when you're 21? Life's hard enough. When you get hooked up like that with a woman, you're stuck. They live at his parent's house out in the San Fernando Valley. He's happy as a pig in shit, trying to get by on $3,500 a month from County Fire.

"You have to come out and see it," Luis says. He stands up and gazes out over the lawn as if the deer were there now.

Between bursts of traffic, I can hear the sound of the surf crashing on the beach on the other side of Pacific Coast Highway. "I don't even have a girlfriend, let alone a family," I say, "and I'm not driving all the way over here to see a herd of deer."

"That's your trouble. You don't even have a girlfriend," he says. "You can't go through life alone."

The humidity is in single digits. I have no spit. The sweat dries on my body so fast I can't even feel it.The dry Santa Ana wind has been blowing for two days, sucking the moisture out of the air. It starts in the high desert out near Vegas and comes at night blowing toward the ocean. First it's a gentle breeze, which rustles through the trees. By the next morning, the palms and cypress are bent horizontally and you wonder if your roof will blow off.

Containing any wildfire is nasty work. The Santa Anas can move at 60 miles per hour and even faster in the canyons. It's almost impossible to stop a wind-driven fire and when the devil winds blow, three or four thousand acres can burn in an hour. Flying embers can start a spot fire half a mile away. It's not like some small pissant blaze that starts when a space heater catches fire in a bedroom.

Wildfires have personalities. Some of them creep around in the brush and try to lull you into a sense of overconfidence. They hide until they gain strength and then try to overwhelm you when you least expect it. Other fires come right at you from the get-go, no tricks and nothing fancy, just an all-out assault. When the hills around Malibu burn, the fire plays Russian Roulette. Sometimes it burns one house to the ground, leaving a pile of smoking debris and twisted metal while the homes around it are untouched. Other times, it burns everything in its path, leaving a trail of total destruction.

An incident commander once told us, "When you think you have an area under control, don't forget to tell the fire." A wildland fire is never out until it's controlled, contained and cold-trailed.

Today a major fire is burning north of the 101 Freeway and the county is bringing in extra resources to contain it before it jumps the highway and burns down through Malibu to the ocean. The air is filthy, a layer of brown scum fills the sky and the sun is a rotten orange. Bits of ash drift down, settling on roofs, cars and surfboards. Up on Malibu Canyon Road, a sign at the Presbyterian church says, "On Fire for Jesus!" Is someone trying to tell us something?

We flew down from Camp 8 this morning in the Bird, one of the new Sikorsky Firehawks that the county uses. The Bird began as a Blackhawk attack helicopter, modified for the Sultan of Brunei. When he canceled the order, she found a home in Los Angeles as a fire helicopter. Resting on the Pepperdine lawn with her yellow belly and tail, blades hanging down, she resembles an enormous wasp.

Jake strides across the grass and says, "I was looking forward to going to the beach and seeing some chicks today."

"C'mon Jake," I tell him, "you wouldn't miss a fire this size." This was supposed to be a day off for our crew. If the call hadn't come early this morning, we'd be down on the sand playing volleyball.

As soon as the inspection of the pond is completed, we're headed back to the inferno.

TWO
Saginaw, Michigan

I GREW UP IN NORTHERN MICHIGAN where "hot" and "dry" were not words we ever used to describe the weather. If it didn't rain, it snowed. I was an unhappy, scared kid with an empty spot in my chest. Where other boys felt love from their fathers, I felt nothing. Moments of happiness were rare for me and when they came, they didn't last.

My father was a firefighter. He was also a shit. We lived in Saginaw, where he was part of an engine company at the Hess Avenue Fire Station. He wanted to be a detective, but when he washed out of the police academy for being "unsuitable," he became a firefighter. He once got an award for running into a burning building and risking his life to save an old woman. That was his job and he was paid to do it, but when it came to his family, it was a different story. He wouldn't do anything for Mom or my little sister Vicky, and certainly not for me. He didn't care about us.

Being a firefighter is tough work—it's exhausting and hard on your health. My father coughed a lot and his eyes were always red and irritated. On training weekends, he did punishing workouts. He started with calisthenics, ran three or four miles, then went back to the station to lift weights or run the stairs wearing his turnout gear and breathing apparatus. He was on duty for two days at a time followed by a day off.

Life around our house was peaceful while he was away, but the whole mood changed when he came home; then we all tiptoed around holding our breath. He usually had a few beers or something stronger to drink in order to relax and if we were lucky, he would be too tired to get angry and start anything. "Be quiet and don't bother me—I need some peace," he would warn us before he drifted off to sleep. Sometimes we weren't so lucky. He was unpredictable and his anger was always lurking—it raged inside him and like a fire deep in a building, it could burst into the open without warning. He could get into a bad mood over little things and then blow up. I don't remember what I learned at school in first grade, but by that time I was smart enough to watch my father and stay out of his way until I figured out if he was going to explode. When his mouth tightened and his eyes narrowed, I knew we had trouble.

He yelled at Vicky and occasionally slapped her, but Mom and I were the ones he hit. "You little idiot," he would say and cuff me on the head. Sometimes he would catch me with an unexpected blow and I developed a reflex of raising my shoulders and ducking my head to protect myself. As I got older, the blows became punches to my body.

"You're lucky I don't beat you," he told me. "When I was a kid, my dad beat me with his belt. It was a big, thick one and it hurt, but I never cried." My father grew up in Detroit, the only child of an officer for the Wayne County Park Patrol. When he was five, his mother died and his father raised him. "You couldn't be a weakling," he said, "or the other kids would pound the crap out of you. The only way to survive was to be stronger and tougher and then no one touched you."

My parents argued, if you could call it that. My father did all the yelling and my mother said nothing. "This is your fault, damn it! Can't you do anything right?" he would shout, and Mom would stare at the floor in silence. I watched my father hit my mother and I wanted to help her, but I was too small. Sometimes, when I knew what was coming, I ran into my bedroom and closed the door before it happened. As I grew older, I realized that what Mom called "accidents" were injuries inflicted by my father when Vicky and I weren't around.

My mother was a tall, plain-looking woman, but I loved her and thought she was beautiful. My father called her "an ugly bitch" when he was angry and had too much to drink. She took her punishment without complaining. Mom did what she could to take care of Vicky and me, but she had to protect herself. She used to say, "I need a bucket of invisible paint—it'll solve all my problems." I imagined her painting herself into emptiness; first her legs, then her body and finally her head disappeared until there was nothing left but a hand holding a brush.

As early as I can remember, I knew my father didn't love me, but I didn't know why. If he wasn't angry and shouting at me, he looked right through me. We never spent any time together and I grew up learning things from other kids' fathers. When I was in second grade, my school had a father-son night. I was desperate to have my dad come and tell my classmates about being a firefighter. Even fathers who didn't have jobs went with their sons. I stayed home. I felt abandoned before I knew what the word meant.

I would have happily traded my father for Bobby Eccles' dad, who lost his job on an assembly line at Ford. He stayed home and got fat while Bobby's mom worked at Sears. They lived across the street and after school I stopped at Bobby's house on my way home. By late afternoon, Mr. Eccles was usually drunk, but unlike my father, he was always in a good mood and happy to see me. "C'mon guys," Bobby's dad would say, "let's go out in the backyard and work on the clubhouse. I need some help today."

"Mr. Eccles," I said, "can I ask you a question?"

"What, Greggie?"

"Why aren't you at work?"

"I am at work, Greggie. This is my work, I'm a builder."

We stood outside and held plywood while he cut it and used 10 or 20 nails to fasten two boards together. The next week, he tore everything apart and started over, using new wood or the old parts cut into new pieces.

"We're in a redesign mode here," he would tell us.

I don't know where all that wood came from, but I think Bobby's father drove around at night in his pickup truck and stole it from construction sites. When the clubhouse was finished, we played in it for a few months and then it sat abandoned in Bobby's backyard.

Bobby had a black and white dog named Skippy, which his father found on the street. Vicky and I wanted a dog more than anything. I saw strays in our neighborhood, hungry and afraid, with their tails between their legs. I wanted to catch one, bring it home and feed it, but Dad said we couldn't have a dog because it would make a mess and we wouldn't take care of it.

The nights at our house were bad. I was afraid to go to bed when my father was home because I knew what was about to happen. Vicky and I had small bedrooms upstairs and even with our doors closed, we heard everything. I didn't want to listen to the shouting and the other noises, but I couldn't help it.

Vicky often came into my bedroom crying, carrying Larry, her stuffed bear. She would climb into my bed and whimper, "Why is Daddy mad? Is he gonna hurt Mommy?" Sometimes she held a pillow over her head and pulled it tight around her ears. "Greggie, tell Daddy to stop, Larry's frightened," she would plead. I didn't know what to say to her.

"I'm doing the best I can with this family, but you aren't helping," my father said in a loud voice and then kicked over the chair in their bedroom. "These kids are out of control, and you just sit around here and do nothing," he shouted. "I break my neck at work and you stay home and watch television. What the fuck do I have to do to get some help here?"

"Please, Joe, stop. Stop it," my mother begged.

Sometimes when Mom was silent and didn't say anything, my father would shout, "You bitch, pay attention!" When he got violent, I cried along with Vicky and my stomach started to hurt. I welcomed that pain, because the worse it got, the less the screaming and shouting bothered me. I was terrified my father would come in my bedroom and be angry because we were in tears. It didn't matter; he never came and Vicky and I learned to cry without making any noise. I stuffed the corner of my blanket into my mouth to muffle my sobs.

When the shouting was over, Dad would stomp down to the garage and wake up the whole neighborhood when he tore off down the street on his Harley, heading to Richie's Bar to drink and shoot pool with the off-duty cops and firefighters. Sometimes I woke up in the middle of the night and worried that my father might not ever come home. I was afraid of him, but I didn't want to lose him.

One evening, after Vicky was asleep, I heard my parents talking in the kitchen. I got out of bed and opened my bedroom door. Their voices were low, which was unusual, because when my father said something to my mother, he usually yelled at her and we could hear him anywhere in the house.

"…going up to Mackinaw City on my bike," my father said.

"Joe, spend some time with Greggie on Saturday," my mother said. "You never give him any attention. He's nine years old. A boy his age needs time with his father."

"Don't tell me how to raise Greggie and don't tell me what to do. He'll grow up just fine unless you screw things up."

"For God's sake, Joe, he's your son. Show some interest."

That was all I heard. It was quiet in the kitchen and they came upstairs. I closed the bedroom door and got back into bed. Vicky stayed in her room that night; I don't think she even woke up.

In the morning, my father ate breakfast with us and I have never forgotten what he said. "Guess what, Greggie? I've got a surprise. Tomorrow I'm going up to Mackinaw City on the Harley and I'm taking you with me. It's time the men do something together." I couldn't believe it. I looked at my father and he was smiling at me. I felt so special. "We'll ride up, stay overnight and see what there is to see."

My mother was frying eggs and her tears spilled onto the stove. She looked up at me and said, "See what a good father you have? He loves you."

This was the most exciting thing that had ever happened to me. I had never gone on a trip with my father. Vicky sat wide-eyed at the table and I grabbed her stuffed bear and ran around the kitchen shouting, "Ha-ha, I'm going to Mackinaw."

"I wanna go," Vicky whined. "Do I get to go?" She began to cry. "Larry, gimme Larry."

"Sit down and finish your breakfast," my father said to me. He pulled Larry from my hands and dropped him on the table, knocking over a pitcher of milk. He swore and then said to Vicky, "And you—you shut up."

I spent the whole day thinking about the trip. I went over to tell Bobby I was going to Mackinaw City with my father, but his family had gone on a camping trip for the weekend. Skippy went with them.

THREE

Auburn, California

THE DIRTY WHITE STATION WAGON had a diagonal red stripe and "Cal Fire" on the door. The driver leaned over and rolled down the passenger side window. "You Gregory?" she asked.

"It's Greg."

"Hi Greg, I'm Angel. You're here for the rodeo, right?"

"The rodeo? I here for firefighter training."

"Yeah, that's what I'm talking about. The training program in Auburn, we call it 'the Rodeo.'" Angel waved me in. She was a hefty woman with a tanned face and black hair pulled tight into a tiny ponytail. She wore a dark blue uniform and black boots. On her shoulder she had a red, gold and blue patch with the outline of the State of California and the words "Cal Fire." She might have been the same age as my mother. The back of the wagon was stuffed with coils of fire hose, shovels and bottled water. Several radios hung below the dashboard, which made it hard for me to stretch out my legs.

"Thanks for the ride," I said. My head was spinning. I was in Sacramento, California, two thousand miles away from my home and my father.

"Not a problem. I drive up a couple times a week."

I settled into the seat and angled my legs under the dashboard. "What's Auburn like?"

"Oh, it's a nice town. The population's about twelve thousand, including the horses. It's headquarters for our Nevada-Yuba-Placer Unit."

I had no idea what that was and realized how little I knew about what I was getting into. "So what's it like to work for Cal Fire."

"Are you used to regimentation?"

"What does that mean?"

"It means we're a paramilitary organization."

"A paramilitary organization?"

"Yeah. That means you do things on schedule. You get up at 5:30 a.m., fix breakfast for your captain and crew, clean up, go out to PT—"

"PT?"

"Physical training. Then there's tool and equipment maintenance and then washing down the engine and then—"

"What about the firefighting?"

"Yeah, that too. We respond to anything that catches fire. Can you carry fifty pounds of fire hose on your back up the side of a mountain?"

"I never tried."

"You'll learn."

"Can you?" I asked.

"Can I carry fifty pounds of hose? Damn right I can," she said, glancing over at me. "Did you bring boots?"

"Yes." I looked at her uniform again. I tried to imagine myself dressed like an off-duty cop. "Is this what I'll be wearing?"

"When you're not in the middle of a fire. You'll get a clothing allowance and the first thing you do is buy your uniform. How about cooking? Can you cook?"

"No."

"You'll learn."

Angel was a real piece of work. "How many seasonal firefighters are there?" I asked.

"Statewide, about two thousand five hundred. A lot of them come back every year."

"Statewide?"

"Our response area runs from San Diego over to Nevada and up to the Oregon border. We don't train everyone in Auburn."

"So I could have gone to Southern California?"

"I suppose so. Your application came through Sacramento, so they sent you to Auburn."

"How many guys are training with me this week?"

"This week, I think nine of you. The Rodeo goes on for several weeks."

The late afternoon sun cast long shadows as we turned onto the highway. After two days on the bus from Saginaw, a night on a cement bench in Denver and the cramped coach seat on the *Zephyr,* I was tired and struggled to keep my eyes open. Bursts of static and messages coming over the radios couldn't keep me from dozing off.

Mom and Vicky were eating breakfast in the kitchen. I stood near the door to the garage and watched as their chairs lifted off the floor and spun around above the table, faster and faster, like an amusement park ride. They were frightened and screaming, but no sound came from their mouths. I wanted to help them, but I couldn't move.

"Hey, rodeo boy, wake up, we're here." Angel nudged my shoulder with the palm of her hand. "Do you want to eat or should I just show you where to sack out?"

"I'd like to turn in. Thanks for the lift, Angel."

"Good morning, my name is Captain David Cooley, " the man standing before me said in a Western drawl. "Welcome to the Cal Fire training program for seasonal firefighters."

Captain Cooley was a big man; he was about as tall as my father and had the same strong physique. The resemblance ended there. My father's eyes were impenetrable; they were like mirrors reflecting back at you. Cooley's eyes smiled. You could tell he wouldn't put up with any shit, but you could also see that he was a nice guy. He had gray hair, cut short.

"You all look good in your uniforms," he said as he surveyed the nine of us with wrinkles in our new blue shirts and pants. "As members of a paramilitary organization, you'll respect rank and address officers as 'sir.' When you speak in the classroom, you'll stand up."

Every other word here was "paramilitary." Was this part of my father's job? I had been to his station for Christmas parties and to a few other events, but I knew so little about his work. I lived in the same house with him for 19 years and understood nothing about his life. He had done a good job of shutting me out.

"This afternoon," Cooley said, "you'll be issued fire gear—Nomex protective clothing and fireline equipment. We'll teach you how to use it. It's your responsibility to keep your body, your clothing and your equipment in working order." He looked at each of us. "If you aren't in shape now, I guarantee you will be soon. You've got to be in condition to do the things required and you have to be able to carry everything you need. This isn't a job for wimps."

I was having trouble concentrating on what Captain Cooley said. I kept thinking about home. I wanted to talk to Mom and let her know where I was. I wanted to hear her voice. I couldn't ask Angel to let me use the phone; she would see it as weakness and I knew Dad wouldn't allow me to call collect. I needed a cell phone, but had less than $100 in my wallet.

"The next time I see you," Cooley went on, "I want you wearing your fire boots." He put his foot up on a chair, loosened the strap around his cuff, and pulled his blue pant leg up to reveal a worn but polished black fire boot that laced halfway up his shin. It had a thick sole and a wedge-shaped heel like a cowboy boot. "These are White Smoke Jumpers, the best you can get," he said.

The boots I had were for construction work; they were nothing like the ones Cooley wore.

"Start wearing your boots three to four hours a day. You'll be spending a lot of time in them and it's important to break them in. You need to work up to wearing them 10 hours without pain or blisters. Sometime when you're out at a fire, you'll thank me. One other thing: don't let anyone convince you to put duct tape on your feet to protect them. It's hell when you have to peel it off."

Cooley put his foot down and his pant leg caught at the top of his boot. I thought that really looked cool.

"During this week, you'll learn things in the classroom and in the field. We'll teach you some of the basics of firefighting and about safety and survival. Your first job with Cal Fire will be to assist fire crews and perform maintenance and housekeeping activities at the fire stations."

I looked at the eight other new firefighters sitting in the room with me. Could these guys cook? What were their specialties?

"Finally," Cooley said, "I hope by the end of the season, you take away some sense of tradition. Generations of the same family serve in the wildland fire service. My father worked for California Department of Forestry and Fire Protection—they called it CDF back then; my grandfather, Earl Cooley, was in the Forest Service. He was the first parachute jumper to dive into a forest fire. That was 1940, in Moose Creek, Montana. Someday you may have a son or a daughter who will be proud to follow in your footsteps."

I sat up a little. I had already gone beyond my father's footsteps; I had come to California to be a wildland firefighter.

We stood on the cement, holding our new Nomex fire gear. The forest was 20 feet from the edge of the parking lot at the Auburn facility. This was definitely not the California I had pictured. I imagined palm trees and the beach and great-looking girls. I dreamed of driving a Porsche convertible to a club on the Sunset Strip. This was the middle of the woods, just like Saginaw and the Upper Peninsula.

"Okay guys, listen up. I'm Captain Hunt. Here's the drill. You have to get your protective gear on in sixty seconds or less. That means the pants and jacket, the wildland gloves, your helmet, goggles and shroud. And it means no exposed skin when you're finished." He pulled a stopwatch out of his jacket. "Lay all your stuff on the ground and let's give it a try."

I struggled. It was hard to pull the pants up over my jeans. The straps of my daypack got caught on my jacket sleeves. My helmet fell off. I put my gloves on and then couldn't fasten the shroud around my face. I forgot to pull my goggles down off my helmet. On my fifth effort, I did everything in 95 seconds, my best time. The smaller guys were able to put their gear on faster. Keith Magnuson, a kid from Fresno with red hair and a red face, did the best. I watched with awe as he slipped on his jacket and pants as if he were covered with grease. He did it in the right sequence, putting his gloves on last. He turned in a circle for inspection—an alien showing no skin, face covered with a shroud and eyes magnified as he looked out through his goggles. He took 65 seconds to do it.

Later in the afternoon we learned to use the fire shelter, or the "Shake and Bake," as Captain Hunt called it. "If a fire comes roaring up the side of a mountain at you," he said, "you'll have thirty, maybe sixty seconds to deploy and your life will depend on being able to do it."

The shelter looked like a giant piece of tin foil, folded up like an accordion. We carried it in a canvas case clipped to our belts.

"Once opened," Captain Hunt said, "get your arms and legs through the straps in each corner, wrap the shelter around your back and lie face down on the ground, arms stretched above your head, heels toward the oncoming fire.

The shelter will capture some breathing air underneath. Make sure you have water and wait for someone to tell you it's safe to come out. Keep the edges of the shelter in place under your body. Finally, it doesn't hurt to pray."

It was hard enough to pull the fire shelter out of the case, use the ripcord to tear off the plastic cover, open it, wrap it around my body and lie on the ground, all in 30 seconds while standing in the parking lot. I tried to imagine doing that with a wall of flames rushing at me.

"At twelve hundred degrees, the aluminum oxidizes and turns dark," Captain Hunt said. "At one thousand six hundred degrees, the inner skin starts to melt. The good news is that the foil reflects 95 percent of the heat."

Six of us ate dinner in the Auburn mess hall. Whoever prepared the food knew what he was doing. We had a large bowl of salad with sliced vegetables, chicken stew served from an enormous pot, rice, and peaches in syrup for dessert. We lined up at the buffet table with various other Cal Fire personnel and filled our plates. Two tired-looking fire crews filed in, followed by a group of mechanics who taught engine maintenance and several men wearing side-arms, badges and stormtrooper boots. Not quite part of the crowd of veterans, we found a table on the edge of the room.

"What's with the guys with guns?" I asked.

"I think those are arson investigators," Arne Magnuson said.

"This is beyond paramilitary—it's like the freakin' armed forces," Bobby Davis, a tall skinny kid with a bad complexion, said. "We might as well be in the Army."

"If you were in the Army," Magnuson said, "someone would be shooting at you. Remember that."

"So you came out here all the way from Michigan?" Ken Banks asked me. He was one of the people Cooley had described—his father was a Cal Fire battalion chief.

"Yeah," I said.

"That's cool," Magnuson said. "I've heard about guys coming down from Washington and Oregon, but I never heard of anyone coming all the way from Michigan."

"What're you doing after the fire season?" Banks asked. "Are you going back to school? Working as a seasonal is a great way to pick up eight or ten grand to pay tuition."

"I'm done with school right now," I said. "I'm not sure what to do. I'd like to go to Southern California."

"If you're still interested in being a firefighter in November, try L.A. County," Magnuson said.

"L.A. County?" I asked.

"Yeah, they've got camps for wildland firefighters in Los Angeles," Magnuson said.

"My dad's in the Forest Service," Travis Foster said. "He says there's two kinds of seasonals, the guys just trying to pay for their tuition and the ones who want to become full-time firefighters." Foster was a big, soft kid who looked like he lived on donuts. If you jabbed a finger against his puffy pink skin, it might leave a permanent impression.

"So, which one are you?" Banks asked him.

"Me?" Foster said. "I'm not excited about seeing a wall of fire coming up a mountain at me, if that's what you mean."

"My dad's a firefighter for the City of Modesto," Tony Petruno said. Petruno was big too, but he was lean and looked tough. His skin was tanned from hours outdoors. I could imagine Petruno as a firefighter, no problem. "He loves it," Petruno continued. "He wants to be the first one at every fire. If there's a big fire on his day off, he'll go down to the station and suit up. He gets upset if he misses something."

"That's not me," said Foster.

"My dad's a firefighter in Saginaw," I told them, "but the only thing he likes to chase is women. I never heard him say he wanted to go to work on his day off."

"C'mon," Petruno said. "Every firefighter loves what he does. He wouldn't risk his life and put up with all the crap if he didn't."

"What's on in the morning?" Foster asked.

"A three-mile run and then we're gonna work on a progressive hose-lay," said Magnuson.

"Another run? Jesus," said Foster.

"What's a progressive hose-lay?" I asked.

"Your father's a firefighter?" Banks said.

"Yeah, and...?" I said.

"And you don't know what a hose-lay is?" Banks said.

"No, I don't. Am I supposed to?" I looked across the table at him. Banks might as well have said, "You're stupid." He glared back at me. Conversation stopped at our table. The guys were waiting to see if things were going to escalate.

"You'll find out in the morning," Banks said.

"OK, men," Cooley said, "we call this the *Tulare Drill*." We stood by the side of a road, looking out over a hard dirt field. A 100-foot length of 1½-inch wildland hose connected at one end to the engine was stretched out in the field. Dressed in full fire gear, each of us carried a backpack with two more 100-foot rolls of the same hose, along with nozzles and clamps.

"One at a time, you will run to the end of the hose," Cooley said. He pointed toward the field as if he were aiming a pistol. "By the time you get there, it'll be charged with water. Clamp the hose and take off the nozzle the way we showed you. Attach one of the coils you're carrying, reattach the nozzle and extend the hose. When you've stretched it out, repeat the process with your second coil."

"How much does a charged hose weigh?" Petruno asked.

"You'll be wrestling with something that weighs about a hundred pounds," Cooley said.

Impatient to get started, the driver at the wheel of the engine hit the accelerator, sending exhaust fumes into our faces.

"Imagine you're trying to get the hose to a burning house," Cooley said. "The owners will lose everything if you take too long. Any questions?"

Foster went first. When he stopped to attach his first coil, he fumbled with the clamp. He took off his gloves.

"Foster, never, *never* take off any of your gear during a fire," Cooley shouted. "Put your gloves back on."

While Foster fiddled with his gloves, the clamp popped off his hose and water under pressure sprayed everywhere. The jet hit Foster in the chest knocking him down. He was drenched.

Cooley ordered the pump turned off so Foster could reattach the clamp and muttered, "Christ, what's wrong with this kid?"

Foster managed to connect the first coil. As he extended it and the water in the hose became heavier, he turned and tried to pull it by walking backwards.

"No, Foster," Cooley shouted, "You're at a fire—you can't walk backwards, it's too dangerous!"

Foster turned around and struggled to pull the hose along the ground.

"Put it over your shoulder and move forward," Cooley yelled.

After more blunders, Foster attached the second coil and extended the entire hose.

"Foster," Cooley shouted, "those poor people lost their clothes and all their furniture while you were dicking around."

By the time nine of us had dragged a charged hose and learned to use the clamps, it was late morning. Cooley declared the exercise complete. "OK guys, take off your Nomex, drink some water, and let's get something to eat. This afternoon, we'll work on wearing breathing apparatus."

It felt good to get my helmet and fire gear off. We stood around the engine, drinking from our canteens and I noticed that Foster, Magnuson, Davis and an older guy named Keith Bradsher were looking at me and laughing. After a minute, Petruno, Banks and two others had broad smiles on their faces as well. What was going on here? I felt like a kid who had come to a party with his fly open. Now even Cooley was smiling and as I looked at him, he turned away.

I wiped the sweat off my forehead. My hand was black. I rubbed my forehead again with my other hand and looked at it. It was covered with black, greasy crap. I looked at myself in the side-view mirror of the engine. My face was covered with the black stuff and it was all over my hair. I looked at the inside of my helmet and found the headband covered with a black substance. Each time I had touched my forehead, I had smeared it around my face. "Is this supposed to be funny?" I shouted. "Who the fuck did this, goddamnit?" Everyone gave me blank looks, trying to hide laughter. "Who put this crap in my helmet?" I demanded. "Banks?" I don't know why I singled out Banks, but I walked toward him, my fists balled up.

"Kowalski," Cooley said, stepping in front of me. "Cool off. It's only powdered graphite and Vaseline. It'll come off." He laughed. "You'll just have to scrub a little."

I stood by the engine and glared at the whole group. Everyone, even Cooley was in on it. "Fuck you guys," I said.

Things were tense in the mess hall at dinner that night. I managed to come in late, load up my plate, and eat by myself instead of sitting down with the rest of the guys.

We spent the last day learning tool proficiency. We assembled on a hillside covered with brush and learned to cut a 3-foot fireline "down to mineral soil," as Cooley described it. We used the Pulaski, a tool with an ax blade and a pick, to chop and dig out brush and roots. We used the McLeod, a combination hoe and heavy rake, to scrape and clear the ground. We used our shovels and each of us got to practice with the 21-inch Stihl chainsaw, cutting small trees and branches.

"You've each got twenty minutes to act like a hot shot and work out your frustrations using the saw," Cooley told us, and gave me a look.

We learned to work in a line: the saw; two Pulaskis; three shovels; three McLeods. Cooley kept shouting, "Get your dime, keep your dime," reminding us to work 10 feet apart. Like an awkward yellow centipede, we moved through the brush, leaving a trail of fallen branches and a swath of dirt.

My anger over the graphite and Vaseline had cooled, but no one admitted to doing the deed. I had lost interest in making friends with any of these guys. The Rodeo was over.

Cooley pulled me aside at the end of the day. "Greg," he said, "you're a big strong kid and I know you can do the physical work, but you're screwed up way too tight. Your captain will want to know how you react under stress before you get out to a fire. You'll be living in close quarters for the next five or six months and—"

"Captain Cooley, I—"

"Let me finish, Greg. The graphite trick gets pulled all the time, and everyone takes it in stride. You can't blow up over a little joke. You have to ease up. Can you do that?"

"Sure," I said.

"Good. Tomorrow Angel will drive you up to the Colfax station."

"An Indian cemetery?" I was back in the wagon with Angel, heading to Colfax.

"Yeah, the Colfax Indian Cemetery," she said.

"How big is it?"

"Twenty-four graves, I think."

"And it's the biggest thing in town?"

"Actually, it's about the only thing in town. There's only seventeen hundred people."

"What am I going to do out here? I haven't even got a car."

"Well, you'll be at the station four days a week. That only leaves three days and nights."

"Three days a week in Colfax, looking at an Indian cemetery?"

"I wouldn't complain. You could've been assigned to Iowa Hill. They don't even have regular electricity; everything's on generators up there. Besides, maybe you'll be called away on a fire or a train wreck. Placer County has a lot of train wrecks."

"Sounds like Colfax is the train wreck."

"Here's my advice, Greg. Captain Tucker doesn't like people with attitude, so get over it."

FOUR
Mackinaw City, Michigan

I WAS SO EXCITED that I barely slept Friday night. I was going on a trip with my father—the two of us on his motorcycle! Before we left in the morning, he said, "We're traveling light, don't bring a lot of stuff." I took my parka, the blue sweater I got for my birthday and the leather bag of quarters I was saving for new ice skates. On the way out, Mom stuck my toothbrush in my coat pocket.

My father's Harley was a 1984 Electra Glide, which he bought from the Michigan State Troopers. It was white and still resembled a police motorcycle, but the red lights and siren had been removed. He spent a lot of time working on the engine and polishing the chrome. He was proud of it and sometimes when people saw him riding it, they thought he was a cop. I think that's the way he wanted it.

We rolled down the driveway and Mom yelled, "Be careful, have fun!" Vicky watched us from the front steps. As the Harley accelerated down the street, I held on for dear life. The rear seat was too big for my butt and I was afraid I would slide off. After an hour on the road, we stopped for food at a convenience store. My father was still in a good mood. He bought two Detroit Pistons caps and gave one to me.

The trip took almost three hours and I was starting to get tired. At last, we arrived in Mackinaw City and cruised around. It's called a city, but it's not; it's a town, much smaller than Saginaw. We rode by a veteran's monument, a fort and a big lighthouse. We saw restaurants, fudge shops and stores that sold T-shirts. On our way to the motel, we passed the Thunder Falls Family Waterpark. It was the end of September and most of the shops and the

Waterpark had closed for the season. The streets were quiet.

This wasn't my first visit to a motel. Mom's mother and father came once a year from Chicago to visit us and stayed at the Holiday Inn in Saginaw. "I don't want your folks around the house," my father said whenever they arrived. "If they have to see you, visit them at the motel and leave the kids at home." Mom took Vicky and me to visit our grandparents anyway; it was one of the few things she did to defy my father. It was always a day of excitement when we saw them. We ate breakfast in the coffee shop and went to their room to open the presents they brought from Chicago. They stopped sending gifts to the house because my father threw them in the trash. Vicky and I thought it was great fun to get all our birthday and Christmas presents on one day.

Once when they visited, my grandparents pulled Mom out onto the small patio and asked if she wanted to bring us to Chicago to live with them. I pretended to be busy, but listened to them talk. "I can't leave him," Mom said. "He has good qualities and he takes care of us. He's just stressed out. His work is so dangerous."

"The man's a louse," my grandmother said. "You're in denial and eventually you'll regret it."

When I asked my mother what "denial" meant, she told me it was a word for adults.

The Mackinaw Motel wasn't as nice as the Holiday Inn. It was a one-story, U-shaped cinderblock building. Half the rooms faced the street and the others faced a vacant lot where a burnt pickup truck was half-hidden in the weeds. Tan paint had begun to peel off the ouside walls, revealing a gray undercoat and only half the letters were lit in the neon sign over the entrance. Across the street there was a hostess bar with windows painted black.

My father parked his Harley and we went in. A man sat behind a thick piece of scratched plastic, watching a television set on a small desk. He wore Army camouflage pants and a dirty gray sweatshirt. His skin was white and he looked like he had never been outside. He was eating a hamburger and when we came to the window, he stood and wiped his mouth on his sleeve.

"We want a room for tonight," my father said. "Two beds; we'll be out in the morning."

"It's twenty-two dollars for the room, payable in advance. There's a three-dollar deposit for the room key and if you wanna watch television, there's a nine-dollar deposit for the remote."

My father opened his billfold, took out two $20 bills, and said, "We only need one key. He paused, looked at me and said, "Let's have the remote."

"Your room's number twelve. You can get to it from the parking lot or down the back hallway. There's ice and vending machines and we got some video games and a pinball in the arcade. You gotta be out tomorrow by eleven. There's free coffee in the morning." He cracked a wide grin that showed brown, uneven teeth and said, "Don't forget to visit our world-famous swimming pool out back." He winked at my father as he slid the key and the remote under the plastic window.

My father handed me the remote and said, "Don't lose it."

Outside, we walked past two women who had just arrived on matching pink motorcycles. They looked at us and my father stopped and stared back, hands on his hips. Women were always giving my father looks. At an early age, I was aware that women were attracted to him and sensed his interest in them. One of my mother's friends once described him as a "thirty-eight-year-old hunk." Sometimes my mother would watch him doing something and say, "Your father's so handsome." He was over 6 feet tall and had coal-black hair. I knew I was going to grow up to look like him.

My father's mood suddenly changed when he saw the women. "Go on to the room Greggie," he said, and handed me the key. "I'm going to have a little chat with these ladies."

The room was about the size of my bedroom at home. It had two narrow beds, an unpainted nightstand with an electric clock bolted to it, a mirror and a dresser with a television set on top. The toilet, sink and shower were separated by a plastic curtain with boats on it. Tiny bars of soap and a few towels lay on the sink. Lime green curtains covered a window facing the parking lot and street. A picture of cowboys riding across a desert and a sign advertising Thunder Falls Water Park hung on the wall. I jumped on one of the beds and turned on the television. The picture was black and white and fuzzy.

My father came in and said, "Stay here and wait for me. I'm going for a ride. I'll be back in a couple of hours." The window vibrated when the three motorcycles left the parking lot.

I was almost 9 years old and not afraid to be alone. When my father traveled to Detroit overnight for training classes, my mother sometimes went to a friend's house and Vicky and I stayed home by ourselves. Staying with a 5-year-old sister was the same as staying alone. Once, when my father called in the evening from Detroit, I had to tell him Mom had gone to the grocery store. He didn't call back and Mom was back the next morning before we woke up.

By dinnertime, my father still hadn't returned and I was hungry. I had $6 in quarters in my leather bag and went out into the hallway to see what I could find to eat. The lime green carpet matched the curtains in the bedroom and smelled bad. I found the vending machines, bought a Kit Kat, chips and a Coke and ate on the floor.

Sounds came from some of the rooms. I heard a shower. A man and a woman argued. I couldn't understand what they said, but the guy sounded pissed, like my father. I heard two televisions, one tuned to a Detroit Lions game, the other announcing a track meet at the Olympics in Korea.

I finished my Coke and went out to see the swimming pool. It was empty and the bottom was covered with leaves, branches and empty soda bottles. Plastic lounge chairs lay in a tangled pile near a boarded-up snack-bar. I sat down at the edge of the pool and imagined that my feet were dangling in warm water. I closed my eyes and I was on vacation at Disneyland. Vicky and I had been on the rides and had eaten popcorn and ice cream. We were having a wonderful time, but I couldn't picture my mother and father there with us. We were by ourselves and Vicky was getting scared. I told her not to worry, but I was frightened too. Some of my friends had parents who were divorced and I wondered what would happen if Mom and Dad split up. Vicky and I might be left alone without anyone to take care of us. We would be orphans.

I began to shiver sitting by the empty pool and decided to check out the arcade. It was quiet when I walked back through the hallway. The man and woman had stopped arguing and the television sets were silent. The arcade was just a motel room with its door removed. The walls and the ceiling were painted black and the carpet was the same lime green. Two floor lamps with purple bulbs gave off a dim light. Screens from the video games glowed in bright colors and against one wall, standing by itself was the pinball machine. I'd never fooled around with a pinball machine, but had seen the older kids from school playing one at the Saginaw Mall. I thought the flashing lights, bells and other sounds made by the big steel balls crashing around inside were very cool and had to try it. I wasn't tall enough to reach the flippers and went into the hallway to find something to stand on.

As I walked back toward the vending machines, a man came in from the parking lot. "Hey kid, where you going?" he said. He stepped in front of me. One of his shoes was held together with duct tape. He wore dirty brown pants and his belt was a necktie threaded through the loops and tied in front.

I was afraid to look at his face. "I'm trying to find a chair."

"A chair, a chair, he's looking for a chair," he sang.

"I'm gonna play the pinball machine but I'm not tall enough."

"You're gonna play the pinball machine? Got any money?"

I held up my leather bag.

"Well, the little turd has money. Let's have it."

"It's my money, it belongs to me." I turned away from him.

"I said, let's have it, kid." His filthy hands pulled at the bag. The thin leather strap around my wrist snapped and he had my quarters. He shoved me and I hit the wall head first and fell onto the carpet.

"Hey," I cried, "that hurt. Give my money back!"

"Shut up, you little pecker, or you'll be sorry." He walked down the hall and out into the parking lot.

I sat on the floor. My wrist hurt where the leather band had broken and my head was pounding. Tears came and the more I cried, the more I wanted to cry. I couldn't stop. I felt awful; I was frightened and alone and the money I had been saving for ice skates was gone.

A door opened wide enough for a man to stick his head out. "Hey, keep quiet, you little brat," he growled.

I got up, still crying and went back to the room. Inside, I wrapped myself in the bedspread and fell asleep watching a Western. The television screen was full of gray snow when I awoke. It was the middle of the night and the room was empty. The night's events came back to me and I was terrified. Where was my father? Had he forgotten to come back and gone home without me? I tried to remember if I had done anything during the day to make him angry and leave me at the motel. Did he have an accident? I once saw a motorcycle crash near our house. The bike lay twisted in the middle of the street, chrome pieces and glass scattered everywhere. The rider was hurt, lying on his back, crying out in pain. The rough pavement had ripped open his leather pants and jacket.

I saw blood on his clothes and on the street.

I looked through the curtains to see if my dad's Harley was outside. A few cars were parked in the lot, but the space in front of our room was empty. From the window, I couldn't see if the motorcycle was down by the office. I ran out of the room and hurried to the office. Across the street, the flashing lights at the hostess bar cast strange shadows.

The same guy with the bad teeth and white skin was behind the plastic window. He sat at the desk with his back to me, facing a dark television screen. He was rocking back and forth and when he heard me, he turned around. "Hey, it's three in the morning. What're you doing in here at this hour?" He pulled up his pants.

"I'm looking for my father. I wanted to see if his motorcycle was out front."

"Well, it's not, is it," he said, and tugged at his zipper. "Now get out of here and go back to your room."

I walked back through the parking lot. I was so frightened, even the possibility that I might run into the man with the duct tape on his shoe didn't seem to matter. In the room, I lay on the bed looking at the ceiling. I was sure I had done something to make my father desert me. He wasn't coming back and someone would have to call Mom. I looked at the cowboys in the picture hanging on the wall and tried to make them move by closing one eye, then the other.

In the morning, when I got the nerve to go to the office, the man was gone and a woman was at the desk talking on the phone and looking at a magazine. I was afraid to interrupt her and sat in the office staring out the window.

Without hanging up, she looked at me. "Do you need something?"

"I'm waiting for my father."

"I don't suppose you drink coffee," she said. "How about some milk?"

"Sure."

She pointed to the pitcher by the coffee machine and returned to her conversation. I poured some milk into a paper cup. It was warm, but I was hungry and drank it anyway. While she looked at her magazine, I took some sugar cubes from the bowl and put them in my mouth.

A family came to check out. They had a girl about Vicky's age and while they stood at the window, she turned, looked at me and stuck out her tongue. It had green gum on it. On the way out, she opened her mouth and dropped the gum on the floor.

Moments later, my dad rolled into the parking lot on the Electra Glide. I squeezed my eyelids closed, afraid I would start to cry. A couple of tears escaped and ran down my cheek, followed by a torrent. My father walked into the office, looked at me and asked, "What're you crying about?"

I was so happy to see him, I couldn't say anything.

"You ready to go?" he said. "Are you hungry?"

I shook my head no.

"Grab your coat and let's get on the road. We can eat on the way home."

I ran to the room and got my parka. I was so thankful to see my father that I was trembling.

On the ride back, it was cold and my father's breath smelled like beer whenever he turned his head to talk to me. It took forever to get home and we didn't stop to eat. He dropped me at the house and went on to the station.

"How was the trip?" my mother asked when I walked in.

"It was OK."

"Where did you stay? At a motel?"

"Yes."

"Was it like the Holiday Inn?

"No, it wasn't a Holiday Inn, but it had a swimming pool and a pinball machine."

"That sounds nice. What did you guys do?"

"We rode around. Dad bought me a Pistons cap."

"I think it's wonderful that you and your father did something together."

Vicky, who had been listening, started to whine, "I wanna go on the Harley."

Under the cover of Vicky's tears, I locked myself in the downstairs bathroom, turned on the water in the sink and sat on the top of the toilet. I wanted to tell my mother what had really happened, but we never talked about the Mackinaw trip again.

The following week, while I was at school, my mother fell down the stairs. She hurt her back, bruised her hip and had difficulty walking for almost a month. She also had bruises on her face, which she said happened when her head hit the steps.

FIVE
Colfax, California

ANGEL TURNED OFF HIGHWAY 80 and drove up a tree-lined driveway. "That's Captain Tucker," she said, pointing to a man with his back to us. He wore a blue T-shirt with "Cal Fire" on it.

I took a deep breath. I thought I would look back on this morning and remember it as the beginning of my life as a firefighter. This would be the place where the boy from Saginaw disappeared and the man from California emerged. The men I met here would be my friends for life.

Captain Tucker walked toward the wagon as I got out to greet him. "Welcome to the station, Greg," he said. "You're from Michigan?"

"Yes, sir."

"Long way to come."

"I wanted to see the Indian cemetery."

"Sounds like Angel's been prepping you." He bent to look in the window of the station wagon. "Hi, Angel," he said.

"Hi, Jerry."

"C'mon Greg, I'll show you around," Captain Tucker said. The station at Colfax wasn't anything like the two-story brick building where my father worked in downtown Saginaw. It was a small house in a forest clearing with three tiny bedrooms, one bathroom, a kitchen and a living room with a television set and rusted weight-lifting equipment. Across the tree-lined driveway, Captain Tucker kept an office above an oversize garage which held a single engine.

Angel departed without saying goodbye.

"Your shift runs Sunday through Wednesday," the Captain said as we walked back out onto the empty driveway. "You'll be working with David

Ramirez—he's our engineer, and with Ray Hibbert. He's a seasonal."

"Is this his first year?"

"No, it's his third."

"Where's he from?"

"Emigrant Gap, up Highway 80. He'll help you get into the routine. Ever use a rescue saw?"

"No sir."

"Every day we check the generator, pumps and hydraulic tools." He stepped on a large pinecone, nearly lost his footing and kicked it into the forest. "The breathing apparatus and wildland hose has to be inspected and we've always got tools to sharpen."

"We used breathing apparatus and hose at the Rodeo," I said.

"Good. How about rope work?"

"Rope work?"

"Rappelling, that kind of stuff?"

"No sir."

"How about cooking breakfast, can you do that?"

"I'll learn."

"We start at seven. After breakfast we do ninety minutes of PT and then move on to the equipment."

"Does that mean we eat at seven?"

"Yeah, so you'll be up earlier. I hope you enjoy it here, Greg. A single engine station is like a family."

I was sure I would enjoy it as long as it wasn't like the Kowalski family. "Captain, where should I stay when I'm off duty? I don't even have a car."

"You can't stay here. There's no extra room."

"Have you got any suggestions? Should I stay in Colfax?"

"You could rent a room in town, but I've got another idea if you're interested."

"Sir?"

"Bald Mountain. It's a fire lookout. You could stay there for free and do some maintenance work."

"A fire lookout?"

"Yeah, you know, a tower. There's a place to cook and sleep."

If this was the beginning of my new life as a firefighter, living by myself in an observation tower wasn't part of the plan.

"It's not in use right now. It needs some paint and a clean up," Captain Tucker continued.

"Sounds lonely. I can't see myself living in the forest. Maybe I should just stay in Colfax—"

"It's really beautiful, Greg. You'll like it," the Captain insisted. "You'd be doing Cal Fire and me a big favor. The place is empty."

"I don't know."

"There's one hundred and seventy-five steps. Climbing's good exercise. Give it a try, Greg."

"Where is it?"

"Six miles from here. We can work out some transportation."

"Okay," I said, knowing I was making a big mistake. "I've got to go see about a car as soon as I get a paycheck."

"Good boy," Captain Tucker said, and clapped me on the back. "C'mon, I'll introduce you to Ray."

We walked around to the back of the house. Ray Hibbert was on his hands and knees, looking at the undersides of the leaves of a tomato plant. When he saw us coming, he stood up and brushed the dirt off his pants. "Can you believe it, Cap'n, I've got Cabbage Loopers."

"Well, you better spray them. By the end of the summer the whole garden'll be gone."

"Damned pests," Ray grumbled.

"This is Greg Kowalski. Greg's from Michigan."

Ray was at least 4 inches shorter than I was, but solid. His neck was as wide as his head and his body resembled a tree trunk—a Redwood tree trunk. It looked as though someone had put a bowl over his head to cut his thick hair. He stuck out a hand the size of a baseball glove and said, "Hey, Greg."

"Greg's going to bunk at Bald Mountain on his days off," Captain Tucker said. "Call Auburn and tell them we've got someone to do the maintenance."

"Will do." Ray turned to me and said, "Sure you want to stay up there?"

"Is there a problem?"

"No, but why not just camp out? The weather's pretty good."

"Camp out? Three days a week? You've got to be kidding. I'm not a camper and I don't want to entertain a bear in my tent."

"Bears are kinda fun," Ray said. "As long as you hide your food."

The beaches of Southern California never seemed farther away.

The next morning, Captain Tucker joined me in the kitchen at 6:30 a.m. and gave me a quick lesson on preparing eggs. He wanted his cooked in the microwave—three in a bowl, with a little milk. "David eats Granola every day. He won't touch eggs," Captain Tucker told me, "and Ray will eat eggs scrambled, fried, boiled, or any other way, so fix whatever you want."

For my first meal, I fried potatoes and bacon, which was slightly burnt but edible. The toast was easy because the kitchen had a toaster. I put too much coffee in the machine and had to toss it out and start over, but the second batch was fine. Breakfast wasn't great, but I was proud of it and no one complained.

After breakfast, we did some stretching and went out for a one-hour trail run. Captain Tucker set the pace and led the way. I figured I could do anything Ray could do and ran behind him on the narrow path. David brought up the rear. He and Ray were physical opposites; David was a thin wiry man. We ran at a rapid pace and when we finished I was tired, but not exhausted. Ray's body was not made for running. He was panting and soaked with sweat. His face was bright red.

"Cool down and drink some water," David said. "Then we'll go over the equipment."

After the color of Ray's face returned to normal, we joined David outside the garage. He placed the rescue tools on the ground and wiped the oil from his hands with a rag. "They're pretty simple," he said. "The cutters are like big chompers and the spreader and ram are used to pry open metal." He picked up the cutter and showed me the sharp pointed blades. "We use these on vehicles. Usually the roof's crushed, or the dashboard and steering wheel have collapsed into the passenger compartment." He put the cutter down. "Everything runs off of this souped-up lawn mower engine connected to a hydraulic pump."

"So, did you do a lot of hunting and fishing back in Michigan?" Ray asked me.

"No," I said.

"I like bass fishing," Ray said, "and camping. I work for my father. There's Class IV rapids around here and we run rafting trips on the American River."

Ray rubbed his hand over his ribcage. "Last year our raft was thrown against some rocks and he broke five ribs. We haven't done any tours this year so I'm thinking about joining full time and pulling in some regular pay."

I couldn't imagine Ray in a raft. The thing would sink. "Where do you find girls around here?" I asked him.

"There aren't any."

"So, what do you do for excitement?"

"Tomorrow I can show you how to use the ropes to get down the side of a mountain. That's excitement."

I was busy during the day, but the nights at the station dragged on forever. Unless we watched television—and the reception wasn't great—there was nothing to do except go to sleep. Some evenings I sat around listening to Captain Tucker, David and Ray. The conversation was dull. David was quiet; he just sat there and didn't say much. Captain Tucker and Ray spent a lot of time discussing bass fishing and gardening. I learned more about Cabbage Loopers than I ever wanted to know. By 9 p.m., it was lights out.

I could lie in bed for two or three hours before falling asleep. The bed was too short and my feet hung off the end. I was restless and thrashed around and by morning the sheets and covers were on the floor. I was homesick. It was less than a month since I had left Saginaw, but it seemed like a year. I tried to picture what Mom and Vicky were doing. I thought about my father and tried to imagine working every day with him, shoulder to shoulder, as Ray must have done with his dad on the river. I wondered what life would be like if my father loved me. Sometimes, as the night wore on and I couldn't go to sleep, I searched my mind for happy moments from my childhood.

One night, after lying awake on top of the bed for several hours in the dark, I got under the covers and my leg touched something. I sat up, turned on the lamp and lifted the sheet. I saw gray fur. My heart was pounding as I jumped to the floor and yanked the covers back. Someone had put a dead squirrel in my bed. It looked like it had been run over. Its tail was still bushy, but its body was flat as a pancake and its legs stuck out in four directions. The paws still had sharp nails. The head was in one piece and the mouth was open, showing tiny sharp white teeth. The eye sockets were empty. I lifted the flattened animal by its tail and dropped it on the floor. There was no blood on the sheets, but the fur had begun to fall out.

Ray was the only one who could have done this. It must have been some kind of goddamned hillbilly joke. I had promised Cooley that I would not lose my temper, but this was different. I was so angry I started to shake. I wanted to take the squirrel into Ray's room, wake him up and cram it down his throat. I lay on top of my blanket and clenched my fists. I was still awake when the sun came up.

In the morning, I cooked up scrambled eggs, bacon and toast. As a special touch, I took one of Ray's tomatoes from the garden and added it to our breakfast. I thought his plate looked particularly appetizing with scrambled eggs inside a triangle of crisp bacon and, in the center on top of a slice of tomato, the head of the squirrel looked up with empty eyes. "Enjoy your breakfast, Ray," I said and clenched my teeth.

"What the hell?" Captain Tucker said. He pushed his chair back from the table. David looked at Ray's plate, laughed and continued to eat his Granola. Ray sat holding his knife and fork and stared at the squirrel head.

I sat down and began to eat my eggs. "Is there a problem with breakfast?" I asked.

Ray stood, emptied his plate in the trashcan and went outside without saying a word.

"Greg," Captain Tucker said, "what the hell is this?"

"It's just payback," I said. "He—"

"That's disgusting, Greg. Don't ever do anything like that again," Captain Tucker got up, dumped his uneaten eggs on top of the squirrel head in the trash and followed Ray outside. I continued to eat while David lingered over his coffee.

That afternoon, I had a chance to use the Captain's telephone. "Operator, I need the main number for the Los Angeles County Fire Department."

Captain Tucker forgot to tell me there was no running water at the Bald Mountain Tower. He lent me his pickup to go shopping on Wednesday afternoons when I went off duty and I bought food and bottled water at one of the small markets in Colfax. Wednesday evening, the Captain drove me up the narrow fire road to the base of the tower and dropped me off. I bought a backpack but still had to make several trips up seven flights of stairs with the water and my other supplies.

The tower was 17 feet on a side and the walls were mostly glass. An Osborne Fire Finder, mounted on a table in the center of the cabin, allowed a lookout to locate a plume of smoke using sights which rotated around a glass-covered map. Someone had spilled coffee that had seeped under the glass and obliterated the southern half of Placer County. A dozen antennae bristled on the roof, but the communications equipment including the telephone, had been removed. A two-burner stove, a microwave and a small refrigerator in a corner made up the kitchen. Two Army cots were placed end to end along one wall under the windows. Since there was no water, my toilet was a Porta-Potty at ground level, hidden in a stand of pine trees. I was glad my family didn't know about this. My father would laugh and tell me what a fuck-up I was.

For a few days, I was bored and lonely and was tempted to tell Captain Tucker I would find a place in town. I tried to imagine that the Bald Mountain fire lookout was a lifeguard stand at the beach and that I was looking out over white sand and water. I tried to picture girls rubbing lotion on their bodies, their bikini tops rolled partway down. It didn't work. All I had was a long-range view of the top of the forest, which resembled a green and brown shag carpet. Here and there a power transmission tower rose up, but there was nothing else to see.

Ray had told me fire observers lived alone in these towers for weeks at a time and by the third week, I was becoming accustomed to the isolation. On the wall next to the stove someone had posted a seasonal fire lookout job description from the California State Personnel Board. The section describing "Special Personal Characteristics: *willingness to work alone in remote areas*," had been underlined. I could do it. I would live like a recluse; I didn't need anyone. There was no way the men at Colfax were going to be my lifelong firefighter buddies.

On Friday, when the B-crew from Colfax was on duty, they ran up the fire road and climbed the tower stairs for early morning PT. Captain Tucker sometimes came up with them. From above, I could see them when they were halfway up the road, but heard their voices sooner, echoing in the quiet forest. When they came puffing up the stairs on their first lap, I stood outside eating breakfast.

"Morning guys, great day!" I would say. On their second trip to the top, I called out, "We've got espresso. Singles? Doubles?" On their third and last effort, I told them, "Sorry, we're out of coffee." I got some nasty looks from faces dripping with sweat and snot. No one thought I was funny, but it didn't bother me; I didn't care.

I didn't work hard on the tower maintenance. I cleaned up the interior, washed the windows and began to scrape and paint seven flights of stairs and railings. I worked two or three hours a day, which left plenty of free time. I thought about Kirsten waiting outside class for me, wearing her short plaid skirt, white blouse and white socks rolled down to the tops of her loafers. I remembered walking home with her, making jokes while she laughed and brushed her black hair out of her eyes. I was with her again in her bedroom when she stood with her back to me, unbuttoning her white blouse. Kirsten wasn't important to me at the time, but I would have loved to see her now. I missed her.

After a month, I received my second paycheck and David drove me into Auburn to a used-car lot. "You know, Greg," he said when he picked me up, "you're a prisoner in that tower, just like in old England." I had no idea what he was talking about, but was thankful for the ride. Auburn seemed like a big city after four weeks at the Colfax Station.

David and I wandered around the car lot until a salesman approached us. "We've got a lot of nice cars here," he said.

"What about the blue Wrangler?" I said. "The one with the dented rear bumper?" I wanted to ask him where the Porsche dealer was. What I really wanted was a red Turbo Carrera, not a blue Jeep with a banged-up bumper.

"It's a '93. We just got it on the lot. The mechanical stuff is okay, but it needs some body work."

"How many miles?"

He checked. "Sixty-eight thousand."

"How much with no body work?"

"You a buyer?"

I told him, "I need wheels," and told myself, "forget the Porsche."

"It's a six-cylinder. It cost about fifteen thousand new. The tires are good. We give you a sixty-day warranty on mechanical." He paused and was probably wondering how much he could get out of me. "I could give it to you for twenty four hundred."

"Am I supposed to bargain?"

"No, take it or leave it."

"David, what do you think?" I asked.

"You need transportation, don't you?" he said.

"I can give you five hundred now and pay seven hundred fifty a month," I said to the salesman.

"Do you have a job?"

"I work for Cal Fire. I'm here for the season."

"No problem—firefighters are very reliable," he said. "We've sold several cars to Cal Fire employees. We can work it out."

"I'll take it."

"Congratulations," David said. "Your first car."

"Whoop-de-do, I'm a car owner." For the first time in my life, I was earning money, enough to buy a Jeep if not a Porsche. I didn't know anyone my age in Saginaw who could buy a car using his own cash and credit. That had to count for something.

The salesman steered me toward his office. "Come inside and fill out some paperwork. You need insurance. We can help you with that. Have you got a permanent address?"

I had decided to stay in the tower. I was probably turning into a sicko— but I was actually beginning to enjoy it. I gave the salesman the Colfax Station address.

On a quiet Sunday morning in the middle of August, we responded to a report of a vehicle that had gone off Yankee Jim Road and fallen into one of the canyons on the North Fork of the American River.

"I'm not sure exactly where it is," Captain Tucker yelled to us as we ran to the engine. "It happened west of Pine Lake Drive."

David sat up front, and Ray and I rode in the back of the engine, in the open crew area. We sped two miles south down Highway 80 to the Yankee Jim turnoff. Once on Yankee Jim Road, we climbed into the mountains. The American River in this area was fast and dangerous. Over the years it had cut deep and rocky canyons, the sides of which were covered with dense brush.

Captain Tucker slowed as we wound around tight, narrow turns going up the deserted two-lane road. We came around a bend and saw a silver Jaguar convertible parked on the shoulder overlooking the canyon. The driver's door was open. A man sat behind the wheel, his hands covering his face. Captain Tucker cut across the road and parked the engine behind the Jaguar, trying to stay out of the downhill traffic lane. The man seemed unaware of us, even though we had arrived with our siren on. "Oh my God," we heard him say as we approached.

"Sir, hello?" Captain Tucker said, and shook the man's shoulder. "Can you tell us what happened?"

The man seemed surprised to see us, four firefighters in wildland gear standing around his car. "It went off the road, there." Without turning his head, he pointed behind him toward a sharp turn up the road.

"A car?" Captain Tucker asked.

"A black Jaguar."

"How many people in the car?" David asked. The man gave no response. "Sir, how many people in the car?" he asked again.

"One. It's my brother," the man said, looking straight ahead. "Help him."

"Your brother went off the side of a cliff and you're just sitting here?" I said to myself.

Captain Tucker must have heard me, because he gave me a quick, angry look and said, "He's in shock. Wait until it sinks in." He went to the engine and radioed for assistance.

The man in the Jaguar repeated in a monotone, "Help him, help him."

David stayed with the man in the car while Ray and I walked up the edge of the road, trying to see into the canyon through the brush. "I can't see anything down there, can you?" I said.

"I don't even see any tire marks," Ray said. We could hear the rough water of the river below.

Captain Tucker maneuvered the engine around so that the front bumper, which had a winch, was close to the edge of the canyon. "Greg, stop the downhill traffic!" he shouted.

David opened a compartment on the side of the engine. "Ray, help me with the ropes," he said, and took out a black nylon harness. Ray pulled coils of yellow rope from another compartment while David helped Captain

Tucker put on the harness.

I walked up the road, lit two fusees and placed them in the middle of the bend to stop traffic.

"Awful quiet down there," David said.

"I'm going over to take a look," Captain Tucker said. David threaded the nylon rope through metal loops on the harness and looped one end around the drum on the winch. Ray fed the line back out as Captain Tucker walked backward over the side of the canyon and disappeared in the trees.

I watched the guy in the Jaguar put his hands back on the steering wheel and bury his face in his arms. Since we had arrived, he had not looked at the spot where he said his brother went off the cliff.

David checked the winch. Ray looked over the edge and tried to track Captain Tucker's descent. The glow of the fusees on the pavement left red circles in my vision while I attempted to imagine the scene below. The brother had to be badly hurt, maybe dead. The steering wheel and dashboard might have crushed his chest. The glossy black paint of the Jaguar would be scraped by tree limbs, the front bumper and grill demolished by boulders and the windshield shattered.

I watched a CHP officer arrive in a patrol car, followed by another in a Bronco. The first blocked the road below and ran up to the man in the Jaguar. The second officer stopped next to the engine. He got out and declared, "There's an H-30 crew on the way."

"What's an H-30 crew?" I asked him.

"Helicopter rescue," the officer said.

We heard the guy in the Jaguar telling the first cop, "My brother was following me. I saw him in my rear view mirror. He went off the road at the curve. Help him."

The cop had his notebook out. "How fast were you going?"

"I don't know. Help my brother, for God's sake, get my brother."

The officer asked to see his driver's license. An EMT crew in an ambulance and a Placer County Sheriff's car arrived with two deputies. A Jeep coming downhill stopped and two men and a girl wearing a tank top got out and stood in the middle of the road watching us. Another car stopped behind the Jeep, and the driver lowered his window to get a better view. One of the sheriffs told the people to stay behind the flares. The paramedics stood by the man in the

Jaguar, urging him to get out of the car. He refused. The road was filled with blue and red flashing lights.

Captain Tucker hoisted himself back up onto the road. "Farther down it's a sheer drop. I couldn't see anything but broken bushes."

Another engine arrived from Iowa Hill. Additional sheriffs arrived. We were a helpless crowd of rescuers standing by the roadside. Eight Cal Fire firefighters, two CHP officers, four Sheriff's deputies, two paramedics and a growing crowd of spectators on the far side of the flares listened to the man in his Jaguar pleading, "Help my brother!"

We heard it before we saw it. The staccato of a small helicopter echoed through the hills. Soon we saw a black and white CHP rescue helicopter with a red tail. It circled twice above the canyon and descended to eye level. As it hovered, a flight officer in a helmet and tan jumpsuit climbed out onto the strut. We watched him attach his harness to a cable hanging from a winch mounted above the door. He stepped off the strut, swung free in the air at the end of the cable and sank below the trees. Moments later, the helicopter gained altitude, retracted the loose cable and began to make slow circles above the canyon.

Once the H-30 crew arrived and assumed responsibility for the rescue, everyone on the road relaxed. Most of the guys knew each other and began to share bits of conversation. Two of the sheriffs discussed a female deputy. One of the paramedics said he was hungry. The Iowa Hill crew laughed at a joke. The CHP officer from the Bronco said, "No one could survive a drop like this." We waited on the road and paced back and forth.

Ten minutes passed.

The noise of the helo increased as it descended again, lowering the hoist cable. We watched with anticipation to see what would happen. In less than a minute, the flight officer came up alone, a brown spider dangling at the end of a strand of web. As he twisted around to face us, he drew a finger across his throat and shook his head. He climbed onto the strut, back into the helicopter and it flew out of the canyon.

Now the dead man's brother was paying attention. He had seen the flight officer come up alone. The paramedics tried to move him onto a gurney positioned next to his car. He jerked away from them, threw himself facedown on the pavement and began to sob. He pounded his fists and smashed his forehead against the asphalt. "No! No!" he shouted. The EMT crew and one of the sheriffs restrained him.

The CHP officer emerged from his Bronco and said in a low voice, "They said the car's crumpled up like a tin can. It's a four-hundred-foot drop onto sheer rock. The driver's head is in his lap.Broken neck. Broken back."

We stood around while the medics tried to calm the man and the sheriffs began to fill out forms. The other CHP officer opened one lane to traffic, waving the cars past the smoldering flares.

"Let's go, guys," Captain Tucker said. "Nothing left for us to do here." He nodded to the Iowa Hill crew as he got into the engine.

It was all so matter-of-fact. Our daily routine had been briefly interrupted by the loss of a life. A man had sailed off the road in a car. One minute everything was normal, the next minute someone was wiped off the face of the earth. A sudden transition from life to death had happened here on Yankee Jim Road an hour ago. Now we were headed back to Colfax to resume our schedule, sharpen our tools and clean our engine. Everything would be as it was earlier, except that some guy we didn't know and never saw was lying dead, crumpled in a Jaguar, hanging on the side of a canyon. "That poor bastard," I said to Ray.

During my 23 weeks as a seasonal, I rode in the back of the engine with Ray Hibbert to nine wildland fires, five structure fires, six vehicle incidents including an overturned cement truck and several cases of shortness of breath. There were no train wrecks. The wildland fires in our area were minor and I was never away more than two days. The B-crew went down to Riverside County to battle a major blaze that lasted 15 days. Ray went with them while I remained at the station for two weeks and worked overtime. The incident on Yankee Jim was the most significant event for me. I wondered about the brother who survived.

My last paycheck came on Wednesday before Thanksgiving and I hung around for the dinner at the station. Captain Tucker's wife prepared a turkey at home and brought it over to us on Thursday afternoon. Ray and I and Tom Bancroft from the B-crew prepared salad, mashed potatoes and baked zucchini from Ray's garden. We bought a pumpkin pie in town.

After dinner, I said goodbye to everyone. David Ramirez was the only person in the group I would count as a possible firefighter friend. "Let me know how you're doing," he said. "I'll probably see you on a fireline somewhere."

Captain Tucker wished me good luck and said, "You can always come back next summer if you're not happy with L.A. County."

I knew that wouldn't happen.

Ray and I shook hands. He didn't look me in the eye, but I knocked him on the shoulder and said, "Take care of yourself, Ray."

"Likewise," he said.

Mom, Dad and Vicky would be finished with dinner at home by now. The evening air in Saginaw would have an early winter chill and if the sky were clear, the stars would give off a cold hard light. I went out to Captain Tucker's office to use the phone.

"Hello, hi Dad, it's…Dad…hello?"

SIX
Saginaw, Michigan

IN MICHIGAN, KIDS STARTED SKATING as soon as they could walk. Eight-year-olds played organized hockey games on the frozen ponds, lakes and outdoor rinks in Saginaw. I was bigger than others my age and my size helped me on the ice. I don't know where it came from, but everyone said I was a natural. I loved the game. The ice was hard and unforgiving, like my father. I could go up against it and cut into it with my skates.

By fourth grade, I played with skaters in the Squirt category and when I turned eleven, I skated with the Pee Wees. At first, my father encouraged me to play. He said it was macho and that it would toughen me up. When I started Pee Wee, he came to a few of the early games. I thought he liked standing around with the other fathers. They slapped each other on the back and bragged about their sons. I felt good when I saw him standing behind the glass. Hockey was one of the few things I excelled at and I thought I had achieved something that made him proud of me. It didn't last long. After a couple of months, he lost interest and stopped coming to watch me and Mom had to pick me up after the practices and games.

The month before my 14th birthday, things got serious in the hockey department. I had developed into a strong left wing and the Bantam Division of the Saginaw Blades invited me for a tryout. The Blades, with their blue and orange uniforms, were part of the Little Caesar's Amateur Hockey League sponsored by the City of Saginaw. They were a "travel" team, which meant they competed against other teams in cities around Michigan. Anyone who could skate would kill to play for the Blades. I had a real Detroit Red Wings practice jersey, which I wore sometimes even though it was too big for me, but if I could wear my own Blades jersey, the winged wheel would never come out of my drawer again.

Saturday, the day of the tryouts, Mom took me to the Saginaw rink. It was an old building. Inside it had hard plywood seats, but that didn't keep spectators from coming to the Blades' games. "Good luck hon—do your best," she said, as I hauled my hockey gear out of the back seat of her Taurus. "Your father'll come by and pick you up after lunch."

I had been on the ice at the Saginaw rink a few times, but never imagined that someday I might skate for the Blades. At least 100 kids came out that morning. I had skated on teams with some and played against others. The tryouts were seeded and the better players skated first. The coaches stood around the rink, pressed against the glass watching us. I skated in the second group and was finished by 10 a.m. Mr. Carlson, my Pee Wee coach, flashed the thumbs up to me when I came off the ice. "Nice job, Greg," he shouted.

"A piece of cake," I yelled back. I felt happy, confident of my skating. I was always up for a physical challenge. I sat around and watched the other kids and waited. By noon, the ones on the ice weren't any good, and they knew they wouldn't make it. A truck delivered pizza and soda and we stuffed ourselves while we waited for the team selections.

"Ladies and gentlemen," the voice from the loudspeaker echoed through the building. "The City of Saginaw thanks you for your support of amateur hockey and our own Blades team. We had many good skaters here today, more than we could select. Thanks to everyone for participating." I held my breath. At that moment, nothing was more important than being picked for the Blades. "Starting with the Bantam selections," the announcer said, "we have the following players: David Peterson; John Buska; Greg Kowalski…"

We screamed, jumped on the ice and skated around, arms held high, waving our hockey sticks. We skated around the net, we skated backward, arms linked, to the blue line. A center from my Pee Wee team, Renni Braun also made the cut. We gave each other high-fives. Renni whacked me on my shoulder pads with his stick. It was a great moment and it was happening to me. Nearly all the parents had spent the morning at the rink watching and waiting for the results. As more names were read, some rushed forward to congratulate their sons, while others stood silent in disappointment. My father was nowhere in sight and I began to wonder if he had forgotten to pick me up.

Mr. Wilson, the Bantam coach, came over to shake my hand. "Great to have you on the team, Greg," he said. "I've seen you skate, you're good." The praise kept coming. I felt so happy. "Where are your folks?" Coach Wilson asked. "I need some signatures and a check."

"A check?"

"For the expenses."

"What kind of expenses?"

"It's two thousand dollars a year, plus the cost of overnight travel."

"Two thousand dollars?" I said. It might as well have been two million. No one had mentioned expenses. The excitement of the day drained away and I began to feel sick to my stomach. While the other parents signed papers and talked to the coaches and officials, I skated around by myself and waited for my father. The chill from the ice crept up my legs into my chest.

He arrived a half hour later, came down to the edge of the rink and said, "Let's go."

"I made the team, Dad," I said, standing on the ice. "I'm on the Saginaw city team. You have to talk to Coach Wilson. They want some money."

"Money, for what?" my father said.

"To play on the team."

"They want money? They should pay us."

"Dad, I have to play."

"How much do they want?"

I stepped off the ice. Unsteady on my skates on the rubber mat, I clutched my father's arm, but he pulled away. "They want two thousand dollars," I said.

My father looked at me and laughed. "Get your skates off." He went over to Coach Wilson, who was talking to a group of parents. "Are you out of your mind?" my father said, interrupting the coach. "Who has two thousand bucks to pay for a thirteen-year-old to play hockey?"

Coach Wilson was caught off guard. "Mr. Kowalski? We—"

"Forget it," my father said, "We don't have two thousand dollars for this bullshit." He turned to me. "Let's go, Greg." He started toward the exit.

"Dad!" I screamed.

When we got home, my father refused to talk about the hockey money and told my mother, "Keep your damn mouth shut," whenever she tried to discuss it with him.

Renni called and wanted to know if I could come over to his house after dinner for a celebration with some of the other guys. I told him no. "What's wrong, Greg—you don't sound so good," he said.

"We don't have the money," I said, "I won't be playing." Renni started asking questions and arguing, as though I were the one who had made the decision. I hung up. He may have called back later; I was in my room slapping the bed with my hockey stick and thought I heard the telephone ringing.

While the other guys celebrated and dreamed about playoff games, I spent most of the weekend thinking about how much I hated my father and imagining ways I could punish him.

On Monday, Coach Wilson came to school to talk to me. "Greg, I've got the money for you," he said. "The scholarship fund will contribute a thousand dollars, and Darren Hansen's father will pay the rest. We want you on the team."

"Who's Darren Hansen?" I asked.

"He's a substitute. His father owns a stamping plant. They live on Davis Drive next to the Country Club. I convinced him the team has a better chance if you play."

"I can't believe it," I said. Someone else was willing to pay so I could play hockey. Another father had stepped in to help me.

"Tell your mother to come see me," Coach Wilson said. "She can sign you up. I'd prefer not to see your dad."

"Thanks, Coach Wilson."

"You have to call Mr. Hansen and thank him. I'll give you his number." Coach Wilson started to walk away. He turned and said, "Greg, you may not want to tell your father what's going on here. He might get angry."

I couldn't wait to get home and tell Mom I was playing for the Blades.

"We'll just call it a full scholarship and not mention the money from Mr. Hansen," she said. "It'll be our secret."

When my father heard about the scholarship, he said it proved he was right, there was no reason to fork out $2,000 of our own money for me to play hockey.

Zilwaukee School had 350 students from kindergarten through eighth grade. With my new status on the Blades, I hung out with the other jocks, and we were the coolest guys in the school. We swaggered around the halls and no one dared to challenge us. During lunch hour, a crowd of girls circulated around our table saying stupid things and trying to get our attention. After school, some of them hung around, waiting to see if we would stop to talk to them.

At the beginning of the season, the Blades elected Renni and me co-captains of the team. A week before Thanksgiving, one of my teammates crosschecked me during practice. My head hit the ice and I lay unconscious for a few minutes. The paramedics from my father's station answered the call and rushed me to St. Mary's Hospital.

I was on a bed with a curtain around it in the emergency room. I had a concussion, needed four stitches and had chipped my front tooth. My father had to leave work to pick me up. "What happened?" he said.

"I hit the ice."

"Why?"

"I'm not sure. Someone crosschecked me." It was the first time we had even discussed hockey since the day Mom and I told him about my scholarship.

"Did you do anything stupid?"

"I don't know, Dad, I don't remember anything."

"How do you feel?"

"My head hurts."

The ER doctor came to see me before I was released. "Stay in bed for a couple of days," he told me, "and don't skate for at least a week. The stitches can come out in ten days."

"Let's go. I've got to get back to the station," my father said.

I had a terrible headache and felt unsteady as I tried to stand up. They had to wheel me in a chair out through the waiting room. My father said something about insurance and emergency-room treatment I couldn't hear and ignoring the arrow pointing to the patient discharge window, he pushed me through the main doors to his pickup.

I spent a week in bed before my vision cleared up. I never remembered being knocked to the ice.

"Mom, we're eight and two," I said one morning at breakfast. "We're one of the best Bantam teams in the league and we're going to the playoffs."

"That's wonderful," she said. "I'm so proud of you."

"Do you think Dad could come and watch? That would be so great. He hasn't seen me play since I was a Pee Wee."

"I'll talk to him. I'm sure he'll want to come."

We advanced to the final round of the playoffs and my father never showed up. Mom came to all four games and even Vicky came for the semifinal round.

The morning of the championship game against Bay City, Mom drove me over to Zilwaukee School to catch the team bus. When we arrived, most of the team was already there. Duffel bags full of equipment and pads lay in a pile on the cement and three dozen sticks were lined up against the back of the bus. To me, it felt like a Stanley Cup game.

My mother must have been reading my mind as I got out of the car. "Don't worry," she said, "we'll be there before the puck drops. Your dad promised he would come."

We spent the 30-minute bus ride to Bay City trying to outdo each other with descriptions of imagined feats and heroic goals. We were ready to run the Bears off the ice. When we arrived an hour before the game, the parking lot was already filling up. People were standing around outside looking for extra tickets.

The visiting team's locker room was clean and spacious—I had never seen anything like it. We had individual lockers, a blackboard to diagram plays and a trainer's table for taping ankles. "You guys are the best team on the ice," Coach Wilson told us as we stood around him. "We can win this one if everyone does his job." While Coach Wilson discussed final strategy, we heard the Bears through the wall in their dressing room. They were shouting and banging the lockers with their sticks. "Check them at the blue line," Coach Wilson said. "Don't give their wings a free run into our end. First and second lines, I want to see you play your most aggressive game." The coach wrote and underlined "DIG FOR THE PUCK" on the board. "Hit them hard, and dig, dig, dig for the puck," he said. I looked at Renni, Jon Buska, Joey Woodward and some of the others. We were so pumped-up we were about to explode. "The third line will give you some rest, I want to run the Bears ragged, tire them out. We're stronger than they are—we can outlast them." Coach Wilson paused for a moment and then shouted, "Who's the best?"

"The Blades! The Blades!" we shouted and hammered the butts of our sticks against the metal lockers.

This was the first Little Caesar's championship game played at the new Bay City Arena, which featured a suspended four-sided electronic scoreboard, seats with upholstery and special shatterproof glass around the boards. It made the arena in Saginaw look pathetic. When we skated out on the ice to warm up, parents and girlfriends were shouting and cheering. I remembered a movie I saw about gladiators walking out into an arena, looking up at the mob of Romans shouting for blood. The ice was a pool of white light surrounded by ascending rows of spectators shouting for blood. The noise of the crowd echoed in the building. I was a gladiator and I was ready for the kill.

Several of the girls from Zilwaukee were in the fifth row, waving blue and orange Blades scarves. While we skated around, taking shots at our goalie and thumping him on the shin pads, I looked for my parents. I knew where they were supposed to sit, but their seats were empty.

Halfway through the first period, I saw people standing up to let my mom and dad step past. By that time, our team had calmed down and we started to connect with our passes. I was skating on the first line. It was our toughest game and we were evenly matched with the Bears. There was no relief as we went end to end, both teams hitting hard and displaying amazing stick handling. Each time we skated down the ice toward my parents' seats, I looked up at my father, hoping he was watching my coordination and speed. I was sure I was playing the best game of my life because he was watching me.

At the end of the first period, there was no score. We skated off the ice and I looked back to see my father. He was talking to the man sitting next to him. He looked like he was enjoying himself.

We drank water in the locker room and listened to Coach Wilson. "You're doing great," he said. "Don't lose your concentration. Forget about the crowd, focus on the puck." Our goalie, Terry Mead, was having trouble with his pads and the trainer was trying to tighten the belts. I was feeling about as good as I had ever felt during a game.

We went back out on the ice. The Bay City Zamboni had laid down a new coat of ice. It looked like a sheet of glass. In the first minute of the second period, the Bears scored a goal against my line and the announcer shouted "GOOOOAL" over the loudspeaker. I was angry. We weren't organized, we were just skating around and letting them through. When the puck went in, I looked up at my father. I couldn't see his face clearly, but I was certain he was glaring at me. I had let him down.

Two minutes later it was another "GOOOOAL," this time against our second line. I began to feel a sick feeling in my stomach. I wanted to get off the bench and do something.

"Let's go, guys!" Renni shouted as our line came back on the ice.

A Bears defenseman blindsided Renni and smashed him into the glass. He lay on the ice until Coach Wilson and our trainer helped him up. Renni was taken off the ice and I could see he was badly hurt. The Bears took a penalty and we scored a power-play goal in the first 30 seconds. The announcer calmly said, "Goal," but part of the crowd stood up and erupted in cheers. I looked up; my parents were still there.

The Bears came back to full strength and I moved over to replace Renni at center. In the air-conditioned arena, on the cool ice, I was soaked in nervous sweat. The Bears were momentarily confused by the change in positions. I intercepted a pass at the blue line and sailed in alone on the Bears' goalie. My shot went into the upper corner of the net for an unassisted goal and the score was tied. The crowd went crazy and the noise seemed to go on forever. It was the best move I had ever made on the ice. The announcement of the goal was drowned out by the sound from the Saginaw fans. My teammates skated over to give me bear-hugs. Coach Wilson stood up on the bench and flashed a victory sign. I looked up at my father. He wasn't waving, but he was still there. He had seen me do something remarkable.

Between periods, we found out Renni had been taken to the hospital for X-rays on his shoulder. "All right, guys," Coach Wilson said as we skated out for the final 20 minutes, "take control of the play."

"This one's for Renni," I shouted.

In the third period, the crowd never sat down. As both teams desperately tried to get the puck into the net, the shouts of "Blades!" and "Bears!" made it impossible to hear anything on the ice. I was feeling invincible until I went back to the bench and looked up to see my parents were gone. I couldn't believe it. I thought maybe they had gone out to get something to drink, or that my mother had to use the restroom, but they didn't come back. They were gone. I felt numb. The score was tied and we had eight minutes left to play.

John Buska was called for tripping and we took a two-minute penalty with 90 seconds to play. I wasn't on the ice when the Bears scored on a last-minute power play. The announcer didn't hold back. "GOOOOOOOOAL!" he shouted, "GOOOOOOOOAL!" Half the crowd went ballistic, the other half was dead-silent. The Bears skated around with their sticks held high. When that puck went in, all my excitement and enthusiasm drained away. I felt sick to my stomach.

We were unable to do anything as the last seconds faded away and it was over. We lost three to two. I was certain I could have scored if my father had only stayed until the end of the game. We sat on the bench with our heads down as the Bears skated a victory lap around the rink. Then we had to suffer through the traditional line-up for handshakes with the opposing players. Several of the Bears said, "Nice game," or "Way to go." We didn't say much and left the ice while the Bears accepted the trophy.

In the locker room we sat on the benches, still wearing our skates, leaning on our sticks with our heads down. Coach Wilson was disappointed but congratulated everyone and shook our hands. His last words to the team were, "Keep your heads up, men, you can be proud of the way you played. We'll win it all next year."

Second place felt like last place. We rode back to Saginaw in silence. I looked at Darren Hansen. He had managed to get a few minutes on the ice at the end of the second period and probably thought he had a great season.

SEVEN
Malibu, California

I DROVE THROUGH THE SAN JOAQUIN VALLEY under a clear midday sky. Orchards and farms stretched in every direction. At the end of November, the land was green. Oranges, heavy on the trees, bent branches halfway to the ground. In Michigan, the sky would be gray and full of rain, the spring growth still months away. Now that it was over, I felt better about my season with Cal Fire. Maybe my father was wrong—I might have a future as a firefighter.

The traffic on Interstate 5 was light on the day after Thanksgiving. Beyond Bakersfield, a long climb over the mountains in the Los Padres National Forest took me to the top of the Grapevine. I was less than a hundred miles from Los Angeles and even closer to Malibu. I was on the way to "Baywatch," California. My Wrangler wasn't happy; it struggled up the hills, rattled on the way down and tried in every way to tell me it didn't like long trips.

Coming across Malibu Canyon Road in the late afternoon, I covered the remaining miles through winding canyons. At the bottom of a long descent, the road dead-ended at Pacific Coast Highway. On the other side was the ocean, stretching out to an indistinct horizon. The water reflected a dozen shades of blue and silver, seagulls walked in the surf and pelicans flew overhead. I pulled to the side of the road, lowered my window and for the first time, inhaled the mist and salt smell of the Pacific Ocean. After all the pictures on television and all my dreams, it was exactly the way I had imagined it.

Pepperdine University covered the hillside on my right. Houses lined the white beach along Pacific Coast Highway and the surrounding hills and bluffs. For the first time in months, I felt happy. Instead of worrying about what was going on at home, I imagined telling Mom, Vicky, Bobby and my other friends about my first view of Southern California.

I drove south through Malibu, following the directions to Fire Suppression Camp 8 at the top of Las Flores Canyon. I turned off Pacific Coast Highway and my Jeep labored up a five-mile climb to a spot where the top of the mountain had been cut off. Before I saw a sign, I saw one-story structures, red fire vehicles in parking stalls and a huge fire helicopter that looked like a Blackhawk. Up here, the ocean was only a blue triangle visible through the canyon to the west. Higher mountains on three sides of the fire camp reflected the setting sun, showing red, gray and white rock under patches of green vegetation.

A windsock, communications antennae and a water tank with the L.A. County Fire Department insignia covered a hill by the entrance to the camp. I parked under a flagpole flying the American flag and the flag of the California Republic with the grizzly bear in the center. A 6-foot-high image of a rattlesnake curled into a figure eight, with the words "Air Attack – Camp 8," was painted on the side of the nearest building.

As I got out of the Jeep, a firefighter walked out of one of the buildings, hands in the pockets of his blue jacket, collar turned up against the cool late afternoon air. "Can I help you?" he asked. The name "Bratton" was stitched on the jacket. He was the camp superintendent.

"Captain Bratton, hi, I'm Greg Kowalski. I'm one of the new Fire Suppression Aides."

"Hello, Greg." He stepped forward to shake hands. He was average-sized, but seemed to move with an air of authority and confidence. His blue-green eyes considered me. "Don't get ahead of yourself," he said. "You're not an FSA yet. There's a few formalities and you still have to survive a four-week training camp." An old white boxer-mix with black jowls, an under-slung jaw and red-rimmed eyes ran out and wagged a stubby tail. A smaller brown mutt stood a few feet back. "Camp security," Captain Bratton said, looking at the dogs. "You're early—things don't start until Sunday evening."

"Yes sir, I know. I thought I would check things out and find a place to stay."

"You spent the season with Cal Fire, right?"

"Near Sacramento."

"Your background check isn't complete yet, but we've confirmed you're not a psychopath."

"No, sir."

"It's good to have guys with experience. We've got two coming in from the Forest Service."

"How many all together?"

"Including the three of you, twenty-four. Half'll wash out before the academy's over. We'll take two or three; La Cañada and Camp 9 will each take three or four."

"I got some good experience this year," I said. I didn't mention learning to cook squirrel head and eggs.

"There's still plenty to learn," the Captain said. "Are you in good shape? Most of the guys say this is the hardest work they've ever done. We had a Marine drill sergeant drop out last year."

"They worked us hard at Cal Fire. I carried a lot of fire hose."

"The name used to be California Department of Forestry and Fire Protection – CDF. That name was better because of the jokes. You know what we called CDF?"

"No, sir."

"Can't Do Fire." He smiled and bent down to pet the white boxer. Cooley would be pissed if he heard that; he might even lose his temper. "So, you need a place to stay for the weekend?" the Captain asked.

"Yes, sir."

While we talked, another man joined us. He was the first firefighter I had seen with both names on his clothes—Jerry Dunham. "This is Mr. Dunham," the Captain said. "He's one of the engineers here. He'll set you up for tonight. Jerry, this is Greg Kowalski. Greg's the one from Cal Fire. He needs a bed." Captain Bratton shook my hand again. "See you Sunday, Greg."

"Thank you, sir." I heard the engines of the helicopter rumble and watched it lift off from behind the buildings, gain altitude and disappear over the mountains. "Where's the helicopter going?" I asked.

"The Blackhawk?" Jerry Dunham said. "We call it the 'Bird.' It's headed back to the base in Pacoima. County has three and they're sent out every morning for fire response; one comes here."

"How often do you use it?"

"There's a lot of emergency medical response calls. If it's a fire, it depends on where it is. There's a lot of valuable real estate out here. We had a fire down on Malibu Road last October. The Bird dropped our crew on the ground twelve minutes after we got the call."

"It must be awesome flying to a fire in a helicopter," I said.

"Sometimes we take crew trucks if the fire's in the hills around here," Jerry Dunham said. "When we fly, we're Crew Eight-One; when we're on the ground, we're Crew Eight-Two."

"Eight-One sounds good to me," I said.

"By the way," Jerry Dunham said, "Did you ever hear the joke about CDF?"

"Sure, Can't Do—"

"It stands for the three worst grades you can get in high school." He smiled at me. "C'mon, I'll give you a quick tour. Know anything about this place?"

"No."

"It was a Nike launch facility, built in the fifties."

"What's a Nike launch facility?"

"Underground bunkers up here held Nike anti-aircraft missiles during the Cold War."

"The only Nike I ever heard of is the shoe."

"It was part of what they called the 'Ring of Fire' around Los Angeles. We still use one of the vaults for our woodworking shop; it has five-foot thick cement walls and a huge hydraulic lift. They used it to raise missiles; we use it to lower plywood."

"How long has Camp 8 been here?"

"Since '74. The missiles were removed and the Feds gave the facility to the county for a fire camp." We walked out onto a cement pad. "This is the 'Grinder.' You'll work your butt off here every morning. We start every morning with stretching and calisthenics." He pointed to the building where Captain Bratton had emerged. "That's the cap's office, meeting room and administrative area. The building in front of you is the mess hall and kitchen. On the left is where we sleep. We've got a weight room and a TV and rec room in there too. If you're on duty, those rooms are off limits until eight in the evening."

I looked at the three single story cinderblock buildings, each surrounded by planters. In the fading light, I could still see red, orange and purple flowers as well as ferns and other plants I had never seen before, growing around the buildings. Palm trees were everywhere. At one end of the Grinder, a fountain sprayed water into a pond. I couldn't believe this was a fire facility. I had seen worse-looking motels.

The white boxer and the brown mutt appeared out of the shadows and ran up to Jerry Dunham. "It's too dark now to see Disneyland," he said. "It's just beyond the helipad. It's our smoke facility and obstacle course."

I followed him to the middle building. The dogs accompanied us but stopped at the door. "They have the run of the camp but they're not allowed in here," he said.

"I love dogs. What are their names?" I asked.

"The boxer is Duke. He was found out on the Vegas highway by a film director who lives in Malibu. He gave him to the camp. The other one is Sadie. She lives part time at a house up the street. They chase the coyotes away at night."

"We had wolves in Michigan."

"The coyotes aren't really a threat. They just get into the trash and sometimes kill cats. It's the rattlesnakes you have to watch out for. Western Diamondbacks."

"I've never seen one."

"You'll hear it before you see it. They're aggressive and they like heat. In the early morning they'll be out on the rocks and the blacktop soaking up the sun." We went inside. "This is where the FSAs sleep when they're on duty." He pointed down a long hallway of doors. "If you sign a Stay Over Agreement, you can spend the night here when you're off duty." He knocked and opened the first door. I saw two beds, simple wood bureaus, a desk, and two surfboards in silver cases reaching almost to the ceiling. A black Body Glove wetsuit hung from the outside of a closet door. The room was a mess. The beds were unmade, the covers and a pillow were lying on the floor and the desk was covered with newspapers, magazines, paper cups and a half-eaten energy bar. "Welcome to the Bay of Pigs," Jerry Dunham said. "That's what we call it because it's such a mess." We walked to the end of the hall to see the showers and a latrine. It looked like a military barracks I had seen in a war movie.

"Where do you want me to sleep?" I asked him.

"For the next two nights you can share a room with Jake Mangan. He's staying here full time while he looks for a new apartment. Sunday night, when you become an FNG, I'll put you in the dorm with everyone else. We're still setting it up."

"What's an FNG?"

"A Fucking New Guy. That's what you are during the academy. If you make it through, you're just a New Guy for the next year. You'll have special duties around the camp your rookie year."

"Like an initiation?"

"Yeah, an initiation. You want to have dinner with us?" I know Jake's around, and Hector and maybe Art."

"Sure, I can always eat."

"Art's a guy you can learn a lot from. He's been in the camp seven years and he's a crew leader." We walked to the mess hall in the early evening light. "He just finished swift-water rescue training and he's getting ready to move on."

"This place sure isn't like a station," I said. "Nothing like what I saw at Cal Fire, either."

"No, the camps are special. You'll learn the routine once you become part of the family. We're a brotherhood. We do a lot together and we take care of each other, especially at fires."

Another promise of another family. "How long do guys stay in the camp?" I asked.

"At some point, everyone moves on. They move up to other jobs in County Fire, or they join some other fire department. We just lost one of our FSAs to Culver City. Hector's the only one who isn't going anywhere. He's 38 and this is as far as he wants to go. C'mon let's eat."

The sign on the mess-hall door told everyone to "SUCK IT UP – NO EXCUSES." I hadn't eaten lunch and the smell of food cooking made my mouth water. At one end of the mess hall was a kitchen area with a large stainless steel stove, a refrigerator, an old sink and a couple of counters covered with wood chopping blocks. Two dozen large metal pots and pans hung from hooks. I saw a door to a walk-in freezer and an open food pantry bigger than my bedroom in Saginaw. The shelves were filled with cans, bottles and cartons of food. Cases of Gatorade were stacked to the ceiling.

Three rectangular folding tables each had space for eight. One entire wall was covered with a glass case filled with pictures of wildfires, engines, helicopters, crews in full gear, volleyball teams in shorts, various dogs including Duke and Sadie, a single firefighter surrounded by a black border and in the center, a black circle with a white rattlesnake coiled in the shape of an eight.

Following Jerry Dunham, I took a paper plate and some silverware from a tray. I ladled peas from a big stainless steel pot. A second pot had baked beans; the third had overcooked barbeque ribs. Large bowls of salad and peach halves in syrup finished the dinner. A pot of barbeque sauce sat on the table along with plastic jugs with various juices and every kind of ketchup, mustard and sauce. "The food's pretty good here," Jerry Dunham said. "We have twenty or more at a meal, so we order from institutional restaurant suppliers. When you order peas, you get a five-gallon container." The camp intercom erupted in static and his name was called. "Excuse me," he said. He grabbed a rib and left his plate on the counter.

I sat down across from three other guys at a table.

"You a New Guy?"

"I hope so. I'm Greg Kowalski." I stuck out my hand.

"How are ya? I'm Jake Mangan." Although the evening was cool, Jake wore a blue short sleeve Camp 8 – Air Attack T-shirt and blue cotton pants. His chest and arms showed a lot of muscle. On his bicep, he had a tattoo of a flame inked in red and outlined in blue. His face was rugged and he had thick blond hair. He shook my hand with a strong grip. I pictured him in a supporting role on *Baywatch*. "This is Hector Wells. He's our Indian. And this is Art Victor," Jake said.

"Native American, Jake," Hector said. "How you doin'?" Hector had dark eyes and skin, black hair going gray and he was wearing a blue sweatshirt with a hood hanging down in back. Hector didn't stop eating and didn't bother to shake hands.

"Hey Greg," Art said as we shook hands. Even at the end of November, everyone had a deep tan. Art had white stripes across his temples from his sunglasses.

"Where you from?" Jake asked.

"Michigan."

"Oh yeah?" he said. "I have a cousin who lives in Detroit. Got any fire experience?"

"Six months with Cal Fire."

"My dad was a CDF Captain in Riverside," Jake said. "He did search and rescue for years."

"I saw the CHP Search and Rescue in action this summer," I said.

"He loved those old Super Hueys," Jake said. "He said the best time in his life was when they lowered him down on a cable from a hovering helicopter."

"What's he doing now?" I asked Jake.

"He died of cancer two years ago."

"Sorry to hear that. My dad's a city firefighter in Saginaw."

"Appreciate him while he's alive," Jake said.

"He's a prick. He's so mean, he'll live forever."

Art reached for one of the toothpicks in a paper cup on the table. He turned it between his fingers, inspecting it carefully before peeling off the cellophane.

"When my dad died, I went out and got this." Jake pointed to his arm.

"That's some tattoo," I said.

"Wait till you see the tattoos on the women down the road," Jake said.

"The women down the road?"

"The inmates at Camp 13," Art said. "It's a county fire camp for female prisoners."

"The foremen carry escape cards," Jake said. "Each card has a picture of an inmate and a complete physical description, including tattoos."

"That's cool," I said.

"What's cool," Jake said, "are the descriptions of the tattoos and where they are. If I were a female inmate, this flame would be on my pussy." Jake flexed his bicep.

"That's not your pussy?" Hector asked.

"I think I'm gonna share your room until Sunday night," I said to Jake. "That's what Jerry told me."

"It's Mr. Dunham," Art said. "And the other engineer is David Mendoza. He's Mr. Mendoza to you, even though we call him Dozer."

Jake smiled. "Get used to it—that's the way it is until the academy is over."

"Mr. Dunham," I repeated.

"Have you got a lot of stuff?" Jake said.

"Everything I own is in the back of my Jeep."

"I broke up with my girlfriend," Jake said. "I'm looking for a new place. Something cheap. I need someone to share the rent. If you make it through the month and you're interested, we could talk about it."

"What would it cost?" I asked Jake.

"Furnished, it could run seven or eight hundred a month, each."

"I'd have to think about that."

"You've got to have a place," Jake said. "What if you have a girlfriend? You can't bring her here. You live here five days a week and get your food and clothing for nothing. By the end of the year, with overtime you'll bring in at least three grand a month. You can swing it."

Three thousand dollars a month was twice what I was paid as a seasonal. I wondered how much money my father earned.

"No one can live here full time," Jake said, "except maybe Hector. Right, Hector?"

Hector chewed on a rib.

"Wells doesn't sound like an Indian name," I said to Hector.

"Hector's a 'Cur Darlene,'" Jake said. "He went off the reservation and came to live in Southern California."

"A what?" I asked.

Hector put the rib bone down on his plate. "My father was a full-blooded Coeur d'Alene. I grew up in Kootenai County, Idaho."

"We have the Chippewa tribe in Saginaw," I said. "They have animal and bird names. I went to school with some kids whose last name was Brave Bear Hunter." They were strange people—a total mystery. I never understood what they were talking about.

"My father's last name was Wildshoe," Hector said. "He was a blackjack dealer at the casino in Worley."

"So how come your last name is Wells?" I asked.

"After he drank himself to death, my mother moved our family to Spokane. I'm only half Native American—her name was Wells—and that's the name I use."

"Why would you give up your father's name?"

"It was easier than Wildshoe," Hector said without elaboration.

"How long have you been a firefighter?" I asked him.

"Since they invented fire," Jake said.

"I was in the Forest Service for six years," Hector said. "Before that, I worked on BLM and National Park Service handcrews. We worked on the Indian Trust Lands up in Idaho. We had lightning fires twice a week."

"There's a lot of American Indians on the wildland crews up North," Art said.

"The families depend on the seasonal firefighting work," Hector said. "There aren't that many jobs on the reservations."

Hector was 38 and his only home was a room in the Bay of Pigs. He didn't have a father, had given up his last name and was 1,000 miles from his tribe. He was rootless. Jake's offer to share an apartment sounded better. I didn't want to end up like Hector. "Sure, " I told Jake, "if you find a place, let me know."

"You been on a helicopter?" Art asked me. "Do you like flying?"

"I've never been on a helicopter or an airplane," I said.

"Well," Art said, "we spend plenty of time getting on and off helicopters. It gets the adrenaline going. We do canyon insertions, one-skid landings, hover-jumps, stuff like that."

"I've seen guys jumping out of helicopters in Vietnam movies," I said.

"Wait till you're standing on top of a mountain," Art said, "and you have to unload tools from the tail of a copter hovering two feet off the ground. We've got some damn good pilots."

"How many here have been to college?" I asked.

"We've got one college boy in our crew," Art said. "Red Eye. He attended Cal State Dominguez Hills for a year. You?"

"No," I said, "just high school in Saginaw."

Art went on, "Red Eye didn't like Cal State, he always wanted to be a firefighter."

"Let me guess why he's called Red Eye," I said. "My dad's eyes were always red from smoke irritation."

"I don't know where the name came from," said Art, "but he's black and his real name is Shawn Rhoze. Don't go calling him Shawn. He'll get pissed."

"You look like you're what, six-foot?" Jake said to me.

"Six-one."

"You play volleyball?"

"No, hockey."

"Hockey? Forget it, this is a desert," Jake said. "We play volleyball on Sunday afternoons at the beach. We wash the trucks in the morning and if nothing else is going on, we get down to the beach around two. You been to the beach yet?"

"Just what I saw coming down Pacific Coast Highway."

"It's called 'PCH.' You'll be good at the net. We need tall guys. Except Hector. He's useless. Right Hector?"

Hector stared at Jake.

Jerry Dunham didn't come back to dinner. When we finished eating, Art dumped the paper plates into the trash and put the glasses and silverware into an old dishwasher. Jake threw me a cloth. "You might as well get started. We wipe down the tables, the counters and the stove. The food and drinks go back in the refrigerator, then we sweep up the kitchen."

"We did this at Cal Fire," I said. "I've got the wiping down to a science."

EIGHT
Saginaw, Michigan

I THOUGHT ABOUT LEAVING HOME all the time. Living with my father was wearing me down. It had to come to an end. The shouting, the threats, the physical punishment—the constant fear I had done something wrong and the knowledge I couldn't do anything right. It went on month after month. When I was younger, I imagined running away, hitchhiking or jumping on a train, but I never had a destination. By the time I was a teenager, my dreams of escape focused on California. The West Coast looked great on television. Baywatch was my favorite program even though I wasn't much of a swimmer. I imagined working as a lifeguard and living near the ocean. I would give up hockey, wear shorts and get a suntan.

By the time I was a senior at Saginaw High, my life was coming to a dead-end. I didn't play hockey my last year. Even though I loved the game, I didn't have the heart; it just seemed like too much trouble. Coach Wilson and Renni came to talk to me, but I wasn't interested. I felt like I was sinking in quicksand. I couldn't move. The only positive thing about my last year was Kirsten, a good-looking junior I started seeing at the beginning of the year. She must have really liked me, because she went out with me even though I wasn't a big jock anymore.

I had to decide what I was going to do at the end of the school year but had no clue. My grades were decent, but I was no genius. No one in our family had gone beyond high school. Our teachers urged us to continue our educations and some of my classmates began to apply to college—to the University of Michigan or Michigan State. Several planned to go to junior college, while others intended to enlist. Bobby Eccles joined the Marines. Saginaw Beauty

Academy was a popular choice for the girls. I didn't know what to do. I couldn't see myself going to college. We didn't discuss my future at home. My father told me to get a job, but didn't offer any ideas or assistance. My mother suggested I talk to the guidance counselor at school. I drifted through my senior year until I got some unexpected help in December.

Each year the Saginaw Fire Department had a Christmas dinner for the crews and their families. My father never missed a chance to be with his "team," and Mom, Vicky and I were overjoyed to attend. It was a chance to go out somewhere and have fun, confident my father wouldn't lose his temper and start shouting at one of us. It was one of the few things the Kowalskis did together, which meant we all arrived in the same car.

At the Christmas party, my father was always in a good humor, even cracking jokes. He was a different person, relaxed and happy. The firefighters at the station seemed to like him; he was one of the boys. I couldn't understand how he could be so nice to everyone around him and be so mean to us. After the party, he went out with his friends and by the time he came home he was drunk. Then he was the person we knew.

As long as I can remember, a framed poster of a firefighter hung near the front door of the station. The guy wore a turnout jacket, yellow Nomex pants, boots and goggles up on his helmet. His face was covered with soot except around his eyes. He was reaching out. I was a little boy the first time I saw the picture and I looked closely to see if it was my father. It wasn't, but for years, I imagined that it was and that he was reaching out for me. For a while it was my favorite image. Each year at the Christmas party I stood gazing up at it and it seemed the firefighter was looking directly at me. As I grew older, I began to hate the poster. It wasn't my father. My father never reached out to hold me. The poster was a fake. I began to avoid looking at it and hurried past it with my eyes on the floor.

The wives of the Saginaw firefighters all knew each other. They had a bowling team and a book club and once a year organized a fundraiser at the station. My father didn't want my mother wasting time with the other wives and he wouldn't let her attend any of the events. She did manage to bake a cake or cookies each year, but my father delivered everything to the fundraiser himself. At the Christmas party, my mother didn't know anyone except Vicky and me.

I looked forward to seeing Mike Bentak, my father's captain. Mike never missed a chance to talk to me. Whenever he saw me, he wanted to know how I was getting along and asked about the hockey team. He seemed to know that my life at home wasn't happy and tried to encourage me.

The year I was a senior, we were late to the Christmas party because my father was unhappy with Vicky's choice of clothes. My mother had helped Vicky choose a dress which she said looked festive, but my father said, "You look like a 15-year-old slut," when he saw it. We had to wait while Vicky went upstairs in tears to change. When we arrived, everyone was already in the meeting hall eating turkey and listening to Christmas carols played over the public address system.

When an ice-cream cake dessert came, my father went outside with some of his friends to smoke cigars and Mike Bentak pulled me aside. "Greg," he said, "what are you planning to do after graduation?"

"I'm still working on it, Mike, I really don't know."

"What would you think about becoming a firefighter?" he asked.

A firefighter. It was an unexpected question. "I've thought about it, Mike. I asked dad a couple of times, but he never encouraged me."

"I don't know if your Dad likes being a firefighter," Mike said. "Most of us live to go to fires. I'm not sure what motivates him."

"He'd probably be really proud if I became a firefighter."

"Well, I've got an idea," Mike said. "How old will you be in June?"

"Nineteen."

"Great, that's a year over the minimum age." He reached into his jacket and handed me an envelope. "If you're interested, here's an application for the wildfire training program at Cal Fire. It's a six-month seasonal job in California."

California! Mike's idea was a complete surprise and I was thrilled. I didn't know what to say.

"You can do this," Mike said. "It takes physical work and the ability to handle emergencies."

"Like a hockey game," I said.

"You'll be out in the boondocks—not a lot of people."

"It's OK, Mike." I felt deserted most of the time anyway.

"My sister's married to a Cal Fire man in Sacramento. Wait about three days so I can tell them the application's coming, then send it to this address.

Indicate your father's a firefighter—that'll help." Mike winked at me. "Let's see if we can make a battalion chief out of you."

"Mike, this is incredible, thanks."

"Don't say anything to your old man until you hear from them, OK?"

"He'll be proud of me when I tell him, Mike."

"He's touchy. We don't want him screwing things up."

My Christmas gift from Mike Bentak was a chance to escape from home and do something that would please my father. I couldn't get over the fact that Mike had done this for me and I wasn't even his son. If Mike had been my father, my life would have been so much different. I couldn't even imagine all the things we would have done together.

For weeks, I checked the mailbox as soon as I got home from school. If the mail hadn't been delivered, I found excuses to stay near the front door or out in the yard. In early March, I found a letter buried in our junk mail from the State of California, Department of Forestry and Fire Protection in Sacramento. It was a thick envelope and I prayed that was a good sign. My hands shook as I tore it open and pulled out a packet of papers. A letter addressed to me offered a seasonal firefighter's job. No personal interview was required because I was in Michigan, but I had to pass a physical. They wanted me in Auburn, California by May 31, to train to be a wildland firefighter. Where was Auburn? I had never heard of Auburn.

The next morning, after my father left for the station, I waited for my mother to come down to the kitchen. She had become quieter as she got older. Over the years, her brown hair had turned mostly to gray. Her face was wrinkled and she had dark circles under her eyes. When she was younger, she was a tall, strong woman but now she seemed smaller, shrunken. She hardly spoke to my father and didn't even say much to Vicky or to me. It had been years since she stepped in to protect us from my father's outbursts. Mom was disappearing into herself. On days when Dad was home, she stayed in the bedroom the entire day with the door shut. She wouldn't come down to the kitchen until he left the house. For years, she had carefully polished his badge and the brass buttons on his dress uniform, but those days were past. He complained because she wasn't making breakfast for him anymore, but it didn't seem to matter. She looked tired and complained of being unable to sleep. When she did sleep, she said she had terrible nightmares.

The morning I waited to talk to her, she came downstairs at 9:30 a.m. and made her morning drink of coffee with half-and-half and sugar in her favorite mug. With an expressionless face, she sat down at the table.

"Mom," I said, "I'm in. I'm going to California, the end of May."

"You're *in?* In what?" she asked. She looked at me with tired eyes.

"I'm in the State of California wildfire training program. I have a job as a firefighter."

Her eyebrows went up. "You've got a job in California?"

"Mike Bentak helped me. He knows somebody at the Forestry Department."

"Mike Bentak!" my mother said. "Is that what was going on at the Christmas party? Your father will kill him."

"Mike's his captain Mom. Besides, Dad doesn't even have to know he was involved."

"You know how your father is, when he finds out he'll be angry and take it out on someone. If he can't give Mike hell, I'll end up hearing about it. It'll be my fault, like everything else."

I wondered why my mother always acted this way. She thought everything was her fault. "This has nothing to do with you, Mom. This is my idea. It's my plan." When the idea of going to California first came up, I thought my father would be pleased, but now I realized Mike was right; Dad was going to be angry, which was his response to everything and he'd probably screw things up.

"You're serious about this?" Mom said.

"California is offering me a job as a firefighter."

"Where are you going?"

"Auburn."

"Where?"

"It's near Sacramento. All I have to do is show up in Sacramento."

"How do you plan to get there?"

"Greyhound." I felt like dancing around the kitchen. "Californ-i-a here I come." I didn't tell her it took almost three days and the bus made 42 stops.

Vicky came in, went to the cupboard and took out the Frosted Flakes. "What about California?" she asked.

Vicky must have been listening to my conversation with Mom from the other room and came in to hear more. My mother sipped her coffee and said,

"Vicky, Greg and I have things to discuss, take your cereal into the living room."
My mother turned to me. "Do you have any money? Who's paying for this?"

"It costs a hundred eighty dollars to get there. I've got some money saved. I'll have enough left to get by out there for a few days. I don't expect any help from Dad."

"Do you actually have a job?"

"No, but I'll be hired when I get there. It's like a football training camp. You live there while you learn to be a firefighter." I let this sink in for a moment. "What do you think?"

"This is so sudden," she said. "I always knew someday it would be time for you to leave, but I didn't think you would go all the way to California. I imagined you somewhere nearby." She took a deep breath and blew it out. "Will you miss graduation?"

"No. I leave on the twentieth."

"What about Kirsten?"

"What about her?"

"What does she think?"

"I haven't told her."

"You haven't told her? Isn't she going to be upset?"

"She'll get over it. I'll tell her before I leave."

My mother exploded. "Greg, you're growing up to be just like your father. She's your girlfriend! You're leaving for California and you haven't told her? Don't you think you owe her that?"

"It's no big deal, Mom, she'll get over it."

"You don't even care about Kirsten."

"Sure I do, Mom, I—"

"Have you slept with her?"

"C'mon Mom."

"Have you?"

"Maybe."

"Is she going to come around here after you're gone and tell us she's pregnant?"

"Jesus, Mom."

"You know that's why I married your father. Because I was pregnant with you. I thought he loved me. I found out he only loves himself."

My mind raced. *I was an accident! My parents didn't want me.*

"Well, I guess this takes care of what you're doing next year," my mother said. "Go ahead, it's time for you to leave. But you tell your father, don't expect me to do it for you." She rubbed her eyes and went back to her coffee and newspaper.

Vicky came back into the kitchen and put her bowl of half-eaten cereal in the sink on top of the pile of last night's dirty dishes. I was sure she heard everything Mom said.

"Greg—" Vicky started to say.

"Mind your own business," I told her. "You don't say a thing to Dad about this."

"You're going to California?"

Later that week, I told Bobby Eccles what my mother had said about marrying my father. "I was an accident. They didn't really want me."

"It's no big deal," he replied. "Who cares if your mother was pregnant before she got married? People in Hollywood do it all the time, sometimes they never get married. No one cares."

"I care. My parents didn't want me. I was a mistake."

"That's bullshit."

"If they were married to other people, they'd be happier."

"That's crazy talk, Greggie," Bobby said. "If your mother didn't get pregnant, you wouldn't be here."

"Maybe that would have been better for everyone. And don't call me 'Greggie,' that's what my father called me when I was a kid."

"Man, you're weird."

The day came when I told my father about California. I had rehearsed and imagined so many conversations with him that the words no longer meant anything. Late one afternoon, he came in through the garage and dropped his pack on the kitchen floor. He looked exhausted, his face blackened by soot. He had come directly from a fire and had that burning odor firefighters sometimes bring with them. Mom was bent over the stove making mac and cheese. He looked at it and said, "I've been at work for forty-eight hours and risked my life today. The least you could do is have a decent dinner ready."

She didn't say anything and wouldn't look at either one of us.

I knew it was the wrong time to talk about going to California, but I thought I might never find the courage again. I had to tell him at that moment. My stomach had ached all day in anticipation of the conversation and now I didn't know if I could even speak. Vicky sensed something bad was about to happen and left the kitchen.

"Dad," I said.

My father turned to me. "What?"

My mind emptied. I forgot everything I planned to say. "Dad," I blurted out, "I'm gonna be a firefighter. In California."

"A firefighter?" His face didn't change. He stood there for a moment and stared at me with his red eyes. I wondered if he was going to hit me. He pulled out a chair, sat at the table, leaned back on two legs and said, "You, a firefighter? In California. You've got to be kidding."

"No, it's true. I'm gonna be a firefighter."

"Well, at least I'm finally getting rid of you, you pain-in-the-ass. When you go, take everything you need because you're not coming back."

NINE
Malibu, California

D AY ONE. EVENING. Camp 8 Academy Orientation.
On Sunday evening I met some of the other new recruits. We sat
around in the empty mess hall after dinner waiting for our orientation meeting.
Harris said he was a longshoreman. Fowler, who came down from Northern
California, told me he had worked for the Forest Service. Several had construc-
tion jobs. One worked in a grocery store.

At 7 p.m., we went to the classroom. I felt jittery, the way I did before a
hockey game. Someone sat down next to me and extended a hand. "I'm Luis."

"Greg Kowalski."

"Nice to meet you."

"Likewise. What's your last name?"

"Zambrano."

Twenty-two of us sat and waited. The door opened. Duke and Sadie came
charging into the classroom, followed by Captain Bratton. "Evening, gentlemen," he said. "Welcome to the academy." He stood in front of us and scanned
the room with his blue-green eyes. "I want to tell you what's ahead in the next
four weeks. Has anyone been in the Armed Forces?" Three raised their hands.
"You men will get this. Until the academy's over, each of you will begin and
end every sentence with 'sir.' Is that clear?"

"Yes, sir," a few ragged voices responded.

"What?" Captain Bratton erupted. "Loud and clear, everyone: 'Sir, yes sir.'"

"Sir, yes sir."

"Again, louder," he demanded.

"Sir, yes sir!" we screamed.

"Better. Now, if any of you aren't feeling well, if you aren't one hundred percent physically, this is the time to be honest and speak up, because you won't make it through this academy. If you're hurt or sick, don't start and you can come back. If you fail and wash out, you go to the bottom of the list and you may never return." He paused. "Does anyone have the flu, or a bad knee or back, or anything else that will be a problem?"

No one volunteered. I looked around. I was one of the tallest in the group, but most of the guys were big, with strong necks and thick arms. We had no small guys and with the exception of two who were overweight, everyone looked fit. No one looked like Foster at the Rodeo.

"I just want you to know, the next month here will be no vacation. If you're not prepared to bust a gut, that's another reason to go home now. Everywhere you go in camp, you will run, not walk. You will carry your water bottle with you at all times and you will stay hydrated. There will be days on the fireline when you have a gallon and a half of water in your banjo to last twelve hours and you never know when that may happen. If you don't start out hydrated, you won't get through that day. Every toilet in the camp has a pee indicator, so you can check the color of your urine." There was an undercurrent of laughter in the group. "Hey, this isn't a joke. If your pee is dark yellow, you're dehydrated. The darker it is, the more water you need to drink. Got it?" Captain Bratton eyed the group again.

"Sir, yes sir!" A couple of guys glanced down at their laps.

"Good. Next, whenever you run past a firefighter in the camp, you will shout, 'Timber-by.' Who knows what that means?"

Duran raised his hand.

"Yes, Duran."

"Sir, firefighters say that on the fireline when they pass someone, sir."

I had never heard anyone say "Timber-by" when I was a seasonal. We always said "Bump-by," or just "Bump."

"Right Duran," Captain Bratton said. "It alerts someone if you're coming by with a sharp tool or a piece of equipment." The Captain walked to one side of the room. Everyone's eyes followed him. A sign with a black background was painted on the wall. A large skull wore a fire helmet. Above the skull, red letters outlined in flames said: "Look, Listen and Learn," and below, "Or Cook, Sizzle and Burn." "You guys are in this together. Learn to function as a group and to watch out for each other. I want you to pair up. Pick a buddy and take care of him during the academy. Try to make sure he gets through it."

I glanced at Luis. He was listening carefully, even taking some notes, He seemed like an intense, serious guy. When he looked back at me with dark eyes, he nodded. We never spoke about it, but at that moment we agreed to get each other through the academy.

"We'll give you everything you need here," the Captain said. "Tonight we'll issue clothes and boots, and give you haircuts. You can choose a hair style."

"Sir, Scott sir."

"Yes, Scott?"

"Sir, what are the choices of hair styles?"

"What?"

Scott hesitated. "Sir, what are the choices of hair styles, *sir?*"

"Shaved, number one clipper, that's the choice."

Scott had long hair. He tried to smile.

"You'll have class instruction in here," the Captain said. "All of your study materials are on the table. Please sit in the same place each day." The door banged open. "This is Mr. Arias. He'll be leading the physical training."

Raphael Arias strode to the front of the room. "The physical workouts are tough," he said. "Every morning between seven and eight we do calisthenics and stretching. Be out on the Grinder before seven, ready to go, no excuses. Whatever exercise we're doing, sit-ups or push-ups, you'll call out the total number followed by the number of the repetition you're doing, like, 20-6. That's 20 total push-ups, and you're on number 6. When you finish any physical effort, you'll yell out, 'Air attack.' Any questions?"

"Sir, no sir!"

"We were supposed to have twenty-four FNGs, but two didn't show," Raphael said. "Half of you won't make it. The whiteboard at the back of the classroom is the Wall of Shame." He pointed and 22 heads turned. "If you wash out, your name goes up on that board as a reminder to the guys who are still here."

Smiles were replaced by nervous looks.

"You'll be divided up into three squads. Your squad leaders will be the three men who have some fire experience. Duran and Fowler are from the Forest Service. Kowalski is from Cal Fire. Hold up your hands please."

Everyone's gaze shifted to us. It took me by surprise and for a moment, I felt like I was co-captain of the Blades again.

"One final thing, Captain Bratton said. "You're not allowed to pet Sadie or Duke until the academy is over. Understood? Okay, that's it for tonight. Mr. Arias will take you over to get your clothes. By the way, if you're down in Malibu, don't go telling any of those pretty girls that you're firefighters, because you're not. For the next thirty days, you're FNGs, nothing more."

"Sir, Scott sir." He waved his hand around in a circle.

"Yes, Scott?"

"Sir, what's an FNG, sir?"

"Fucking New Guy. The firefighters here are FSAs, fire suppression aides, and that isn't you Scott. Pick up a water bottle on the way out and put your name on it. I want to hear 'Timber-by' on the way out."

"…Timber-by!"

Day Two. Morning. The Grinder.

We were bald when we showed up on the Grinder. No one looked good with a shaved head. Everyone's head looked like a cantaloupe, somehow much larger without hair. One guy, Loya, had a huge forehead and his head was the size of a watermelon. He looked like a space invader. Fowler had a scar running down the side of his scalp.

We started with sit-ups, then push-ups, jumping jacks and finally leg-raises, lying on our backs holding our legs 3 inches off the cement. After the calisthenics, we stretched and Raphael led us on a fast trail run. By the time we started, it was already hot and dry and the path turned steep 10 minutes out of the camp. A mile out, a guy named Barth tripped, twisted his ankle and couldn't go on. After another mile, two others, Meehan and Garcia, couldn't cut it. They dropped from the group, gasping for breath. I looked back at them and saw them start back down to the camp. I couldn't believe two guys quit on the second morning after a half-hour run.

Three were gone, 19 were left. Barth could come back for another academy.

"…Air attack!"

Day Three. Afternoon. Fire Orders and Watch Out Situations.

An instructor from Camp 2 at La Cañada talked about the fire safety rules everyone had to know. "Men," he said, "you're going to be working in one of the most dangerous fire areas in the world. The scrub and brush in Southern California is full of oils that burn four hundred degrees hotter than anywhere except Australia. You do not want to find out how hot a sixteen hundred degree fire is, believe me."

He talked about each of the 10 Standard Fire Fighting Orders and the 18 Watch Out Situations, calling them the "Tens and Eighteens." "These were written from experience, to protect you. Understand them, memorize them and review them from time to time. Don't ever be afraid to speak up if you think a situation is unsafe and violates one of the rules."

A couple of the guys were having a whispered conversation at the end of the table. "Hey, pay attention," the instructor said. "This is important. It's little things that get you. Shit happens when you let your guard down and you think, 'no big deal.' That's when you get hurt. Questions?"

"Sir, no sir!"

"Remember, the wildland is predictable only when you understand how unpredictable it is."

"…Timber-by!"

Day Four. Afternoon. Disneyland.

"On your butts, lay your water bottles in front of you," Raphael bellowed. He stood in front of us wearing the same blue shorts we had all been issued. He wore no shirt; his upper body was muscle with not an ounce of fat on him. He had big quads. "I want 20 sit-ups. Ready?"

"Sir, yes sir!"

"Louder!" Raphael yelled back. Jake and Red Eye stood next to him.

"Sir, yes sir!"

"Let's go," Raphael barked, as he, Jake and Red Eye got down and joined us doing sit-ups.

"20-1, 20-2, 20-3…" we shouted. "…20-20. Air attack!"

"Stay on your butts," Raphael cried. "Now, on your backs, legs 3 inches above the ground." We lay on our backs holding our legs up until they started to tremble, our stomach muscles tightening to the point of hurting. Captain Bratton walked around checking to see if anyone's heels were touching the cement. Dozer stood to the side watching us, his cap pulled low over his eyes.

"Up," shouted Raphael.

"Air attack!"

"Fifty jumping jacks," Raphael barked, as he started.

"...50-31, 50-32..." It was beginning to hurt.

"...Air attack!"

"Stretching, touch your left toe," Raphael ordered. "Hold."

"...Air attack!"

The workout went on. Duke and Sadie wandered out and sniffed at us as we did our exercises.

"Stretching, touch your right toe, hold."

"...Air attack!"

"On your faces. Give me forty pushups," Raphael demanded. "Toes and hands are the only things touching the cement. Your foreheads touch your water bottle when you come down."

At "40-21," Decker started to groan next to me.

Captain Bratton walked over, stood over him and bent down to look Decker in the face. "Decker, can you do this?" he asked. Decker groaned again and at 40-28, he collapsed on the cement.

"Keep going," Raphael shouted to us and ran over to Decker. "Decker, stand up. Stand up and watch the rest of the guys. Stand up."

Panting from exertion, Decker struggled to stand. As he stood next to me, I could see the sweat running down his legs, dripping onto the cement. The others were grunting as the count went on. The push-ups were killers. My arms were cramping and my shoulders ached. I tried to check on Luis, but couldn't see him. At "40-37," Sadie and Duke began a wrestling match on the cement next to me. Duke was on the bottom, Sadie on top. They growled, slobbered, nipped at each other and finally rolled into me. I collapsed onto the cement.

"Kowalski, keep going, keep going or stand up like a wuss," Jake yelled at me.

I kept going.

"...Air attack!"

We stood and gasped for air. Some of the guys rolled their shoulders, trying to shake off the cramps. Captain Bratton walked out in front of us. He carried a clipboard. A stopwatch hung from his neck. "Drink some water, fill your bottles and take a rest," he ordered. Art brought out five-gallon water cubies. We lined up, refilled our bottles and sat cross-legged on the cement, still breathing hard.

"OK," Captain Bratton said. "Now we're gonna visit Disneyland. Each pair will hit the obstacle course at two-minute intervals, starting with squad leaders Duran and Fowler. Squad leader Kowalski and Stone will go next. I'll call out each pair and say 'go.' "

"Sir, yes sir!"

Duran and Fowler went off.

"...Kowalski, Stone, go."

I ran down the embankment into Disneyland. Stone, a small, lean guy, was next to me. We ran to the push-up bar. Stone arrived first. Jake watched us. "Sir, Stone, sir," he yelled, and began his pushups, "...15-1, 15-2..."

"Sir, Kowalski, sir, 15-1..."

"...15-15. Air attack!"

Stone ran ahead of me to the steep incline boards to do sit-ups. The Dozer stood and watched us. We shouted our names and struggled to hook our feet under the straps at the high end of the boards.

"...15-14, 15-15, Air attack!"

I followed Stone up a steep hill. I couldn't catch the little bastard. We did 10 chin-ups on the high bars.

"Sir, Stone, sir."

Red Eye stared at us.

"...Air attack!"

We ran up another steep hill, over tires laid on the ground and onto the flat area near the Nike vault doors. Each of us dragged an empty 100-foot fire hose past an orange cone 200 feet away. It was easier than the progressive hose-lay in Auburn.

"Sir, Kowalski, sir."

Art watched us.

We climbed over 4-foot cement walls. Stone struggled and fell behind.

"...Air attack!"

We ran to the 50-pound bundles of fire hose suspended from pulleys. We had to hoist a bundle 25 feet, three times. I was stronger than Stone on this one. I thought about Angel. This was a new torture. I should call her.

Hector acted as if it didn't matter that we were busting our balls.

"Sir, Kowalski, sir."

"…Air attack!"

I was getting tired. My eyes were burning from sweat and my blue T-shirt was plastered to my chest. We ran down a hill to the log covered with more truck tires. We sledge-hammered the log with 10 swings over the right shoulder and 10 over the left shoulder. Stone was smart. He shortened his grip on the handle and took shorter swings. Jerry Dunham stood there, drinking Gatorade.

"…Air attack!"

We started up the steep hill to the water tank. Stone ran past me as if I were standing still. I slid back. I couldn't get any traction and clawed my way to the top on all fours. Stone was already there. A firefighter I'd never seen before sat on top of the water tank and looked down at us. Railroad ties hung suspended from chains. We had to do five overhead presses and we were finished.

"Sir, Kowalski, sir, Stone, sir. …Air attack!"

From the water tank, it was down a short paved driveway, past the front flagpole and back out onto the Grinder. Stone passed me and finished 10 feet ahead.

"…Air attack!"

"Nineteen minutes, eight seconds for Stone," Captain Bratton shouted out. I sat on the cement. Sadie rushed over and started to lick the sweat off my legs.

Decker got as far as the 50-pound hose hoists and quit. An hour later I watched him load his things into his old VW. He turned, nodded his head in our direction, got in his car and drove out of the camp.

"…Timber-by."

We had 18 men left. I lost two from my squad.

Day Six. Morning. Arduous Level Run.

"…Timber-by."

Captain Bratton announced a four-mile run for everyone including the FSAs. "It's up Rambla Pacifico at the 'arduous level.' Everyone carries his full fire pack."

"Sir, yes, sir!"

This run was the worst test yet. Jake, Raphael and the other crewmembers immediately ran out ahead of our group of FNGs. Only Hector and Art stayed back with us. As we ran, I tried to stay near Luis. I could hear his ragged breathing and urged him to keep going. He struggled and started to fall back. We carried water bottles, fire shelters, helmets, radios, fusees, banjos and even a roll of toilet paper, which Dozer called "Mountain Money." It was all supposed to weigh about 45 pounds, but the pack seemed to weigh a ton; it seemed so much heavier than the coiled hose I had struggled with at Colfax.

Halfway up the road, Wyatt staggered to a stop, sat down in the middle of the road and threw up. As if Wyatt's failure affected him, Hermann went on for a moment, dropped his pack and stopped. I looked back to see Captain Bratton pull up to them in his truck. Fowler shouted encouragement to the rest of us. Luis was still moving. I looked over at him and he held one fist in the air and screamed, "Air attack!"

I pushed my body almost to the point of shutdown. My lungs were burning and my legs ached. We were all reaching the limit. At one point, we got closer to the crew, but we couldn't catch them. I tried to run faster, but couldn't. I didn't see Tibbits stop and drop his pack. By the time that happened, he was behind us.

"...Air attack."

Hermann, Wyatt and Tibbits were gone, 15 FNGs were left.

Murphy thought an insect flew into his ear during the run. By the time we returned to camp, he was certain something was crawling around inside and it was beginning to hurt. Jerry Dunham loaded him into the captain's truck and drove him down to the Malibu Urgent Care Center on PCH. A doctor checked Murphy's ear and found nothing. Murphy was back in camp two hours later, looking sheepish. Jerry Dunham said the visit cost the county $250.

Day Seven. Afternoon. Lessons Learned.

The class consisted of watching a series of Forest Service videos called *Lessons Learned*. Each focused on a particular fire and began with a Forest Service Ranger telling us that between 1926 and 2000, 400 wildland firefighter fatalities had occurred.

The "Wenatchee Heights Burnover" video left an impression on all of us. Rick West, a fire chief with 20 years' experience, narrated it. He described a wind-driven fire burning on a 100-degree day near apple orchards in Washington

State. "I found one of my wildland engines in a hazardous position at the top of a canyon," he said. "It was manned by a green crew at its first major fire. They were trapped on a narrow road. The wind picked up and ten-foot high sage brush close to the road was starting to burn."

He recounted how he drove his Bronco as far as he could and then ran to assist the engine crew. He directed them to retreat through an adjoining apple orchard while he covered them with a hose from the engine. Apple orchards were used as safe zones, he explained, and fire usually stopped at the first two or three rows of trees. His crew escaped.

"The fire came down on me," he said. "In the smoke and heat, I was trapped and I decided to try to survive in the engine. I lay on the floorboards until it was so hot the windshield exploded and I knew I had to get out." He described how he took a deep breath, held his hands over his mouth and nose, jumped out of the truck and ran into the orchard. "Above all, I had to protect my airways. The superheated air would kill me. I felt the heat burning my skin. Shock set in, I knew I was burning, but adrenaline somehow kept me going. As I ran, I noticed my pant legs were on fire, I had no gloves and I saw that the skin on my hands was loose."

At this point, we were starting to squirm in our seats, exchanging quick glances in the semi-dark room. I felt nauseated when the chief described his loose skin. This was the first time I heard someone describe being caught in a fire.

A paramedic arrived from the other side of the orchard and tried to help Chief West, who had to run 20 rows into the orchard before the medic could start an IV and give him morphine. The video described how Chief West was rushed to a local emergency room and then by helicopter and jet to a burn center in Seattle. He suffered second- and third-degree burns on 65 percent of his body. On his back, one piece of X-shaped flesh remained where the heat had been deflected by straps holding his radio.

As the camera moved in closer to Chief West, we saw that most of his ears were gone, his nose was disfigured, his face was a single flap of tight skin and his arms were wrapped in flesh-colored material. He said he was missing the tips of his fingers. He finished the video by telling us, "My life has changed drastically. I can't describe the pain to anyone. Every day they had to scrub the old skin off my body. Every day I had to go to therapy to keep what muscle I had left and to use my joints so they wouldn't become frozen. I am facing more surgeries to rebuild my ears, nose, and fingers. I had to think long and hard before I decided to talk about what happened to me. I decided if I could keep even one firefighter from going through the pain and agony that I went through, it would be worth it." He ended by reminding every firefighter to think about personal safety. "Firefighters sometimes forget to take care of themselves. *It can happen to you.*"

The video lasted 20 minutes. When it was over Dozer turned up the lights and told us to take a 15-minute break. There was silence in the room. We half-shouted, "Timber-by" and went outside.

"You know, cartilage melts," Fowler said. "That's why burn victims have so much damage to their ears and noses. In the Forest Service, we had a guy whose ears melted. After he came out of the hospital, he used to go around and say, 'Talk to me guys, I'm all ears.'"

"…Timber-by!"

Day Ten. Afternoon. Lifeline Specifications.

We were exhausted after a vicious run up Las Flores Canyon in the morning. No one was paying attention to the instructor from another camp who was trying to teach us about nylon rescue rope. "You have to check every lifeline every day for broken strands. It's 100 percent nylon and melts at 480 degrees," he told us.

When we left the classroom, we passed Captain Bratton, who waited outside.

"…Timber-by."

He pulled Bruno aside to talk to him. Raphael had been pushing Bruno hard for the last two days, telling him he had a bad attitude and wasn't working hard enough.

"…Timber-by."

Bruno left camp that evening.

Fourteen FNGs remained.

Day Eleven. Lunch. The Lottery.

We ate at a separate table. At the crew table, Red Eye collected $10 from each FSA to buy lottery tickets.

"What's the pot?" Art wanted to know.

"Forty-eight million," said Raphael.

"What would you do if you won some of that?" Art asked him.

"I'd buy a custom crew truck," Raphael said. "It would have individual leather seats, air conditioning and a built-in icebox. No more ice chests sliding around. And I think I'd put a special air horn on it."

"If I won anything," Hector said, "I'd go to the county and offer to buy the camp. I'd offer them a price they couldn't refuse."

"Good idea, Hector," Jake said. "Then you could spend every night here without signing a Stay Over Agreement." Hector punched Jake on the shoulder. Jake play-acted and fell off his chair.

Jerry Dunham came in. "All right," he shouted at our table, "all FNGs on the Grinder, let's go."

"…Timber-by."

We ran out onto the cement. Before we started PT, Captain Bratton announced that Gordon had been dropped for "academic" reasons.

Thirteen left and counting down.

Day Fourteen. Morning. Crew Trucks.

"…Timber-by."

When my squad prepared to board the crew truck, I pulled the metal stairs out, stepped up, opened the door, got down, took three long steps back, turned and faced the entry. My crew lined up behind me, each man an arm's length behind the other. When we loaded, we double-timed up the stairs, banged a fist on the side and yelled, "Air-attack!" As long as we were FNGs, we had to wear our helmets inside the crew truck.

On one exercise, when King ran into his truck, he forgot to pound the side. Dozer was watching. "Everyone back out," the Dozer shouted. "On your faces. Give me twenty push-ups for King's fuck-up."

"…20-20. Air attack."

The second time, King hit the side of the crew truck hard with his fist.

Day Sixteen. Evening. Dinner at Coogies.

It was Monday evening. Seven of us got together to discuss our survival strategy for the next 10 days. We sat around eating burgers at Coogie's in the

Malibu shopping center. Luis came with us; he hadn't gone home to his wife and kid. Fowler was there, and Duran, Stone, Knight, and Scott.

"Anyone see John Cusak?" Scott asked.

"John Cusak, the actor?" Fowler asked.

"Yeah, my sister says he's supposed to have lunch here all the time," Scott said.

"Well, it's dinnertime, and I don't see him," Fowler said. Fowler was the senior guy in our group with two years in the Forest Service. He had worked in Northern California, near the Oregon border. He told us he got the scar on the side of his head while surfing, when he wiped out and his board hit him. Duran spent one year with the Forest Service in Montana but didn't like the pay and benefits. He didn't seem to know that much about firefighting. Stone turned out to be a good guy. He worked hard and didn't complain. Knight worked construction and was used to the physical stress. He didn't seem to be suffering. Scott put in the effort but was a major pain in the ass. He complained and had to have the last word about everything. I couldn't imagine sitting next to him in a crew truck for several hours. Luis struggled with some of the tough physical stuff but had a lot of determination. Every day he swore to me that he would make it no matter what it required. He said he had to take care of his wife and kid. Every time he told me that, I wondered why the hell he had a kid when he was 20.

"There's not a guy left who can't finish this," Fowler said, "you just have to believe you can do it." With the exception of Scott, the whole group was starting to work together as a team. My father would have been surprised, maybe disappointed. I wasn't living up to my image as a fuck-up. I had made it through as a seasonal and I was surviving the Camp 8 Academy.

On the way out, Luis said "Timber-by" to the waitress.

In the morning, I was surprised to learn that Knight had decided to go back to construction work. "This isn't for me," he told us at breakfast. "I'm just not a team player."

Day Eighteen. One a.m. Bad Dreams.

"Joe, no, please, you're hurting me." Standing in the hall outside my bedroom, I saw the light in my parents' bedroom shining under the door. I listened to my mother's voice. "Joe stop, you're hurting me!"

I awoke to the breathing and snoring of the 11 other FNGs. My stomach was about to explode. I got out of bed, went to the john and then outside. I stood on the Grinder in my underwear and felt the late night chill at the top of Las Flores Canyon. The camp dogs were gone. I heard birds chirping in the darkness. A couple of coyotes began yip-yapping and barking somewhere out in the hills. Soon more coyotes joined in. Dogs began to bark. The yowling went on, echoing through the canyons. Suddenly the coyotes ceased, the last dog barked and silence returned.

I tried to shake the memory of the dream. My father was hurting my mother again. The dream seemed so real. It could be happening now in their bedroom while I stood outside in the California night. I wanted to call home to find out if everything was all right.

Day Nineteen. Morning. Cutting Fireline.

Harris was gone. He didn't say anything to anyone and didn't show up in the morning. He must have gone back to work as a longshoreman. Podesta was exhausted and dehydrated. He reported late to the Grinder and was unable to finish the first set of sit-ups. We were left with 10 men.

After the workout on the Grinder and a three-mile run, we came back to camp. We changed into our yellows and wore cotton pants and long-sleeve cotton shirts underneath. We boarded the crew trucks and traveled up Rambla Pacifico to practice cutting fireline. We spent three hours under a hazy sky hacking a 3-foot line through the thick, 6-foot high brush on the side of the mountain above the camp.

Dozer shouted "spot fire," and we practiced retreating up the line to our safety zone.

Jerry Dunham screamed at me, "Kowalski, it's day sixteen and you're not squared-away yet. You're running with the blade of your McLeod facing up. What happens if you fall? Do you want to cut your hand off?" It wasn't my best day. I still remembered the dream about my mother from the night before and my stomach hurt.

"On your faces," Art shouted, this one's for Kowalski." In the middle of the brush, wearing our full gear, packs and helmets, 10 of us hit the dirt and did 20 push-ups.

"…Air-attack."

Dozer declared the spot fire out and we moved back down the line to continue cutting brush.

"…Timber-by."

Thirty minutes later, when we were at the bottom of a wash, I broke into a cold sweat and got the shakes. Luis made me sit down in the shade, forced me to drink Gatorade and told me I was dehydrated. Jerry Dunham and Dozer ignored the fact that I had stopped. I watched the guys cutting line as they started up the far side of the wash. I was proud to see how coordinated they were and how fast they moved through the thick brush. After a few minutes, I felt better and climbed up the hill to join them.

"…Timber-by."

Day Twenty. Lunch. Female Inmates.

As we ran from the Grinder to the mess hall, a crew truck from the inmate camp arrived. This was my first look at the women dressed in orange. They came to pick up some of the firewood we stacked out behind Disneyland. Except for their uniforms, they looked like ordinary women.

Day Twenty-Three. Morning. Incident Command Orientation.

A captain qualified for Type I interagency fires covered Incident Command. He was patient, serious and spent an hour explaining how major fires were managed, breaking down the organization into planning, operations, air support, logistics and finance. Most important, he told us how to check in so we could be paid when we were sent somewhere to work a large fire.

After he finished, he handed out a test sheet with 25 questions and we were allowed to refer to our training materials for our answers. While we worked, we swigged Gatorade. Sadie wandered in through the open door and walked down the center of the classroom looking from side to side, wagging her tail. When she reached the front, she turned around and walked out. Duke waited at the door.

On the way out, I glanced up at the Wall of Shame. Twelve FNGs gone, less than two weeks to go.

"…Timber-by."

Day Twenty-Three. Afternoon. Helicopter Safety.

Crew Chief Ericson, in his blue flight suit, stood on our helipad, in front of a Bell 412 helicopter. "Come closer men," he urged. "The Firehawks are all committed today, so we'll talk about the four-twelve instead." He turned around and gazed at it. "Has anyone worked around helicopters?" he asked.

No one raised his hand.

"Safety is critical," Ericson said, "don't forget that. When you walk around a helicopter, carry your tools horizontally, below your waist. Be especially careful when you're hot-loading. You don't want to be anywhere near a moving blade." He slid back the side door of the Bell. "Everything on a helicopter costs a ton of money and breaks easily." He thumped the side of the fuselage just behind the door. "The space between this open door and the tail rotor is called 'No Man's Land.' Unless you're unloading tools from the tail, stay away from this spot. Do you know why?"

Everyone's hand shot up.

"Zambrano, why?"

"Sir, because you could be killed by the tail rotor, sir."

"Right. What else, Zambrano?"

Luis gave him a vacant look.

Ericson looked to see if anyone else had an answer. "Because, Zambrano, as I said, everything on a helicopter breaks easily. If you get chopped up by the tail rotor, what do you think it does to the blades?"

"...Timber-by."

Day Twenty-Five. Afternoon. Nearing the End.

We were down to 10 FNGs, but were starting to relax. We were the survivors. We were tough and motivated and we didn't want to lose anyone else. Stone was still finishing ahead of me on the obstacle course, but I didn't mind, I was proud of him. The "Sir, yes sirs" were becoming more natural. Once I thought I actually saw Jerry Dunham and the Dozer smiling at us.

Graduation.

It was a great day; we all felt we had accomplished something important. Chairs were set up in the front parking lot by the flagpole. Two loudspeakers broadcast Clint Black music. We had washed the crew trucks the previous evening and they gleamed at the entrance to the camp. FSAs and engineers from Camps 2 and 9 arrived to join the men from our camp. Forty firefighters in dark-blue uniforms and sunglasses stood around. Sadie and Duke ran from man to man, sniffing at their legs, waiting for attention. Large slabs of meat cooked on the outdoor barbecue, filling the camp with a wonderful aroma.

Around 11:30 a.m., family members, wives and girlfriends arrived. There was a continual stream of cars coming into the camp. Along with the visitors, the big brass also appeared. The battalion chief of the camps, Andy Garvey arrived. His boss, Deputy Chief Lonnie Nelson came, along with Chief Richard Panos. They walked among the FSAs and visitors, shaking hands.

We waited behind the mess hall in formation. When the music stopped, we heard the sound of an approaching helicopter. We looked up and saw the Bird, its landing lights bright even in the daylight. It circled several times at 300 feet and settled on the helipad. At that moment, I thought I had never seen anything so beautiful. I loved the nine other guys standing with me. We had gone through so much together during the last month. These were my friends for life in the Fire Service.

After Art held us up for a few more minutes to give the flight crew from the Bird time to join the audience, we double-timed out to the parking lot and sat in the front row. The FSAs from the three camps stood behind the seated crowd, creating a tight, blue half circle of men.

Battalion Chief Garvey walked to the podium. "Congratulations to the Class of December 1999," he said. "We had ninety applicants, we accepted twenty-four, twenty-two showed up and the ten men you see in front of you are the ones who made it. These men worked hard to be here today." The battalion chief looked at us and clapped. "And I applaud the families and friends who supported and encouraged them." He gestured to the crowd. "You should be thanked and congratulated as well."

Chief Panos told us, "Today you begin your commitment to the Los Angeles County Fire Department, to the Tens and Eighteens and to your team members. Welcome aboard, gentlemen."

Deputy Chief Nelson said to the audience, "When the TV cameras show a wildfire, you'll see firefighters from the flatlands standing around their trucks. You won't see the men from Camp 8, or from Camp 2 or 9. They're the real heroes. They'll be up in the hills and on the sides of the mountains doing the hardest, most dangerous work. When they do come down, the flatlanders will look at them with respect and awe. Welcome, men."

Dozer stepped forward to read out our assignments and hand out our camp patches. "Fowler, Camp 9." Fowler stepped forward, shook Dozer's hand, took his patch, and shook hands with the each of the chiefs. The chiefs put their arms around his shoulders as his parents stood to take pictures. The group clapped as Fowler returned to his seat. Camp 9 took three others. Duran went to Camp 2, along with Stone and Scott the loudmouth. More applause and photos.

Dozer broke into a broad smile as he said, "Greg Kowalski, the man from Michigan, to Camp 8." This was the best camp, the best location. I stepped forward.

My parents would have been so proud if they were sitting with the other visitors. My mother would stand up to applaud. My father would see me in a firefighter's uniform, a member of a trained crew. He would shout, "Way to go, Greg," turn to someone next to him and say, "That's my son." He'd have a camera and keep snapping pictures of me receiving my Camp 8 patch, shaking hands with everyone and smiling as I returned to my seat

In reality, no one was here to take my picture with the brass. I shook hands with everyone quickly. Other people clapped politely, even though none of them were related to me.

Luis was the last and I knew he was coming to Camp 8 with me. His entire family stood. Luis' parents applauded. His wife, flanked by her own mother and father, held little Miguel above her head. Luis waved to them and stopped for a photo with the battalion chief.

"Mr. Mendoza, will you please dismiss the class one more time," Chief Garvey requested.

Dozer stepped forward. Without a word from him, we rose, faced right and began to march across the cement behind him. Everyone clapped. "Halt!" Dozer commanded. "One last time, on your faces, give me twenty push-ups." At his command, the 40 other men surrounding the audience got down on the cement to join us.

"...20-20, *AIR ATTACK!*"

Late in the afternoon, the festivities were over and everyone had departed. I stood out on the Grinder. It was deserted, even Duke and Sadie had disappeared. Dozer came up to me. "Hey, New Guy, do you want to start work tomorrow?" he asked.

"Sure Mr. Mendoza, I've got nothing better to do."

"Are you moving back into Jake's room? It's time you guys found a place to live."

"We're looking, sir."

"Hey," Dozer said, "Drop all the 'sir' stuff, and just call me Dozer."

"Yes sir, uh, Dozer."

"Glad to have you with us." He put his arm around my shoulder.

"Hey, Dozer?"

"Yeah?"

"Can I use the camp phone? I want to make a call."

"Sure."

I knew the telephone number at my dad's station, even though I had never called it. My hand shook as I dialed.

"Hess Avenue Station."

"Hello, this is Greg Kowalski calling. I'd like to speak to my…to Captain Bentak, please"

"Hold on."

"This is Captain Bentak."

"Mike, hello? It's Greg Kowalski."

"Greg, how are you? Where are you?"

"I'm in Los Angeles; I joined a helitack crew. I just graduated their academy."

"That's great Greg, how was the season at Cal Fire?"

"It was good, I learned a lot."

"So you've become a firefighter."

"I think so."

"Sounds like you're doing well. What does your dad think?"

"I don't know Mike, I haven't talked to him."

"He's here today, shall I get him?"

"No, not now. I'll talk to him another time. I just wanted to let you know what I'm doing."

"It's good to hear from you, Greg. I don't have a lot of time at the moment, but I'd love to hear about your experience. Keep in touch, huh?"

"I will, Mike. Thanks for everything."

"Congratulations, Greg."

TEN
Saginaw, Michigan

I TOSSED ALL NIGHT, half-awake, half-asleep. Visions of Greyhound buses, movie stars on red carpets and wildfires on the sides of mountains drifted through my mind. It was the countdown to my departure; I was ready to blast off. I looked at the clock on my nightstand again. It was 6 a.m. In 29 hours, I would be on my way to California. I thought I heard my father in the kitchen. I got out of bed, put on jeans and a sweatshirt and went downstairs. He was about to leave.

"Hey, Dad, today's my last day at home. I'm on the bus tomorrow morning."

"I know."

"I wanted to say goodbye."

"Goodbye." He moved toward the garage door.

"Dad, wait…" He turned to look at me. "Maybe I'll do something heroic, I could be famous. You'll be proud of me."

"A famous firefighter?" He laughed. "There are old firefighters and dead firefighters. That's it."

We were 3 feet apart, eye-to-eye. I had one hand on the back of a kitchen chair. The grandfather clock in the dining room ticked away. Outside, the sound of a truck broke the early morning silence and I heard the *Saginaw News* hit the front porch. "Don't you even care what I'm doing?" I asked him.

"You've got no idea what it takes to be a firefighter. You're not tough enough."

I felt a rage I had never known. As a child, I was afraid of him. As I grew older, I had become more angry and less afraid. Now I hated him, I wanted to hammer him into pieces, I wanted to kill him. I felt like I had stepped into an ice-cold shower. My body tensed and my heart pounded so hard I was certain he could hear it. I let go of the kitchen chair and clenched my fists. I could throw a couple of quick punches and knock him back. I could grab the frying pan on the sink and hit him. I could split his head open. He would collapse on the floor, bleeding, dying, eyes rolled up in his crushed skull.

"You've never even been west of Grand Rapids," he went on. "Don't call home when you're living in some alley and you need money, because we're not answering the phone."

For years, I had been lifting weights, getting bigger and stronger, but I thought he could still pound the crap out of me if we came to blows. I was 6 feet one inch tall, an inch taller than he was, but he weighed at least 20 pounds more, and he was tough, he had the muscle. I wasn't going to punch him that morning; I wasn't going to split his head open. My anger drained away. "Dad, I'm sorry about your life," I said. "I'm sorry you're not happy.I know it's my fault. I'm going to become a firefighter. I thought that would please you."

"You'll make me happy when you're in California and I don't have to put up with you." He turned and walked into the garage.

Trembling, I listened to the garage door open. His Harley revved and rumbled into the street. The garage door remained open. I took the orange juice from the refrigerator, poured the last of it into a glass and crushed the carton. I pressed it in my hands until it was a solid lump of cardboard. I went into the garage, walked out onto the cool gravel in my bare feet, and threw the carton out onto the empty street. "Fuck you, fuck you!" I screamed.

Back into the house, I left the juice untouched on the kitchen counter and went into my bedroom. The clock said 6:15 a.m. After 19 years, my father and I said goodbye in less than a minute. If Mom or Vicky heard anything, they kept quiet and out of sight. The house was silent and after I calmed down, I went back to sleep in my jeans and sweatshirt.

During the morning, I kept my bedroom door closed and packed and unpacked a dozen times. Mom had bought me an olive duffel and a good pair of thick-soled work boots at a surplus store. Cal Fire said they would provide Personal Protective Equipment, which they called "PPE." I didn't have much to take— jeans, T-shirts, sweatshirts, underwear and the boots. I put extra socks in the duffel, took them out and then put them back. I couldn't decide whether to take my winter coat, then decided I didn't need it. The Detroit Pistons hat had been in my bottom drawer for years. I don't know why, but I stuffed it in the duffel. The Red Wings jersey stayed, but a Blades jersey would make the trip. I had a good collection of country and western and heavy metal CDs—too many to take. I packed five that I liked best, including my favorite, Willie Nelson's *Red Headed Stranger.*

By noon, I had finished screwing around with the packing I could have done in a few minutes. I went down to the kitchen. Vicky was gone, but Mom was still at the kitchen table, reading the paper.

"I was waiting for you," she said. "Want some breakfast, or lunch?"

"Sure, eggs would be great."

"Did you say goodbye to your father this morning? I thought I heard you talking."

"Yeah, we said goodbye. He said he hoped I would take care of myself and come home a hero."

A weak smile appeared on my mother's face. "Greg, your father isn't going to change. That's the way he is. Just remember, I love you and care about you." She hugged me.

"Thanks, Mom, I love you too," I said, uncomfortable with the sudden gush of feelings. "Tomorrow, let's not have a scene at the bus station. I'll say goodbye to you and Vicky here, and you can drive me down and drop me off. You don't even have to come in."

"Any way you want it," she said. "Is Kirsten coming?"

"No."

"Have you said goodbye to your friends?"

"I'm going over to Bobby's house tonight around six. We're having pizza and some laughs." The laughs would come after the beer and some dope.

"Don't stay out too late," she said, putting toast on the table.

My last hours at home were ticking away and my mother was still worried about how late I would be staying out.

In the morning, I brushed my teeth twice and still tasted the beer. I decided to shave, even though I had done it yesterday. It would be a few more years before my beard would be as heavy and dark as my father's.

My head throbbed and my pulse echoed in my ears as I stood in the kitchen with Mom and Vicky. Vicky cried and said, "I'll miss you. Call us." She hugged me.

"Bye, Vick." I kissed her on the top of the head. I followed my mother through the garage to her old Taurus parked on the driveway. The morning sun hurt my eyes. "Are you ever getting a new car, Mom? This thing might not even make it to the bus station."

"When your father thinks I need one," she said.

Since my mother's confession about her pregnancy, the prospect of leaving had become easier. She and my father had spent the last 19 years waiting for me to take off. My departure would solve a lot of problems. In the end, it was easy. We drove to the station without talking. I watched my street disappear in the cracked side-view mirror of the Taurus. Out of the corner of my eye, I saw a few tears run down Mom's cheek, but she didn't break down and we made it before departure time without incident. I grabbed my duffel from the back seat, came around to the driver's side and kissed her on the cheek. "Bye, Mom, I'll let you know where I am." I clenched my teeth and tried not to cry.

Mom kept one hand on the steering wheel. With the other hand, she pressed a wad of 10 dollar bills into my shirt pocket. She looked at me and said, "I love you, hon, be careful. I stuck a sandwich and some potato salad in your pack."

That was all, it was over. Half-numb, I walked into the Indian Trails bus station without looking back. I was on my own.

ELEVEN
Malibu, California

IT WAS A WEEK BEFORE CHRISTMAS and another holiday away from home. In Saginaw, festive lights would hang from trees and roofs and people would be shaking snow off their boots at the door, eager to step into the warmth. In Malibu, the sun was relentless and it would be 80 degrees by noon. A few homes had strings of tiny white lights wound around the palms. Decorations and ornaments turned up here and there, but looked forlorn and out of place. It wasn't the Christmas I knew.

Luis invited me to his house for dinner. I wasn't excited about spending the day with his parents and his kid, watching everyone open presents, so I signed on for duty at the camp. It paid overtime.

We were on the Grinder doing our morning calisthenics and push-ups. I'd gotten to the point where I could do it forever. It was just muscle, just pushing, no thinking required. Up and down, up and down. I saw Luis straining in front of me. We still busted our asses, but now we were part of the crew; we belonged to Camp 8. No longer FNGs, we were New Guys.

A breeze came up Las Flores Canyon. When we finished our workout, Jerry Dunham announced, "Three-mile run in the hills today up Backbone Trail, no packs. After the run, we're going to Camp 13 to work on a wall."

"What kind of wall?" Hector asked. "A prison wall?"

"A retaining wall along the driveway," Jerry Dunham said. "Caltrans dumped three truckloads of rock and they need help."

It was less than seven miles to Camp 13, but on the winding roads it took 20 minutes in the crew truck. Luis spent the time showing pictures of his kid to Raphael, the only other married FSA, who had a son of his own. We drove down a steep descent on Encinal Canyon with tall scrub brush on both sides and passed a stone wall decorated with blue and green tile. "That's the Malibu Country Club," Raphael told me, eager to turn away from Luis and his pile of kiddie pictures.

"A country club up here?" I said.

"It's a golf club," Raphael said.

"Where's the inmate camp?"

"We're coming to it," Raphael said.

"A golf course next to a prison camp? We have country clubs in Saginaw but they don't have prison camps across the street."

"This isn't Michigan," Jake said. "This is California. Things are different out here."

At the entrance to Camp 13, "NO TRESPASSING – STATE PRISON" signs hung from a dilapidated 6-foot high chain-link fence. It had gaps in several places and wouldn't keep anyone in or out. Inside, a dozen one-story buildings, a large depot for crew trucks and fire equipment and what looked like a picnic area—tables sheltered by an aluminum roof—all huddled under pine trees. The place resembled a rundown summer camp in a horror movie.

We drove down a long asphalt driveway and I saw 80 or 90 inmates in bright orange prison uniforms with "CDC-PRISONER" marked in black letters on their backs and legs. They stood in groups behind a wide red stripe painted across the middle of a cement pad. Each inmate held her fire pack, helmet and a lunch pail. A male and female officer in the two-tone tan uniforms of California Correctional Officers stood to one side. When we got out of the crew truck, I heard the man reading names from a clipboard: "Alvarez, Rotella, Warren, DiCristofaro, Garcia…" With each name, an inmate walked up to the red line, got a nod of recognition from the female officer and stepped across.

"What's that about?" I asked.

"In the morning they transfer the inmates from the custody of the Correctional Department to County Fire," Red Eye explained.

"They look like mothers and sisters," I said.

"They are," Luis said.

"Mothers, for sure," Jake said.

My own mother and sister were in prison too, but one that didn't require an orange uniform. I was the only one who had escaped. "Any gangs?" I asked. Half the women were white, the rest black or Latinas. I saw a couple of Asians. A tall firefighter with a mustache and the standard dark glasses joined us. "Not here. There aren't many racial issues with the women," he said.

"This is Captain Martins, camp superintendent," Jerry Dunham said to Luis and me. "Bob, we've got two New Guys, Kowalski and Zambrano."

Martins shook our hands. "Welcome. Sorry, we're running a little late today; we had a problem in the kitchen."

The women had all moved to the County Fire side of the red line and began to chant and several linked arms and danced in a circle. "Now what?" Luis asked.

"One of the women is getting paroled on Monday. It's a little ritual they have," Martins said.

"What're they saying?" I asked.

"Happy last day on crew," Martins said.

When the singing stopped, two of the inmates led the rest in a series of stretching exercises, finishing off with jumping jacks and push-ups. It was a moderate version of what we did on the Grinder, but no one called out "Air-Attack."

"Not much security here," Luis said.

"We get the ones who have less than three years left on their sentences," Martins said. "They're not a flight risk. Once in a while someone walks out of here, but we've never lost an inmate at a fire—they have too much pride for that." Martins turned toward one of the buildings. "C'mon, let's get coffee."

"I wonder what goes on here at night," I whispered to Jake. "A hundred horny women and a dozen firefighters."

"Forget it," Jake said. "The women are back on the other side of the camp with the Correctional Department."

We followed Captain Martins inside. At the entrance, an inmate sat at a desk with a computer and telephone. "This is Miss Engel, my secretary," Martins said. She looked up from the computer and nodded. Inside were two tiny offices, a dining room for the firefighters and an open kitchen. Two other inmates were busy bagging lunches. "This is Miss Leonard and Miss Barboza. They cook for the men," Martins said.

On the wall, I saw a photo of a German shepherd in a black wood frame.

Someone had glued blue stars around the edges, half of which had fallen off.

"That's Max," Martins said.

"Camp dog?"

"Yeah, Max was great. Lived here for years. We had an inmate, Jazzy, a drug dealer who looked after him. When she was paroled, she wanted to take Max with her to Bakersfield." Martins walked closer to the picture and stared at Max. "I thought about it, but it didn't seem like a good idea. Then Jazzy showed up here in a purple Rolls Royce. Before I could say anything, she opened the door and Max was in the front seat, so we let him go. As far as I know, he's still in Bakersfield, living the high life."

"The *high life*," Jake said.

What was it about firefighters and dogs, I wondered. Strays picking up strays. My father had to be the only firefighter in the country who didn't like dogs.

We sat at the dining table, talking, drinking coffee and eating the cinnamon rolls that Miss Barboza had baked that morning.

"Cap, we're about ready," one of the foremen came in to report. "We're taking two crews to work on the running trail."

"OK, guys, let's go," Jerry Dunham said. I was enjoying my third cinnamon roll.

We walked back up the driveway. Fifty or more inmates stood around three piles of granite rocks, waiting to begin work. On the other side of the driveway, a neat cement foundation had been poured in a trench. Yellow string, held in place by wood stakes, ran alongside both sides, indicating the line and height for the wall. A few layers of stone had already been cemented in place. Someone knew more about building stone walls than I did. "Who did this?" I asked.

"We did," said one of the women. "What do you think?"

"Looks good to me," I said. Some of these women had futures as stone masons.

Two of the camp's firefighters started up a mixer and began adding water and concrete mix. Our crew started moving the rocks across the road to the edge of the trench. When the concrete was ready, Raphael, Luis and I carried buckets from the mixer and poured the concrete on the wall. The inmates spread it and set the next layer of stones. What a scene. I was a firefighter, working with my crew under a hot December sun in Malibu, building a stone wall at a women's prison camp. Even my father might enjoy this picture—there were plenty of women around.

I watched the rear end of a blond woman as she bent over to pick up stones. She had tattoos on her arms and the head of a snake showing on the back of her neck above her collar. The tattoos made her look sexy in a tough way. She set a large piece of granite into the concrete. "How do you like fighting fires?" I asked her.

She laughed. "Bring 'em on," she said. "It's a buck an hour."

"That's what you get paid?"

"We get two dollars an hour for forty hours a week in the camp. When California burns, we get an extra buck an hour plus overtime." She smiled. "It almost makes you hope for fire." I looked at her and she stared back. "Last year I picked up an extra thousand."

"What did you spend it on?"

"I saved it. I'm out of here in January." She turned and picked up another chunk of granite. She definitely had a nice ass. "I was at Chino for two and a half years."

I walked back to the mixer with my bucket, filled it and came back across the road. "You a serial killer?" I asked her.

She shot me another look. "Me, a killer?" She laughed. "Naw, I was using. My boyfriend and I got high one night and tried to break into a liquor store. We set off an alarm and he drove off without me. I was so stoned I just stood there until the sheriffs arrived."

"Nice boyfriend."

"He was OK. He pimped for me when we needed money."

So she was a hooker. I wondered about her tattoos. Maybe the snake started on her leg, wound around her body, across her breasts, and up the back of her neck. "What happens when you get out?" I asked her.

"I don't know. I've been going to pre-release class, but they just tell us not to do the same stuff that got us in here." She gazed off at the trees for a moment. "Who's gonna hire someone who's been in the can?"

She'd probably be looking for Johns by the end of her first week out.

"What's your name?" she asked.

"Greg." The snake would be a big turn-on for some guys. She probably charged extra.

"Nice to meet ya. I'm Cindy." She gave me one more look. This time it was just a glance from a young girl. It made me uncomfortable.

"My boyfriend wouldn't get away with something like that," the inmate working next to her said. "If he took off without me, I'd cut his balls off."

Cindy hooted. "Honey, I'd have to cut his dick off. He lost his balls years ago."

As the work on the wall progressed, the Camp 13 foremen encouraged the women, addressing each inmate with "Miss" and a last name. The swampers reminded their crews to hydrate and called for brief rest periods every 30 minutes. By mid-morning, it was getting hot and we all moved into the shade for a break to drink water and Gatorade. The cement mixer stopped and two foremen went to get more concrete mix.

"Are all the women in here for drugs?" Luis asked a Camp 13 firefighter named Bates while we stood under a pine tree.

"Meth, heroin, cocaine, welfare fraud, bad checks, mostly non-violent crimes," Bates said. "But see that one over there?" He pointed to a petite woman with a pigtail. "She ran over her husband's girlfriend with a pickup. Didn't kill her, just broke her legs. And Miss Engel," Bates said, "the one inside on the phones? She helped bury a man's body after her husband killed him."

"Remind me not to spend the night here," Luis said.

"My mom wanted to run my father over with her car," I said. "He beat her up all the time and she wanted to kill him." Bates looked at me. "She had it all planned out. She was going to smack him on the driveway while he was working on his Harley."

Luis was staring at me. "You never told me this," he said.

Jake started to smile.

"It wouldn't have worked. She had an old Taurus and my old man's so mean, she would have hit him, the front bumper would have fallen off and he'd still be standing there without a scratch."

Jake was laughing.

It should have happened. Mom, if you had thought of doing that, I would have helped you. I would have buried his body.

"We try to help these women," Bates said. "We're not cops."

While we built the wall, some of the inmates practiced the "throw and go" across the road. A 100-foot-long rain gutter a foot off the ground was filled with sand and fuel oil. When ignited, the flame spread through the gutter and created a line of fire giving off black, acrid smoke. We watched as the women moved in a circle, heads and faces covered with fire helmets, goggles and shrouds. They scooped dirt with their shovels, stepped up to the fire, threw the dirt over the flames, moved out of the way and started around again. The flames died for a few seconds and reignited. The heavy black smoke from the burning fuel oil swirled around them.

"Faster, faster," we heard a foreman shout. "Throw the dirt and go, get out of the way for the next person. Don't dump it; spread it horizontally. Use your wrist and throw it—try to knock the flames out. If you're at a brush fire, you've got to know how to do this."

By noon, our crew and 50 inmates had built a 3-foot high stone wall running 30 feet along one side of the driveway. Aside from some dripping cement, it looked like a professional job. When we broke for lunch, the pile of rocks didn't look much smaller, but we had managed to use up the concrete mix. Wall construction was over for the day.

The crews working on the running trail, including two sawyers carrying Stihls with canvas blade guards, came back into camp. The inmates gathered at the picnic tables and opened their lunch pails. We ate inside with the foremen.

The kitchen dished up nice sandwiches, a large bowl of pasta with meat sauce and the usual canned fruit in syrup. A correctional officer, a trim black woman, joined us. "This is my counterpart, Lieutenant Powers," Martins said. "She's in charge of the other side of the camp."

"The wall looks good," she said.

One of the inmates brought her a bowl of pasta.

"How many women get paroled out of here?" Luis asked her.

"Five to ten a month," she said. "A third of them make it. The rest end up back in prison."

"Only a third make it?" Red Eye said.

"That's good," the lieutenant replied. "Most of them get out, do the same shit and come back. Sometimes we get the same girls back here at the camp."

"You must like working here," I said.

"It beats working in a maximum security ward," she said.

"You worked maximum security?"

"Yeah, for men."

"No way," I said, "how could a woman your size do that?"

"We're trained for the job.Besides, sometimes a woman can accomplish things a man can't."

"In a men's prison? That's hard to believe."

"It's true. They all have mothers and girlfriends, so they listen. Women aren't as confrontational, there's no *mano a mano.*"

"So you could handle a two-hundred-twenty-pound guy who's been lifting weights for years?"

"You'd be surprised. One time, during a riot, the male prisoners shoved me into a storeroom so I wouldn't get hurt."

"The lieutenant is tougher than she looks," Captain Martins said. "Believe me."

I wasn't going to argue with Captain Martins or the lieutenant, but it all sounded like baloney to me. The woman was 5 feet 6 inches tall.

After lunch we were ready to leave. We shook hands with the foremen and as we headed for the crew truck, I said to Jake, "Five-foot-six women don't stand up to six-foot men, no way."

"Forget it, who cares?" Jake said.

"But why would she say that?" I said. "No one would believe she worked maximum security. Women can't stand up to men. It doesn't happen."

"For Chrissake, Greg, it doesn't matter," Jake hissed. He climbed into the back of the truck and said, "Hey, I think I found a place in Canoga Park. It's got two bedrooms, furnished. You interested?"

"Where's Canoga Park?"

"Over in the Valley, off Topanga Canyon. It's forty minutes from camp."

"How much?"

"Seven hundred seventy-five each."

"Let's do it," I said. "I'm getting sick of the Bay of Pigs."

"We could move in January second," Jake said. "What're you doing for

New Year's?"

"New Year's?" I said. "Nothing. I've got nothing planned."

"Well, there's a party we can go to. I'm dating a new chick, Nicole."

Every other girl in California was Nicole. "I don't know, Jake—"

"She says it's OK to bring you."

"You sure?"

"Absolutely."

"This'll be the first Christmas I haven't been at home." I thought of the party at the Central Fire Station in Saginaw and Mike Bentak. My parents and Vicky would be there. Vicky would be wearing something tight and short, and freezing. My mother would have no one to talk to. After the meal my father would go outside in the cold winter air to smoke cigars with his "team." Later he would come home drunk. So much had happened in my life since Mike took me aside last year. "You know what my prick father did?" I said to Jake.

"What?"

"He put an answering machine in at our house. Now whenever I call, no one answers. All I can do is leave a message."

"You're father's a piece of work," Jake said.

TWELVE
Chicago, Illinois

THE BUS LEFT SAGINAW ON TIME. A dozen passengers slept, sat hunched over magazines or stared out the window. It was a sad-looking group. Alone in a double seat, I pressed my forehead against the window. This was the day I had waited for; to get away from my father. It was just another Tuesday in May, but it was a momentous event in my life. I watched with mixed emotions as the bus passed familiar sights. I was thrilled about going to California and relieved to be out of the house, but I was also scared. I had never been away from home for more than three days and that was with the entire hockey team. Now I was leaving for good. What little comfort and support I got from my so-called family was gone. I tried to imagine my future, but all I had were vague visions of California. As many times in my life as I had felt alone, this was the worst.

We stopped in Flint, where a couple boarded, and then in Perry Junction to let someone off. Two hours out of Saginaw, we arrived at Michigan State University in East Lansing. Summer vacation had begun and the college students were going home. They looked different from the crowd at Saginaw High. The guys wore knitted sweaters or jackets and khaki pants, no torn jeans and no running shoes. Their hair was short and neat. The girls had long hair, shining faces and red lips. They were all good-looking. Everyone appeared happy and self-assured. I was certain they had parents interested in their futures and families who talked about the day's activities over dinner. They all loved each other; no one was neglected or rejected. They never fought. I wanted to be part of one of those families.

"...So when I signed up for the biology lab, guess what guy was in the same section…?"

"…We're going to hitchhike from Paris down to Nice and stay on the *Côte d'Azure* for three weeks…"

"…The Lit exam was easier than I thought, you didn't have to do all the outside reading…"

"…We always have a Memorial Day dance at our club…"

The girls gossiped while the guys talked sports, cars and summer jobs. They all came from another planet.

In East Lansing more people boarded, but I kept the seat to myself. I watched cars, trucks and highway signs fly past. My hangover was gone and I took out the food Mom made for me. I ate some potato salad, sat with the turkey sandwich untouched on my lap and wondered if it was the last meal she would ever make for me. I replayed the confrontation in the kitchen with my father and thought about all the things I should have said to him.

An hour later, we stopped for five minutes in Battle Creek. As we pulled away, I imagined Mom and Vicky standing on the front porch waving to me, getting smaller and smaller as the bus headed west toward California. I pushed the seat back, closed my eyes and fell asleep.

The driver announced our arrival in Chicago. The college crowd was still talking, still smiling, still headed for reunions with loving families. When we came to our exit on the Interstate, I saw a sign for the University of Chicago. More happy college kids.

Inside the Chicago bus terminal shining aluminum storage lockers covered half the wall next to the arrival doors. In the time it took to stow my duffel, the college kids disappeared. I had 90 minutes to kill. I walked out to the front of the terminal to stretch my legs and breathe fresh air. It was warmer and more humid than in Saginaw. A maze of freeways and exit ramps filled the sky, blocking the sunlight on one side of the terminal. Across the street, a deserted two-story factory stood with broken windows and doors sealed with metal. Green dumpsters overflowing with trash sat next to the building. The bare frame of a bicycle—the wheels and seat were gone—was fastened to a fence with a thick chain. Groups of men stood on the sidewalk and in the street drinking out of brown paper bags.

Back in the terminal, it smelled like stale popcorn oil in a movie theater. It was dark and depressing, the walls were dirty and pieces of the acoustical tile ceiling were gone, exposing black corrugated metal, pipes and electrical wire. A line of people waited to buy tickets from a single clerk behind a counter.

I bought a bottle of orange juice, sat on a wire bench and watched the woman sitting across from me. She was short and plump with light-brown skin. She wore a tight pink sweater with red sequins, pulled down off her shoulders. Her fingernails and toenails matched the color of the sequins. Black brassiere straps looped over her bare skin. Underneath, she had breasts the size of cantaloupes and each time she moved, they quivered, bulging out of the top of her bra. She wore gold hoop earrings and her eyebrows were straight brown pencil lines drawn out from the corners of her eyes. Her neck was thick and one of her arms had a "GLORIA" tattoo. She bent over several times to reach into her bag and I watched gravity play with her tits. Once when she sat up, she caught me looking at her. Leaning back against the bench, she thrust out her chest. Her nipples made another set of eyes under her sweater. "See anything you like?" she said. I looked away. "I said, do you see anything you like?" she repeated, louder. This time I heard an accent. I went for the luggage lockers. As I moved away, she called, "Hey cowboy…" I glanced back and she puckered her lips and blew me a kiss.

I got my duffel and stood with my back to her.

The bus driver opened the double departure doors and waved us aboard. I sat four rows back and slid over to the window. One of the first passengers, a woman, took the seat next to me. She took a black sleep mask from her purse, placed it over her eyes and reclined her seat as far as it would go.

When our driver boarded the bus, she was already asleep, her stomach rising and falling as breath whistled through her mouth. "Ladies and gentlemen," he announced, "welcome to Greyhound Bus Lines. In about three hours, we'll make a fifteen-minute stop in Bloomington, Illinois. We get to St. Louis at midnight, where we have a one-hour stop. If you want to stay on the bus and sleep, that's OK. I'll be your driver until tomorrow when we get to Kansas City at 5:30 in the morning. Have a good trip."

Rolling out of Chicago, I tried to imagine the scene at home: dirty dinner dishes piled in the sink; Mom in the bedroom, the door closed, submerged in a television program; Vicky on the telephone with one of her girlfriends; Dad at the station or down at Richie's drinking. I wouldn't be there for his next tirade or outburst of anger. I wouldn't hear his criticism and complaints and I wouldn't have to worry about doing something that would set him off. Why didn't I feel happier about all of this? I felt claustrophobic and numb. I was too tired to stay awake and too wired to doze off. I heard the rumble of the diesel engine and felt its vibration through the seat. The masked woman continued to sleep. All I had to read was the Cal Fire pamphlet, "So You Want to be a Firefighter." I had already read it twice at home, got the message that the first days would be difficult and couldn't bring myself to look at it again. I rested my head against the window and watched headlights and taillights on the highway. Everyone had a destination.

When we arrived in St. Louis at midnight, the woman next to me awoke, pushed her black sleep mask onto her forehead and left the bus. Half the people remained asleep in their seats. I used the toilet in the rear, which smelled of urine and deodorizer and went back to my seat.

THIRTEEN
Simi Valley, California

SOUTHERN CALIFORNIA WAS TOUGH TO NAVIGATE—freeways went every-where, looping back, connecting and passing over each other like a bowl of spaghetti dumped on the floor. Wherever I went, I had no idea how much traffic to expect. I was either a half hour early or a half hour late.

Captain Bratton, "TB" to everyone on the crew, invited Luis and me to dinner at his home. He lived in Simi Valley, a town wedged into a narrow basin between the Santa Susana Mountains and sheer yellow and white sandstone hills running along the 118 Freeway. I arrived early and drove around. It was a neat, peaceful middle-class town divided by California Avenue, a street with a wide center median of trees and grass. Jake said cops and other law enforcement officers from all over Southern California lived in Simi.

The better homes, on the north side of town, were on streets and cul-de-sacs filled with SUVs, pickup trucks and powerboats on trailers. The American flag flew from most porches or roofs. Banana plants, birds of paradise and palm trees thrived in the dry soil and grew wild in front yards. On the south side, many of the streets ran off into dirt. The homes were shabbier, the pickup trucks were older and there were no boats on trailers. The wind blew equally hard on both sides of Simi Valley.

TB's home, a cream and brown one-level ranch house on the north side at the intersection of Cloud Court and Marvel Avenue, was easy to find. Luis was waiting for me, sitting in his old blue Toyota with the red front fender. "Hey, how long have you been waiting?" I asked him.

"Just got here. Sylmar's only 15 minutes away."

TB opened the front door while we stood on the lawn. "C'mon in guys, glad you could come." His face and arms were covered with bloody cuts and scratches.

"What happened?" Luis asked.

"I was parasailing at Malibu Bluffs Park. When I came in for a landing, a strong gust dragged me through a patch of bushes."

"Ouch," I said.

"It's not as bad as it looks," he said. "Parasailing is really exciting. You know, scratch a firefighter and you'll find an adrenaline junkie. C'mon in." A large black Doberman, ears cocked, watched us enter the house. "This is Zeus," TB said. "He's protective, so let him smell the back of your hand."

"He's all muscle." I said.

"A ninety-pound three-year-old," TB said.

Zeus sniffed, retreated, but continued to watch us. We walked into a small living room. TB's wife, a delicate woman with warm brown eyes, stood up to greet us. "Luis, Greg, welcome, I'm Jill."

"Thank you for inviting us," I said.

An older woman remained seated on the sofa. "This is my mother, Kathy Irons," Jill said.

"Hello boys," Mrs. Irons said.

"The girls are on a sleepover, so it's just adults tonight," Jill said.

Porcelain figures filled a glass case. A collection of photographs covered the coffee table in front of the couch: TB stood in a dress uniform; Jill sprayed one of her daughters and Zeus with a hose; TB held both daughters on his shoulders; Jill waved from the porch of a mountain cabin; a man stood by a Humvee in combat gear.

"How old are your daughters?" Luis asked.

"Jenna and Jean are seven and nine," TB said. "Jean is nine going on nineteen."

"Tom wanted a son, to go into the fire service," Jill said, "but we had two girls and now the baby factory's closed. Tom's secretly hoping Jean will become a firefighter." Jill went into the kitchen and returned with a tray of glasses, two pitchers and a plate of crackers with cheese. "We've got cranberry juice or lemonade."

Louis looked at everything in the room. "You have a nice home," he said.

"Thank you," Jill said. "So you guys survived the 'Rookie Rock Run.'"

How was it?"

"You mean the run up Rambla Pacifico?" Luis said. "It just about did me in."

I poured some lemonade and took a couple of the crackers. "The what? The Rookie Rock Run?"

Jill looked at her husband. "How many rocks did you add to their packs?"

"Just a couple of small boulders," TB said. "They ran with about fifty-five pounds. It doesn't change from year to year."

I laughed, remembering how the crew seemed to run away from us so easily. "I thought it was heavy, but it never occurred to me that you'd be adding weight. I figured I was just tired."

Luis shook his head. "I saw myself coming in five minutes after everyone else, leaving my name on the Wall of Shame and heading home."

"It's just one of the ways to test you," TB said. "Every year on the first run, we add a few extra pounds to the rookie packs, just to shake you up. On the last half mile, the crew slows down and stays just ahead of you, to suck you into going all out. We wanted to see who would quit. We found out."

"I thought they were slowing down," Luis said, "but I was so exhausted at that point, I wasn't sure."

"You never know," TB said, "when you'll be in a situation that will demand everything you've got. You won't be able to stop and wait for someone to pick you up in a truck."

Luis scarfed down the cheese and crackers.

"It's also about handling pressure," TB said. "We'll keep pushing you until we know you won't come unglued under real stress." His blue-green eyes drilled into me. "What about it Greg?" TB asked. "I spoke to Cooley. He had good things to say, but he said you get angry and lose your temper. That true?"

I was surprised; it never occurred to me that anyone would call Cooley to check on me. I felt embarrassed in front of TB's wife and her mother. "Yeah," I said, "I've been known to get a little pissed off from time to time." I immediately regretted using the word "pissed."

"Get over it," TB said. "If you stay in the fire service, you have to master your emotions." He poured more cranberry juice into his glass. "There'll be times when you're in the middle of total chaos and other lives will depend on you. You have to control yourself and stay in the zone."

"Please," Jill urged. "Help yourself." We took more crackers and cheese.

"Where are you from, Luis?" she asked.

"My parents came from El Salvador. My mother and father walked to California."

"Walked to California?" Jill's mother said.

"Yes, they walked through Guatemala and the mountains of Mexico and over the border."

"So they weren't legal," she said.

"No, and my mother was pregnant with me, but she didn't know it."

"But you were born here?" I said.

"I was born in San Diego. My father worked as a painter. There was an amnesty and my parents got green cards. We're all citizens now."

"Why did you become a firefighter?" TB asked Luis.

"It seemed like a great job," Luis said. His forehead furrowed and he became intent whenever he started to talk about providing for his family. "I have a wife and a little boy. He's almost three. We live in Sylmar with my parents; we can't do that forever."

"The great thing about the fire service," TB said, "is you can work at whatever level makes you happy. You can become a paramedic, an engineer or a captain. If you're ambitious, you can work up to a battalion chief or even an assistant chief. If you live through it and stay in one piece, you can do thirty years, get a pension and retire."

"Hector," I said, "will be the oldest FSA alive."

TB nodded. "He is already."

"Are you from California, Greg?" Mrs. Irons asked.

"No, I grew up in Saginaw."

"Your father must be proud of you, out here on your own," she said.

"Actually, we don't get along too well. I haven't talked to him since I left home last May."

"Have you tried?" TB said.

"Yeah, I've called home, but he won't talk to me. I spoke to my mom twice, for a few minutes when Dad was on duty. Now there's an answering machine at the house and no one picks up."

"That's too bad," TB said. "I'm sure he cares about you. Maybe he just doesn't know how to show it."

"I don't think so. He hates me."

"How can any father hate his child?" said Jill.

"Give your father a chance, Greg," TB said. "Give him the benefit of the doubt."

Give him a chance? Would TB's daughters forgive him if he left them alone in a sleazy motel overnight while he went out whoring?

"Families have to stick together," said Luis. "If you don't have your family, you've got nothing."

"Not every family is like yours, Luis." I said.

"What does that mean?" Luis said.

TB sensed the tension. "Greg, I know a dozen guys at Camp 8 who can be your family."

"Family" was an overworked word in the fire service, but for the first time, I was beginning to think TB could be right.

Jill stood and rubbed her hands together. "Excuse me. I'm going to get dinner on the table. Mom, can you help me?" On the way into the kitchen, she bent and kissed her husband on the top of his head. I couldn't remember my mother ever kissing my father. TB and his wife seemed so happy sitting in the living room of their comfortable home. We never had company for dinner. Our living room in Saginaw was usually the scene of shouting and crying. Our house wasn't comfortable, it was a battlefield.

Zeus followed the women into the kitchen.

"Did you know there's a firefighter memorial in Sylmar?" Luis said.

"Sure," TB said. "For the El Cariso Hotshots, a Forest Service crew."

"I went to look at it. The park's beautiful, so peaceful," Luis said. "Ten of them killed. A fire blew up a canyon."

"It was the Loop Fire," TB said. "1966."

"My wife's very nervous about me becoming a firefighter," Luis said.

"She'll have to get used to it," said TB. "You're going to risk your life every day."

The scent of cooking filled the living room while we sat and talked. I felt like I hadn't eaten in a week by the time Jill came out of the kitchen and asked us to sit down. Hot rolls were already on the table. Jill brought out a platter with a cooked bird. It looked small for a turkey, but it was golden brown and gave off a wonderful aroma. Mrs. Irons followed with bowls of mashed potatoes and green beans. Jill returned with a pitcher of gravy and a dish of butter. It was the best home-cooked meal I had ever seen. My mouth watered and I tried not to stare at the food, so I looked up at the ceiling, focusing on the chandelier hanging from a brass chain.

"Bless this food to our use and us to thy service, in Christ's name, amen." TB caught me off guard with his blessing and I lowered my eyes to the white tablecloth. "Darling, this looks fantastic," he said. "Do you think these guys are hungry?"

"It's the biggest chicken I could find," Jill said. "The turkeys were all frozen. I wanted something fresh."

"I always have a dinner for the New Guys," TB said, holding up a glass of cranberry juice as a toast. "Welcome to Camp 8. I think you're both going to do a great job." We touched glasses. TB picked up a carving knife and cut the chicken apart. A puff of steam came from inside the bird.

"How did you end up out here?" Jill asked me.

"I had to get out of the house," I said. "My dad didn't push me to be a firefighter, but his captain helped me apply to Cal Fire."

Jill put a slice of chicken and some beans on a plate and handed it to her mother.

"You've made a good start, Greg," TB said. "You're only how old? Nineteen? Twenty?"

"Twenty in a couple of months," I said, filling my plate.

Luis helped himself to a large portion of chicken, then loaded up on mashed potatoes. "Was anyone in your family a firefighter?" he asked TB.

"Who wants gravy?" Jill asked, holding up a small pitcher.

"No. My dad was a manager for construction projects. He was a tough guy and we didn't always get along, but I always knew he loved me."

Jill went into the kitchen and came back with more potatoes. "There's two drumsticks here. Anyone?" she said, pointing to the platter. Luis held up his plate.

"When I graduated high school," TB said, "I went right into the Marines. When I got out, I wanted to join County Fire, but there was a fifteen-month waiting list, so I started a training program at Ralph's and went to Cal State Northridge at night. I dropped out of Ralph's when I became a firefighter, but I eventually got my degree in communications." He stopped to eat a piece of chicken and some mashed potatoes. "Have either of you thought about going to college?"

"No interest," Luis said. "I've got to feed my family."

"Greg?"

"I don't know, not right now."

"Think about it. It's important. It'll help you promote in the fire service."

It didn't surprise me that TB had a college degree—he seemed so confident and so much smarter than most of the firefighters I had met.

Luis cleaned his plate. He rubbed part of a roll around to sop up the last of the mashed potatoes and gravy. I thought I saw a look of disapproval from Mrs. Irons. Firefighters were always hungry and ate fast.

"Luis, do you want seconds?" Jill asked. Luis passed his plate before she finished speaking.

"This is really a great dinner, Mrs. Bratton. Thank you," I said, and passed my plate as well. "Whose picture is that in the combat gear?"

"That's my younger brother, Ted," TB said. "He signed up for ROTC, finished college and went into the Army as an officer. He says the heat in the Mideast makes California seem chilly."

"I love the warm weather out here. I always dreamed of coming to California," I said. "When I was a little kid, my favorite program was Baywatch."

"We should start to get some rain soon," TB said. "Then the red-flag days and fire watches are over and we go into winter mode— sandbagging, clearing rockslides and doing fire-station maintenance. We have about three months to relax unless we have floods and mudslides."

"It's really going to rain?" I asked.

"Oh yeah, and when it rains, it pours," TB said. "Every winter a couple of cars skid off the canyon roads and we have to go out at two in the morning and fish people out."

We finished the chicken, beans and potatoes. A single roll remained on a dish. Even TB had cleaned his plate. Jill left a small pile of bones and skin. Mrs. Irons had picked at her dinner, leaving most of it.

"Who wants some coffee?" Jill asked. "And my mother baked a pie. How about coffee and a piece of blueberry pie?"

"Since you're forcing us, I'll have pie, no coffee, thank you," Luis said.

"I'll have pie and coffee," I said.

Jill brought in the pie. It was still warm. TB took a piece and Jill poured coffee for us. Jill and her mother drank tea. "In May, things start to heat up, in more ways than one," TB said. "It's a long fire season, from April to December. I don't know if it's global warming or all the unburned debris in the forests, but every year the fires come earlier and get bigger." TB ate his pie, dropped a piece of crust in his lap, picked it up and fed it to Zeus. "At least once a year we have a monster—one of those interagency fires that burns for three or four weeks and pulls resources from all over the West."

"Enough fire talk for tonight," Jill said. "There's life beyond Camp 8. What's your little boy's name, Luis?"

"Miguel. I never thought I could be so excited about a child. I can't spend enough time with him." Luis went on to give all the details.

"What about you Greg? Any girls in your life yet?" Jill said.

"Honey," TB said, "he's only been here eight weeks."

"Eight weeks is plenty of time," Jill said.

"I'm still searching, Mrs. Bratton."

Jill cleared the dishes from the table. When she returned, Luis looked at his watch, stood up and said, "It's getting late, I think I should be on my way. Thank you so much for the invitation." He gave Jill and her mother each a hug. "The food was fantastic. Mrs. Irons, your pie was delicious."

It was such a wonderful feeling sitting in the dining room. I would have liked to stay longer, maybe forever, but I thought I should leave with Luis. "Thanks for the advice, TB," I said. We shook hands and TB and Jill walked us to the door. Zeus followed at a distance.

"If you want to talk about going to school, Greg, just let me know."

"Drive carefully," Jill said.

TB closed the door and Luis and I stood on the sidewalk. "I want a house just like this," Luis said.

"I want to be like TB," I said.

FOURTEEN
St. Louis, Missouri

"A NYONE SITTING HERE?"

"It's all yours," I said. The light in the bus was dim but unless I was dreaming, a great-looking woman was about to sit down next to me.

"Miserable hour to be getting on a bus," she said. "Where you going?"

"Sacramento."

"California? How long does that take?"

"About a year."

The passengers were all aboard and the driver dispensed with departure announcements. At 1:05 a.m., we rolled toward Kansas City.

"My name's Carol."

I tried to get a good look at her. I saw tight black jeans, a black knit sweater and a brown leather jacket. She opened a black leather purse and in the middle of the night, fixed her lipstick.

"My name's David, David Jordan," I said. It just came out; I didn't even know anyone with that name.

"Any relation to Michael Jordan? You look like a basketball player. " She had a stunning face, a ski-jump nose and short, spiky hair. She gave me a dazzling smile and said, "Just kidding, but you're big enough."

"I'm a firefighter, or will be soon. That's why I'm going to Sacramento."

"Where are you from?"

"Saginaw, land of ice and snow."

"Tell me about it. I grew up in Lake Placid. In the winter the thermometer stayed at fifteen below for weeks and we had twenty-five feet of snow by the end of March."

"Saginaw was never that bad."

"They ran the snowplows over the lake to clear it for hockey. The ice was two feet thick."

"Hockey's my favorite sport," I said, and pointed to the scar over my eye. "Are you coming from Lake Placid?"

"No, I live in St. Louis now."

"Where you going?"

"Out to Colorado Springs. My boyfriend lives there. Actually, my ex-boyfriend."

"How do you find a boyfriend in Colorado Springs when you live in St. Louis?"

"We were together in St. Louis for a year. We started arguing and he moved out. He wanted to go to Colorado, so he found a job as a cook at the Air Force Academy."

"Are you moving out there?"

"No, I'm visiting him for a week." She turned toward me and I saw that she was beautiful. "Are you going through Denver?"

"Yeah. I have to change there. I've been on this damn bus for about fifteen hours, and I'm about to go crazy. You should have seen the beast sitting next to me before."

"Well, I'm not a beast. I can keep you company till Denver." She turned toward the front of the bus. The interior lights dimmed and she melted into the darkness. I thought she had gone to sleep.

"So you're going to be a firefighter," she said.

"A wildland firefighter. My dad's an assistant chief in Saginaw. He's received several commendations. I'm headed for Sacramento for training with Cal Fire."

"Sounds like a dangerous job."

"It is, but my dad would have been disappointed if I had done anything else." *My dad would have been disappointed.*

"He must be proud of you."

"How did you get from Lake Placid to St. Louis?"

"Oh, Lake Placid was a backwater, I hated it. I had a friend in Saranac Lake and as soon as we could, we took off. We went to New York City and trained as dental assistants. When I graduated, I went to work for a dentist on Long Island." She turned in her seat again to look at me. "The bastard was married, but he was always after me. I finally gave in and we had an affair. After a couple of years of banging me in the office and motels, his wife found out. All of a sudden I was out on the street. I found a job in St. Louis. I've been there five years."

Silence again. The diesel gave off a deeper growl as the bus started up a long hill in low gear. In the right lane, a string of semitrailers labored, red and orange lights in a line. I hadn't been away 24 hours and I was already having an adventure, talking to a great-looking chick in the middle of the night on a Greyhound headed for California. This woman wasn't a wreck like my mother, and not a teenager like Kirsten. In the stale air I thought I smelled her perfume. I was getting a boner.

"How long have you been going out with your boyfriend?" I asked. Silence, no response. I leaned toward her and saw that her eyes were closed.

I definitely had a major boner.

FIFTEEN
Malibu, California

B Y MID-JANUARY OF 2000, seven weeks after I arrived at Camp 8, no rain had fallen. The ground was dry and the Santa Ana winds were still blowing. Fire warnings were posted daily and engines and bulldozers were predeployed around the county for immediate response.

On January 5, late in the morning, a grass fire was reported in the hills on Mulholland Highway. It may have started by a spark from the blade of a county tractor clearing roadside brush and spread quickly. The wind pushed the flames toward expensive homes and horse-boarding facilities. Engines from Stations 99 at La Piedra Beach and 71 near Zuma couldn't control the fire and requested additional help.

We got the call during lunch and I was on the way to my first incident as a Los Angeles County firefighter. I wanted my father to see me, riding with crew 8-2, my own "team." We sped up Coast Highway in the truck, blasting our air horn at intersections, watching cars pull over to let us through.

I looked out at beaches jammed with people. A dog chased a Frisbee. Surfers swam among the whitecaps in the rough water. I thought I saw Baywatch's Pamela Anderson by the edge of the water, her body bursting out of her tiny orange lifeguard suit. It was two different worlds—the party on the beach and the emergency response here in the truck.

"Greg, Luis, listen up," Jerry Dunham yelled from the front seat. I was in the back row and could barely hear him over the noise of the engine. "...from onshore wind...pushes fire north and west into the hills...night...turns around... the Santa Anas...in from the desert..." I cupped my hand behind my ear, but it didn't help.

Red Eye leaned over and said, "In the summer, there's a marine layer and cloud cover until noon, but not this time of year." He grabbed the back of the seat as we wound around a tight curve on Kanan Dume Road. "Fuel dries out late in the morning and into the afternoon and fire burns faster as the day goes on."

"Just watch the Channel Seven weather report," Jake shouted from my other side, sticking his elbow into my ribs. "It's a lot easier."

As the truck began the steep climb near the top of Kanan Dume, we received a radio message: "Crew eight-two proceed to Kanan and Mulholland for structure protection at Highland Stable. Crews from Camp 13 have been dispatched." A small cheer went up when we heard it, and Jake and Red Eye exchanged high fives. The mood in the truck, which was always good-humored, became rowdy. We were going to a fire party with the women from the inmate camp.

At the Mulholland intersection, two men were wrestling a frightened horse into a trailer parked on the shoulder. Thick clouds of black smoke drifted across the highway, making it difficult to find the entrance to the stable. The first of the inmate crew trucks sped past us. Visibility was less than 10 feet as we followed them through the smoke, bouncing along a rough dirt access road. Varela, the engineer driving the inmate truck in front of us, radioed that he could barely see. Art slowed and the second truck from Camp 13 rear-ended us. It was only a minor impact that bumped us forward. "Hang on guys, we just took it in the ass from the inmates," Jake yelled. Flames in the low brush and grass around us were 3 feet high and moving fast, but everyone laughed.

We arrived at a dirt parking lot. The access road was on the wrong side to provide a firebreak from the oncoming flames. The wind was pushing the fire directly toward us from the highway. The engine crews from 71 and 99 had their hands full. Through the smoke, we could make out the side of a barn, another building and empty metal corrals, all of which faced Mulholland and the approaching flames. Jerry Dunham jumped from the cab and shouted, "Your safe zone is the parking lot!" We unloaded our tools and Art turned the truck around to face the exit.

The inmates piled out of their crew trucks, wearing their bright orange fire suits with the CDC letters. Some of the women looked frightened, almost hypnotized. "Holy shit," one of them said. Several stood motionless, looking through the thick smoke at the flames.

Inmate camp superintendent Martins ordered, "Line up and get your tools and listen to your crew bosses. Anyone who screws up here goes back to Chino." They formed a line behind the truck, passed out their tools, adjusted goggles and helmet shrouds and headed into the smoke.

Jerry Dunham directed us to the side of the barn to clear brush. We moved through smoke so thick that I could barely see. An orange figure, one of the women, abruptly ran out of the black cloud and we collided like two hockey players. My helmet flew off when my head bounced against the hard dirt. Before I could move, the inmate was up and running again, screaming, "Rats! Rats!" Behind her, two more orange figures came dashing and shrieking. Somewhere the fire had burned through a rat's nest and dozens of gray rats, long tails twitching as they ran, streamed out of the smoke toward me. I struggled to remember if the Fireline Handbook said anything about female firefighters and rats.

I put my helmet back on, pulled my goggles over my eyes and moved toward the barn as more rats charged past. Our crew was lining up to clear brush at the far end. Chainsaws started, each sounding like an explosion. The foremen from Camp 13 reorganized the inmates and they moved in behind our crew, looking like firefighters instead of frightened women.

Martins appeared out of the smoke. He grabbed my arm and said, "Hey Kowalski, help me out." He pulled me into the barn where we saw a woman and two stable hands trying to control a group of anxious horses. A dozen more paced and whinnied in their stalls.

"Thank God you're here!" the woman shouted. "I have a week-old foal in the back. The mare won't budge. Get the foal and the mare'll follow you." She looked at me and yelled. "Can they turn off those goddamn chainsaws?" The smell of smoke was increasing and the animals were starting to panic. She turned and shouted, "Manuel, get halters on them; get them out of the stalls!" She jumped up on a horse. Riding bareback, she urged it out of the barn. As she rode past another worker struggling with two horses, she grabbed the lead ropes and pulled the animals behind her. "The foal," she cried again, pointing to the back of the barn.

One of the Mexicans opened the gates to the stalls. The horses bolted out as soon as their gates swung open. Slipping and sliding on the cobblestone floor, they raced to follow the woman out of the barn. Martins and I ran to the back to get the foal. In a corner, we found a frightened white mare pressed against the wall and a small copy on wobbly legs cowering next to her. Martins opened the gate and began waving and jumping in front of the mother, trying to distract her. "Grab the foal, Kowalski," he shouted.

I edged into the stall while the mare, as tall as I was, did a nervous dance. I moved toward the foal. Without thinking, I got on my knees, put my arms around the frightened animal's legs, ducked my head under its belly, and strained to lift it to my shoulders. It may have been a baby, but it weighed well over 100 pounds. I staggered out of the stall, managing to carry the foal a few steps before it twisted out of my arms and fell to the ground. While it regained its footing, its mother almost trampled Martins coming after it. Mother and baby disappeared through the barn doors and Martins and I followed. Through the smoke, I saw the woman on horseback leading the herd down the access road to Mulholland.

Martins pulled his goggles down over his eyes, turned to me, slapped me on the back and shouted, "That mare looked like my wife the day I bought my bass boat." Martins had nearly been trampled by a half ton of terrified horsemeat, but he was laughing. Before I could smile at his joke, I heard the roar of a helicopter. One of the Firehawks was coming in from the east. When it appeared, it was only 200 feet above the hillside. The rotor wash from the blades hit us as the Bird slowed and its nose pulled up before it released a full load of 1,100 gallons of water between the barn and the oncoming flames. Martins and I were drenched by the wind-driven shower.

I retrieved my shovel and joined the crew. I pulled my goggles back down over my eyes, wrapped the wet shroud across my nose and mouth and stepped onto the fireline between Hector and Luis. Our crew was doing the more difficult initial cutting and scraping. Behind us came an inmate crew, finishing the work on the 3-foot wide cut we were clearing through the brush and grass. Jerry Dunham, working at the head of the line, yelled, "Bump up!" and we moved a few feet farther along.

More engines arrived. Crews laid additional hose lines out to the second building and sprayed the area in front of it. Other inmate crews were now clearing a line near the corral. At the head of their line, two women, both wearing dark-green leg protectors over their orange prison fire suits, used chainsaws.

The women didn't work as fast as we did, but they made steady progress. Together, we managed to clear a decent firebreak around the back and side of the barn, the building, and the corral.

The fire burned dirty, in patches here and there, as it moved past the stable. Jerry Dunham shouted that we were to proceed further down Mulholland to protect the homes now in the line of the advancing flames, leaving Martins and his crews to extinguish hot spots. We headed back to our crew truck and heard another Firehawk overhead. The smoke in the parking lot had already begun to dissipate. In the excitement, I had lost all sense of time. I looked at my watch. In less than an hour, I had been knocked to the ground by a female inmate, nearly overrun by rats, persuaded to carry a small horse and doused by a fire helicopter. Overall, it was a good start to my wildland firefighting career.

We drove out onto the highway and I saw that two sheriff's deputies had joined the woman and stable hands. They struggled to hold the horses, which had been further terrified by the helicopter. For the first time, I got a good look at the woman. She was young, a girl around my age and a knockout. She wore a white shirt streaked with dirt, jeans, leather chaps and boots with spurs. She looked like someone out of *The Horse Whisperer*. We slowed at the entrance to Mulholland and I pulled back the window and waved to her.

"Thanks for the help," she shouted. "Come back and say hello. I'm Deborah."

The crew truck lurched onto Mulholland, we bounced in our seats and Red Eye slapped me on the back. "Whoopee, Greg's got himself a cowgirl."

By late afternoon, the onshore air currents had subsided and the fire lay down. By evening, it was contained. It had burned 110 acres and required 14 engines and 200 firefighters. Because of the expensive homes and the history of fires in the area, fire response was always aggressive. The attitude in Malibu was, "You can never be too rich or too thin, or have too many firefighters." No structures were lost, no humans or animals were injured and it went into the record books as just another brush fire. Only a pack of rats was left homeless.

Two weeks passed after the fire at Highland Farm. The days went quickly and rookie duties at the camp sometimes dragged on into the evening. Some nights I was so exhausted I stayed overnight at the camp and collapsed in bed.

I kept thinking about the girl with the horses and couldn't pass up her invitation to get acquainted. At 7 p.m. one evening, I decided to go see her.

It was cold driving through the hills of Malibu. Not Michigan cold, but colder than I would have expected in Southern California. The heater in the Jeep barely worked and the canvas top had more holes than an old fire hose. I turned off Mulholland onto the bumpy dirt road and my headlights lit up the effects of the fire. The ground was scorched and I saw the silhouettes of singed trees and burnt bushes. A split rail fence was half charcoal. Floodlights lit the barn and horse corrals. One car was parked in the lot where we had stood in the swirling smoke the day of the fire.

I parked and wandered into the barn, feeling stupid showing up unannounced at night. A man brushed a horse outside one of the stalls. He looked up as I entered. "Hi," I said, "I'm looking for Deborah, is she around?"

"Deb, the barn manager? She lives in the trailer at the far end of the parking lot."

I walked back across the lot and, for the first time noticed the trailer tucked under the trees. A washing machine on cinder blocks sat next to it. Light came through closed curtains. Without climbing the metal stairs, I knocked on the door. I got no response and knocked harder.

"Who is it?"

"Fire department, we're here to inspect your stove."

"What?" She opened the door. Her frown immediately turned to a smile. "Well, the fire hero. I was wondering if I would see you again." She wore jeans and a sweatshirt and was barefoot. Her light brown hair was tied up in a yellow bandanna. From the trailer, she looked down at me. She was as pretty as I remembered and definitely belonged in a movie.

"This is the first time I could get over here," I said.

"Welcome to the ranch house. Are you coming in, or are you just going to stand out there in the dark?" I climbed the steps, bent my head and stepped into the trailer. "What's your name?" she asked. "If I'm inviting a man into my trailer at night, I should at least know his name."

"I'm Greg."

"And I'm Deb," she said, extending her hand.

"I remember your name."

"It's nice to see you again. And thanks for rescuing the foal."

"All part of the full service offered by your County Fire Department."

"Sit down. Do you want something to drink? A coke or something?"

The interior was tiny and cramped. I had to bend my head to avoid an air vent on the ceiling. A small dining table and a built-in bench were tucked into one end of the trailer. I barely fit on the bench. "Orange juice would be great." Everything in the trailer was undersized.

She opened a small refrigerator under a double-burner stove. "That fire was so scary," she said. "I've never been through something like that. The horses were totally freaked and the helicopter didn't help."

"That's our transportation to some of the fires."

"We were lucky. When we got out on Mulholland, the sheriffs were there to help us." She sat down with two glasses of juice and tucked some of her hair back into the bandanna. "It took forever to get trailers and by that time the fire had already moved past. The horses were out there for an hour and then we took them back to the barn."

"I'm glad we could help out. That's our job." I looked around the narrow trailer again. "So this is where you live?"

"Yeah, it's my office too. I'm the barn manager."

"How long have you worked here?"

"About two months. I spent a semester at Pepperdine, but didn't like it. I gave riding lessons up here on the weekends and the owner offered me a full-time job. My daddy wasn't too happy when I dropped out of school."

"You looked like a rodeo rider the day of the fire. Where you from? The South?"

"Texas. Outside of Dallas. My father owns a small ranch. I grew up with horses. Where are you from?

"Saginaw."

"Michigan? What're you doing out here?"

"This is home now."

"I'm glad you came by."

"I would have come sooner, but I've really been busy over at the camp."

"I've always had a thing for firemen. You guys are such heroes."

"We're called firefighters."

"OK, firefighters. 'Masters of Disaster,' right?"

"That's the motto."

"How long have you been at it?"

"Down here, about two months. I started last summer in Sacramento with Cal Fire, the old Department of Forestry and Fire Protection.

"Wow, a forest ranger too, quite a package. What else can you do?"

"Well, I'm a hockey player."

"No one plays hockey out here but the Kings. It's too hot. How about horses? Can you ride a horse?"

"I've carried one. Does that count?"

"I think I should teach you to ride—what do you think?"

"That might be fun."

"If I get you up on a horse, you'll be at my mercy."

"Should I be worried?"

"Maybe."

"Are you always this straightforward?" I asked.

"I have two older sisters, both prettier than me. I always had to fight for anything I wanted, including boyfriends."

"Do you have a lot of boyfriends?"

"Oh, dozens. Sometimes they come by at two-hour intervals. You lucked out—I had a cancellation." She got up and turned on a CD player. "What kind of music do you like?"

"We listen to KZLA at the camp."

"I grew up with country western and hate it. How about jazz?" She sat down again across from me.

Sometimes after you look at a girl for a while, she isn't as pretty. The more I looked at Deborah, the better she looked. "How old are your sisters?" I asked her.

"Twenty-one and twenty-five."

"And that makes you…?"

"Nineteen, next week."

"Next week is your birthday? Cool. Maybe we could go out for a movie."

"I'd like that. Would you wear your uniform?"

"Does a uniform turn you on?"

"So does a man on a horse."

"What do you think about this? I'll let you teach me to ride if you teach me how to cook something."

"What?" She laughed and reached to touch my hands. Her skin was rough, and I could feel calluses on her fingers. Her nails were short, no polish. "What a deal."

"Yep, that's it. I have to learn to cook something new."

"I know how to make great turkey chili. It's easy to prepare, even on a little stove like mine."

Deb brought out a candle, lit it and turned off the rest of the lights in the trailer. We sat at the cramped table for two hours. She had a great sense of humor and it was easy to talk to her. She told me about growing up on a ranch in Texas and about her family. Her older sister was married and lived in Houston. The younger one worked for a computer company in Austin. She talked to each of them every week on the phone. Her father called frequently to give her advice about managing the barn. Her mother called to give her advice about men.

I told her about the rookie crap I was going through at Camp 8, and the guys in the crew. I didn't mention my family.

"Do you think you're more like your mother or your father?" she asked.

"Uh, I'd have to think about that. I'm not sure."

"You're how old?"

"I'll be twenty in April."

"You're almost twenty and you don't know which parent you take after?"

"Do you?"

"Sure. I'm like my daddy. I've always known that. I'm happy-sassy like my mom, but I'm most like my daddy."

"Well, my mom isn't happy-sassy."

"Here's a question I always ask guys I meet— what's the best and worst quality you've inherited from your parents?"

"I don't know, I have to think about that one too." I didn't want to get into this discussion.

"You have parents, don't you?"

"Yeah, and a sister."

"How old is she?"

"Seventeen."

"How often do you talk to her?"

"It's been a while. I'm not too close to my family."

"Well, do a little research, I want to know about your folks. My momma says you can learn a lot about a guy from his family life."

"Like I don't have anything else to think about." She didn't need to hear about my family life. "How do I get hold of you?"

"The best thing to do is call the barn. If I don't answer, I'll get the message. Call before you come, I can't have my boyfriends trippin' all over each other, can I?" Deb stood up and brushed my cheek with her lips. "Thanks for coming by."

SIXTEEN
Denver, Colorado

"GOOD MORNING FOLKS, it's five a.m. and we'll be arriving in Kansas City in about thirty minutes. We'll stop for an hour and five minutes. Thank you for traveling with Greyhound."

On the road ahead, it was still dark, almost black, but behind us a golden light began to fill the sky as the sun rose. My first sensation was of something leaning against my left side. A body was curled against me. A head rested on my shoulder. In the middle of the night, Carol had raised the center armrest. I didn't want to disturb her, but she was awake.

"I could use some coffee," she said, sitting up. "Thanks for the shoulder. I must have really slept."

I saw the color of her eyes for the first time; they were pale blue and her skin was the color of a pearl. "I think I'll go wash up," I said.

When I climbed over her into the aisle, she said, "You're even taller than I thought."

The toilet still smelled terrible and I got in and out as fast as I could.

The sun had risen by the time we arrived in Kansas City. I followed Carol off the bus. She was about 5 feet 7 inches tall and had a trim body. We walked into the terminal and sat on stools at the counter in the Traveler's Grill. She turned toward me. I couldn't take my eyes off her. "Well, big boy," she said, "you hungry?" A tired-looking waitress came to take our order. "I want scrambled eggs, dry toast and coffee," Carol said.

"I'll have the same," I said. "And I want orange juice and crisp bacon. Have you got bacon?"

"We've got bacon."

The coffee came first. Carol put three packets of sugar in her cup and I thought about Mom and the way she drank her coffee. I wasn't sure what time it was at home, but soon she would come down into the kitchen, make coffee and sit down to look at the morning paper. Vicky would still be asleep.

I was hungry and didn't care if the food was good or bad. I shoveled it in and finished before Carol even touched her eggs. We sat in silence while she ate. She put her hand on my shoulder and swiveled around again to face me.

"What're you staring at?" I asked.

"Oh, nothing special. I was just thinking how much better-looking you are than Cliff."

"Who's Cliff?"

"My ex-boyfriend in Colorado Springs."

"It doesn't sound like you're looking forward to seeing him."

"It's not going to work—I already know that. I'm headed out there because I couldn't think of anything else to do. I had some time off."

The waitress brought our check and I took it. "I'll buy breakfast." I had never bought breakfast for anyone in my life. I had never even had breakfast with a woman other than my mother or my sister, who didn't count as a woman.

"Thank you," Carol said, "because I'm going to buy you dinner in Denver."

I looked at the check. It was $9.45, not a major drain on my limited bankroll.

"I'll go freshen up," she said. "See you outside."

An hour had disappeared sitting at the counter in the Traveler's Grill and it was time to go. Our new driver, tall and paunchy, stood by the door as we boarded.

"What were you doing in Saginaw before you decided to go out to California?" Carol asked when we were back in our fourth-row seats.

"I was at Michigan State. After my first year, I wanted to start my fire training."

"What were you studying?"

"Oh, the usual stuff."

"Did you have a girlfriend?"

"Sure."

"Were you close?"

"Yes."

"What did she say when you told her you were leaving?"

This was starting to sound like the conversation with my mother.

"She was upset."

"Were you sleeping with her?"

"Yes."

"Are you a good lover?"

"No one's complained." It was true, Kirsten had never found fault with my efforts. I swallowed. My dick was pushing against the front of my jeans. Sweat was starting to drip down beneath my shirt. Carol looked at me in that way girls look at you when they're interested. I tried to picture her naked.

The bus rolled on through Kansas. I looked out the window at the morning sun shining over fields of corn, each plant 3 feet tall. The highway was flat, the land was flat and the horizon was flat. We passed farms with tractors tilling the soil. In places, wheat and alfalfa covered the ground. Endless rows of crops streamed by the window. Cattle stood in mud and drank from water troughs. Wood farmhouses and barns appeared and disappeared like ships on a sea of dirt.

Carol took off her leather jacket and pushed up the sleeves of her sweater, exposing delicate arms with tiny blond hairs. Her skin was almost transparent. The morning melted away. The rumble of the bus, the stale air, the monotonous scenery—none of it mattered while I sat next to her. We were flying toward Denver.

"When do you have to be in California?" she asked.

"By the end of the month. I've got eight days."

The bus stopped in the middle of nowhere, in a land without a single tree. It was Colby, Kansas, a town that looked like a strip mall. A man and a boy, each with a beat-up suitcase, waited to board. "This must be the grain basket of the country," I said.

"The bread basket or the grain belt, I'm not sure which," Carol said. "Let's get off and stretch for a minute." I followed her off the bus. Standing on the sidewalk, she put her hand on my arm. "Here's what we're going to do," she said, moving closer. "When we get to Denver, we'll have drinks and dinner. Then we'll find a hotel near the bus terminal and spend the night together. It's my treat." She squeezed my biceps. "I want a nice hot shower, and then we'll have some fun."

In the time it took her to make her proposition, my body was soaked in sweat again and the inside of my pants was wet. "Let's...uh...do it," I stuttered.

The horizon was no longer flat. Before any part of Denver was visible through the front window, I saw the Rocky Mountains. What began as a jagged blue line in the distance soon became the entire Front Range, bathed in shades of blue, gray and green, rising up from the flat Midwestern plains running into Denver from the east. During the last hour, we made small talk. We looked out the window. Carol's arm on the center armrest pressed gently but firmly against mine. Since she had proposed the evening in Denver and I had agreed, there wasn't much left to discuss. We passed warehouses and trucking centers surrounded by green fields and then the Denver Airport, with its white roof built to resemble snow-covered mountain peaks. At 4:30 p.m., when our driver gave the 30-minute arrival announcement, the only words I heard were "...Mile High City."

Denver was different. Everything looked new. The center of the city was small—much smaller than Chicago or St. Louis. The streets were clean, and trees grew from squares cut in the sidewalks.

"OK, big boy, you carry the baggage," Carol said, pointing to a large black bag with silver tape on the handle, piled with the other luggage beside the bus. I picked it up; it was heavy and had no wheels. I slung my duffel over my shoulder and followed Carol into the a dreary terminal. An American flag covered one wall and every sign was in Spanish first, then English. There were a few people inside. A man slept on a Mexican blanket spread on the floor.

Carol was 10 steps ahead of me, already speaking to a black woman behind the Traveler's Aid counter. "C'mon," she said to me, "I got some directions. There's a hotel three blocks down. This way."

We walked back out of the terminal. Carol crossed 20th street and I struggled to keep up with her. It was warm; the air was crisp and dry and a gust of wind pushed a soda can down the middle of the street. We passed the 20th Street Gym and an adult video arcade advertising "Beautiful Ladies Behind

Glass." Two men with long braided ponytails growing out of shaved heads stood outside smoking. I was breathing hard and struggling to keep up with Carol. Maybe I wasn't in the best physical shape after all. I stopped in front of the video store to catch my breath.

Carol paused and turned. "I can put on a better show than anyone in there," she said, nodding toward the video store.

"I wasn't looking; I'm just out of breath."

"That's the altitude. It's a mile high here."

"That's a relief; I thought I lost a lung."

On the corner of Larimer Street, Carol stopped in front of a Buddhist Temple and looked around. "The hotel must be another block down. Do you want to eat now? I don't even know what time it is, but I haven't had a decent meal since I left St. Louis."

"I can always eat," I said.

We saw a cafe on the other side of the street. As we crossed, I looked down the middle of the empty street at an enormous sign for Coors Field. Beyond, the mountains rose above the low Denver skyline. The cafe looked decent, with a green awning, plants hanging in the windows and the day's menu taped to the door. "Let's see if we can get a drink," Carol said.

Inside, it was empty—too early for dinner. A grill and counter were on one side of the room, tables with purple tablecloths filled the center and on the far side, three booths lined the wall. Carol slipped into the one in the corner. I dropped her bag and sat across from her. As soon as I sat down, she came around to sit next to me. She let her hand rest on the inside of my thigh and an electric current shot through me, radiating out from my groin. I got hard in record time.

She looked down and smiled. "You're ready for this evening. Good boy." Turning to the waitress she said, "Can we get a drink?"

"No, we don't have a liquor license."

"OK, I'll have some coffee—black and sugar. I'm going to wash up." Carol intentionally brushed my cock with her hand as she stood up. With my pants sticking out, I couldn't get up to go to the men's room.

When she returned, wearing fresh lipstick, Carol sat on the other side of the table. I was relieved. When she reached across, put her hand around mine and caressed the inside of my wrist with her fingers, my excitement returned.

"Hang in there, David," she teased. "We'll be at the hotel before you know it."

I ordered a chicken fried steak, not certain whether I would get chicken or steak. Carol ordered soup, a mixed salad and spaghetti. She ate with care, selecting each mouthful with her fork. We lapsed into silence. From time to time, she ran her finger over the top of my hand. The clock over the grill said 5:45 p.m.

I thought about dessert, but Carol asked for the check. When the waitress brought it, she fished in her purse and left a small pile of dollar bills and change on the table. "Let's go," she said.

Picking up our bags, I followed her out the door. It was going to be a night to remember, a night I would tell my friends about. I thought of Willie Nelson singing, "The bright lights of Denver were sparkling like diamonds..."

Walking down 20th Street again, we came to the Centennial Hotel, an old three-story red brick building. Carol held the door open for me and I struggled through with our bags. Inside, a bar filled with cigarette smoke occupied most of the narrow ground floor. On the far side, two stuffed chairs and a coffee table served as a lobby. Hidden under wooden stairs, a man in a red plaid shirt leaned on the registration desk. Carol approached him. "My brother and I need a room."

"How long will you be here?" he asked.

"Let's start with tonight."

"You want twin beds?"

Carol paused for a moment. "Sure."

"I'll need a credit card."

"How much is the room?" she asked, handing him a credit card.

"It's forty-two dollars a night. The rooms are up there," he said, pointing to the stairway. "Room six. Sorry, we don't have an elevator." He swiped the card and handed it back to Carol.

"Can we leave our bags here for a few minutes?"

"Sure, I'll keep an eye on them."

"C'mon David, I'm dying for a drink." Carol took my hand and pulled me toward the bar.

A few men sat drinking and watching a Rockies baseball game on a small black and white television set. The bartender was a dried up little man with one of those mustaches that looks like it was drawn on with a pencil. He wore a Western-style shirt and a string tie. His shirt collar was too large for his skinny chicken neck.

Carol ordered a vodka tonic. "Make it a double vodka."

"You got an ID?"

Carol showed him her Missouri driver's license. I tried to see her date of birth, but couldn't make it out in the dim light.

"What about him?"

"What do you want to drink?" she asked me.

"I mean, let's see his ID."

"Look," Carol said, "we're on our way to Colorado Springs. Our mother is in the hospital with cancer and she's about to die. We're both upset and a drink would ease the anxiety and make it a lot easier to get to sleep. Help us out here."

"I'm not supposed to serve anyone without an ID," he said.

"David, what do you want to drink?"

I had no idea what I wanted to drink.

"Give him a rum and Coke. Don't be stingy with the rum."

A rum and Coke, Christ.

The bartender didn't argue and turned to make our drinks. Carol leaned forward on her stool, put her hand behind my neck, drew me toward her, and kissed me on the lips. I was caught by surprise. She pulled back before I could put my arms around her.

My drink tasted like it was all Coke, and I drank half at once. As it hit my stomach, I felt a warm sensation and realized it did have rum in it. Carol sipped her drink once, stood and walked to the stairs with her glass in one hand, the room key in the other.

"Let's go, David. You're on."

SEVENTEEN
Malibu, California

B EFORE I CAME TO A STOP, Deb was out of her trailer, coming across the parking lot toward the Wrangler. "Hi, Greg. Ready for your riding lesson?"

"Hey, Deb." I climbed out of the Jeep. "Are these boots OK? They're all I have—they're my fire boots."

"They'll do this time. It's not a horse show."

"I'm sorry I couldn't cut loose for your birthday but I'll give you a rain check." I pulled a bag out of the Jeep. "I brought some presents."

"Birthday presents, oh boy!" Deb yanked the bag out of my hand and started to go through it. "Cool. An L.A. County Fire Department Camp 8 hat." She put it on. "Oh, wow, an L.A. County Fire Department Camp 8 T-shirt, size XL." She draped it across her chest. "And an L.A. County Fire Department Camp 8 sweatshirt, size XXL." She swung it around over her head. "Is this a tent or a sweatshirt?"

"Sorry, Deb, firefighters only come in two sizes— extra large and extra, extra large. Happy birthday."

"Thanks, Greg. I can see you spent a lot of time shopping." She gave me a kiss on the cheek. "Time for a lesson. I thought you could ride Killer. How does that sound?"

"What?"

"Just kidding, I've got my horse Merlin tacked up. He's very gentle. You'll just ride around inside the arena to get the feel of being on a horse. Come on." She took my hand and pulled me toward the barn, carrying her birthday gifts in the other hand.

When we entered the barn, I saw a brown horse standing quietly, his head held by two small chains attached to posts. "The saddle looks kind of small," I said. "Where's the thing on the front that you hold on to?"

"This is an English saddle. If you can ride this, you can ride a Western saddle with no problem." She dropped the birthday gifts by a stall.

"Can't I start with a Western saddle?"

"Nope." Deborah unbuckled the horse and handed me the reins. "OK, firefighter, let's walk Merlin over to the arena. She took a brown helmet off a hook and handed it to me. "You have to wear a riding helmet. Try this one."

"I still don't see what I'm supposed to hold on to," I said, glancing at the inside of the helmet to check for Vaseline and powdered graphite.

"You hold on with your thighs. You control the horse with your legs. Good leg action is important." We walked from the barn to the arena, the other building we had worked to protect the day of the fire. Inside, a dirt floor with a white railing around it filled most of the space. Fluorescent lights gave off a faint glow from above. The air was cool and damp and birds flew around inside near the roof. Deb led me over to a platform with stairs. "Hold your arm out—I have to see how long to set your stirrups."

"What's my arm got to do with the stirrups?" I asked.

"That's the way it's done," she said, and reached under the horse to lengthen each strap. "Now step up on the mounting block." She positioned the horse by the side of the platform. "Up you go," she said, pushing my butt.

"What's its name again?"

"*His* name is Merlin. And relax, it's been a week since anyone around here was thrown off a horse and broke his neck. Take the reins in your left hand. Now, put your left foot in the stirrup and swing your other leg gently over Merlin's back."

I followed her instructions and found myself sitting in the saddle. Merlin didn't move. I looked down at Deb. I thought about jumping off Merlin, putting my arms around Deb and kissing her. Jumping off Merlin seemed like the hard part.

"Take one rein in each hand and let's walk out to the center of the arena." She led the horse around in a circle.

"We're moving. Nothing to it."

"Ready to move on your own, Greg? Keep your head up, eyes forward.

Now give him a little squeeze with your lower legs." Merlin began to walk slowly across the arena.

Deb stood aside and looked at me. It was a strange feeling, sitting high on the animal's back, sensing its strength and feeling completely powerless to control it. "How do I steer him?"

"If you want to go right, open the right rein and hold it out a little to the side. Shift slightly in the saddle and look right. It'll shift you body and Merlin will know."

I looked at Deb again. She was so sure of herself, handling the horse and giving me instructions. Merlin moved a few steps to the right.

"Now try going to the left."

"What if I want to stop him?"

"Stop him?"

"I need to know, just in case he breaks loose."

"He isn't going to break loose," she laughed. "If you want to stop, pull the reins back gently."

Merlin and I managed to move around the arena. I wasn't frightened, but I wasn't sure who was in control—Merlin or me, or maybe Deb. I thought of the day of the fire, when I saw her jump onto Merlin's bare back and ride him without a saddle. It looked effortless, but I realized it took a lot of skill, like skating backward at full speed. Merlin and I walked around in the arena making a figure eight.

"Do you want to try a little trot?" Deb asked.

"I think I've had enough for today."

"No way, you've only been riding ten minutes—that's hardly anything."

"What do I do next?"

"To trot, look forward and squeeze him a little with your lower leg."

"The old leg-squeeze—I know that one."

"Say, 'Merlin, trot,' and squeeze until he starts."

I squeezed, and the giant beast started to move. I immediately started bouncing up and down. Every time Merlin took a step, the saddle came up under me like a spring. "Good, Greg, good," Deb shouted. "You have to get the rhythm, and move up and down with the motion of his body. Up and down, that's called posting." Merlin moved another 10 feet, which was 10 more bounces for me, then stopped.

"I think I need some personal training with the up and down body motion, Deb."

"I can see where this is going. Next time we'll do an hour, but we have to get you some boots first." Deb looked fantastic from the rear as she led Merlin and me across the arena. Her jeans were snug across her ass, her blue shirt tight against her body.

The barn was empty when we returned. Deb put Merlin back on the cross ties. I watched while she placed the helmet back on the hook, removed the bridle and carried the saddle and blanket to a storage locker next to the stall. "You could be helping me, you know," she said, walking Merlin back into the stall.

"No way—I'm having way too much fun watching you. Besides, I've had a tough day in the saddle."

"You don't know tough."

"Sure I do." I followed her into the stall and put my arms around her. She didn't resist. She turned to me and I kissed her. She pulled me closer, locking her arms around my back and squeezing hard. I kissed the soft skin where her neck met her shoulder, pulled open the top snap of her shirt and kissed her again.

I could hear her breath in my ear.

"Not here, let's go to the trailer," she whispered.

We tried not to run across the parking lot.

One side of the trailer had a slide-out wall with a small mattress. I was still fumbling with the double-knotted laces on my fire boots when Deb's riding boots hit the floor in the narrow space in front of the bed. By the time I got one boot off, I heard the snaps on her Western shirt popping open. I looked up and she stood in front of me wearing a simple black brassiere and black thong underwear. I put my arms around her, holding her ass in my hands. She kissed me, pushed away and started to unbutton my shirt. I pulled off my other boot without untying the laces and slipped off my pants. I wrapped my arms around her again and she shoved me onto the narrow bed, falling on top of me. Her skin smelled of hay. Thrusting her shoulders back and her breasts forward, she reached back and unhooked her bra. I pulled off her thong and then my shorts. I was still wearing my socks. I rolled on top of her, which wasn't easy on the small bed. She dug her fingers into my ass.

"You have a nice *derriere*," she said.

"So do you." I assumed she was talking about my ass.

"Have you got something?"

"In the Jeep."

"Too far." She rolled over and pulled open a drawer built into the base of the bed. "Use this." She lay back and watched intently as I put on the condom. As soon as I had finished, she took hold of me, spread her legs, urged me on top of her and slipped me inside. Through the rubber, I could feel the heat of her body.

We screwed, or made love, or whatever you call it. It blew my mind. I could never get enough of something like this. Deb wrapped her legs around my waist, her heels pressing into my back. Her breasts were crushed against my chest. Everywhere our skin touched, my sweat intensified the contact between our bodies. She scratched my back and ran her fingers through my hair. Every nerve in my body felt connected directly to my dick. For once, I didn't notice my feet hanging off the end of the bed. We kissed. I ran my tongue over her breasts. I moved against her. She moved with me. Deb began to tremble and sigh. It was all I needed. I came, holding her by the shoulders and pushing myself as far inside her as I could. She let out a squeal, which I was sure everyone on Mulholland Highway could hear. "Is the trailer still attached to the foundation?" I asked.

"It may not be," she said, relaxing but still trembling as she lay beneath me. "Hi-ho, Silver."

I lay on top of her until my heartbeat slowed. We kissed, kissed again and I rolled over, trying not to fall off the narrow bed.

"Way to go, Greg." Her face and neck were flushed. She lay on her back next to me, without covering herself. She had long, thin legs with strong, muscled thighs, a patch of brown pubic hair, a narrow waist, full breasts with large nipples, tanned arms and weathered hands. She squeezed my dick with her hand. I was still hard.

"I'm glad you didn't ask me to slap you."

"Slap me? Why would I ask you to do that?"

"Some women like to be slapped." We lay on our backs for a moment in silence, holding hands.

"I could get some hockey tickets," she said. "We could go see the Kings play."

"That would be fun."

"I have a friend, Gaye. Maybe she and her boyfriend would like to go too."

"I have to be sure I'm not on duty."

"So do you want to stay and have some dinner? We could make turkey chili."

I tried to look at my watch without being obvious. "You know what, I'm supposed to do a bunch of stuff this evening at camp. I can't stay."

"Well that's great. Fuck 'em and leave 'em."

"I'm sorry, Deb, I really have to go. I didn't know it was so late." I pulled on my shorts, put on my shirt and pants and bent to put on my boots. "We shouldn't have wasted so much time with the horse."

Deb lay back on the bed and looked up at me. "So when do I see you again?"

"Soon. I have to check my schedule." I bent and kissed her nipple and then her lips. She tried to pull me to her, but I backed away. "I've really got to go."

Driving back to the camp, I saw a carpet of stars in the clear sky. Our lovemaking made them brighter than usual. I didn't feel the cold air. I was relaxed, happier than I could remember. I thought about how it had felt to make love to Deb, to be inside her. I imagined living with her in the trailer. It was cramped, the ceiling was low, but I could get used to it. We would be a couple, do things together. I would come home exhausted after two days at a fire, walk up the three metal stairs, open the trailer door and say, "I'm home." She would be wearing a bra and panties and throw her arms around me. I would carry her to the back of the trailer and we would make love. Then she would get up and cook dinner.

My happiness was short lived. When I got back to the Bay of Pigs, Jake was awake, lying on top of his bed reading a magazine. "There's a problem," he said as soon as I opened the door.

"A problem?"

"Yeah, the bear got cold."

"The bear got cold? What the hell does that mean?" After the wonderful evening with Deb, I didn't feel like putting up with a bunch of crap from Jake.

"It means, New Guy, that you forgot to take down the State flag and the other flag, you know, the one with the stars and stripes."

"Oh, Shit!"

"Yeah, and to make it worse, Luis wasn't here to do it either. Art had to go out in this freezing weather to do it himself."

"It's not exactly freezing weather."

Jake gave me his evil smile. "It'll be dealt with tomorrow. You ran off to see some honey without taking care of your duties. We can't tolerate that." He dropped his magazine on the floor and turned out the light.

I stood in the dark. "Don't you want to know what went on over at Highland?" I heard no response and knew I was getting the treatment. I forgot about Deborah. I had to worry about my breach of discipline.

In the morning, I was up early. It was 5:45 a.m. and still dark. Deb was still a warm sensation I felt in my body. I dressed and slipped out without disturbing Jake. I wanted to finish my duties before the day's activities began. I raised the two flags. It was early, but the bear would just have to endure the cool morning air. I filled the refrigerators with Gatorade, put water and grounds in the coffee maker and checked the latrine for paper towels and toilet paper. I loaded the food boxes in the crew trucks with granola and energy bars. The chores were getting old. Luis went home at night and I seemed to do more than my share. I didn't mind—I had no family to go home to—but it would be good to get over the bullshit.

Now it was 7:15 a.m. I thought I had time for a cup of coffee before everyone arrived and the day began. I walked back toward the kitchen and the blanket caught me by surprise when it dropped over my head. I couldn't see anything.

"Rookie, you fucked up."

"You froze the bear, now you freeze."

"Greggie, you ran off after a piece of ass and let your crew down." That was Jake.

I crashed down onto the cement walkway, the thick blanket smothering me. "You jealous bastards. You don't even know what a piece of ass looks like," I shouted. I tried twisting onto my stomach, but two guys—I guessed Hector and Red Eye—were on top of me. Someone managed to wrap a rope around my ankles. They rolled me over and over, winding the rope up around the blanket until I was hog-tied.

This time I wasn't going to get pissed off and lose my temper. I remembered what TB had told me one afternoon: "Put up a struggle and don't be a pussy, but don't lose your temper. They're going to test you."

"You jealous bastards," I yelled again. I knew they would tie me into the Stokes basket and I would be "iced." This was my second time, so I knew the procedure and it was going according to the script. Luis hadn't even arrived. He was missing all the fun.

They dropped me in the basket, peeled the blanket away from my head and dragged me out to the helicopter pad. Raphael stood on the service stairs above me. As I looked up at him, helpless, his face was upside down. He poured the first pitcher of ice and water on my head. It ran down my neck onto my chest and my sweats absorbed the water. More ice water arrived. Like an old fire brigade, Art and Jerry Dunham ran with pitchers back and forth to the kitchen and up the stairs to Raphael who performed the delicate task of dumping each load on my head. I suffered through this better than Luis, who had grown up in Southern California and had less tolerance for the cold. There were plenty of days playing hockey in Michigan when I felt as cold as this, though not as wet.

Jake, Hector and Red Eye stood by, taunting me. The wind was blowing and as the "icing" continued, I started to shiver. I was now completely soaked. "You assholes!" I shouted. As I screamed, Hector bent down and threw a handful of flour into my face. The flour went into my eyes and mouth. I inhaled it and began to cough violently as I gasped for air. This was new; I hadn't had the flour treatment. I was choking and trying to curse the crew at the same time. My eyes were full of flour, but I could see Art bending down next to me. I was helpless to defend myself when he smeared peanut butter on my head and face, and then tried to work as much of it as he could into my nose, ears and mouth. I noticed immediately that it was chunky style. I coughed and spit peanut butter and flour which brought howls of laughter.

"Hey, what the hell's going on out here?" I heard TB's voice, but couldn't see him. "This isn't a frat house. You guys are supposed to be firefighters, not college boys,"

That's the end of this, I thought.

"Who's responsible for this?" TB asked. No one said a word—there was silence. The guys were about to catch hell. "Kowalski, you're responsible, you've undermined the discipline of the entire camp." I thought I heard his voice crack in his effort to sound angry. "Release this man immediately," TB ordered. The rope and blanket came off. I climbed out of the Stokes basket, ice water dripping out of my sweats. "Kowalski, on your face," TB shouted. "Give me thirty—no, give me forty pushups. Now. Now! Hurry, we're going for a run before breakfast."

Shivering, I managed to do 39 pushups before TB put his boot on my butt and pushed me down onto the cement. "That's enough. Kowalski, don't ever let the bear freeze again." He stepped back. "OK. guys, you've got ten minutes. We're running four miles with full packs. Let's go."

I ran to our room, dried off and tried to wipe away some of the peanut butter. I was changing into dry clothing when Jake came in to pick up his pack. He was laughing.

When we assembled out on the cement, packs fully loaded, I was still shivering.

EIGHTEEN
Denver, Colorado

I CLIMBED THE NARROW STAIRS carrying Carol's suitcase in one hand and dragging my duffel behind me. My heart hammered. I felt dizzy. My head floated away from my body, I had trouble focusing my eyes and my ears were ringing. I realized that I was either drunk, the altitude was affecting me, or both. At the top of the stairs, Carol held her drink and waited for me in the doorway of room number six.

I stepped past her, dropped the bags and struggled to clear my head. She closed the door, put her drink down and turned to look at me. My dick was hard again. Maybe it had been that way since dinner, I couldn't remember. I put my arms around Carol, pulled her to me and bent to kiss her. It seemed like the right moment.

"Whoa, whoa, not yet," she said, pushing me away. "We've got to follow a procedure here, David, and you're way ahead of yourself." She backed away from me, sat on one of the beds and swallowed the last of her drink. "First, you're going in there," she said, pointing to the bathroom. "Take a shower and clean yourself up. Get all the bus dirt off. Got it?" She removed her leather jacket and kicked her shoes off. "Then I'll shower. By myself. While I do that, you sit here on the bed, OK?"

"OK," I said, taking my toothbrush and toothpaste from my duffel and heading into the bathroom. Her voice had a different tone, more businesslike, but it was a relief not to have to worry about what to do next. The bathroom was bare. A couple of thin bath towels and washcloths rested on the edge of the sink. The shower and tub was a one-piece white plastic shell, which had a large crack running from the showerhead down to the drain.

I stripped. I had worn the same clothes for two days and they were foul. I turned the shower on and the weak stream got warm, but not hot. The water felt good and my head started to clear. My entire body tingled with anticipation and my dick was so hard that any contact would have put me over the edge. I washed myself as best I could with the tiny bar of soap. It lasted a minute before it slipped down the open drain.

I stepped out of the shower and stood naked, watching the water drip from my body onto the floor. I wiped the mirror and looked at my face, verifying that it was actually Greg Kowalski who was about to have this escapade. I brushed my teeth and rinsed my mouth under the faucet. The bath towel was big enough to go around my waist but my erection was no secret.

I came out of the bathroom. Carol studied me carefully and said, "Good boy." She had pulled back the spread on the closest bed. The overhead light was off and a scarf over the lamp on the nightstand between the beds filled the room with a blue tint.

Still dressed, she went into the bathroom. I heard the door lock. Silence. What was she doing in there? More silence. At last the shower went on. I sat on the bed and waited. It seemed like she was in there forever. Finally, the shower stopped and I heard the water in the sink. I was trembling.

The door finally opened and Carol came out. She had a small plastic bottle in one hand and placed it on the nightstand. I didn't know what to look at first. Her breasts were the size of plums, with tiny pink nipples. They were smaller than Kirsten's, smaller than what you see in the magazines, but they looked perfect for her body. Her hair was wet and drops of water ran down her white stomach. On her left hip, she had a small tattoo of a red five-pointed star. My eyes came to rest on her pubic hair. I smelled her perfume.

"Come here, David," she ordered. Cupping a breast, she offered it up to me. "Bite my nipple."

I bent to her and began to suck. Her skin was warm and moist. I put my arms around her, one hand on her back, one hand on her ass.

"Bite, I said, not suck."

I took her nipple between my teeth and bit gently. It became rigid.

"Harder, harder," she urged. She dug her nails into my shoulder. I bit her with more force. "Now the other one," she said. She pushed her breast into my face. I moved my teeth back and forth over her nipple and touched the inside of her thigh. She held my wrist. "No, not yet. Keep doing my breasts."

I went from one nipple to the other, pulling them into my mouth and biting them with my front teeth. She gave a faint cry and twitched each time I touched her.

"Good," she said. "Now, come over here." She threw herself onto her stomach on the bed. She spread her legs slightly, her feet hanging over the edge. "Slap me," she ordered.

"What?" I said.

"Slap me, on the ass, hard."

My hand grazed her.

"Harder...harder."

I heard the sound of my palm hitting her butt.

"Better. Keep doing it...more...come on."

I hit her twice on each cheek, each time with more force. Her skin turned pink, then red. I could see part of the imprint of my hand on her flesh. A small cry escaped from her mouth. "Good—more." I struck her again and my hand stung from the impact. Was she enjoying this? She made another sound and I couldn't tell whether it was a cry of ecstasy or pain. Still face down, she raised herself to her elbows and knees. "Now in," she said. "Stick it in, David."

Nothing I had done before prepared me for this. I had messed around with a couple of girls in high school and one of them gave me blowjobs. When I started going out with Kirsten we had sex, but it wasn't like this. Kirsten lay under me on the pink bedspread in her bedroom, her legs spread and her arms around me as I shoved myself into her. Kirsten barely moved. "That's so nice, Greg," she would whisper. Was it supposed to be the way Carol and I were doing it? I wondered if this was what my father did with his women.

My towel was off. I moved against Carol and barely touched her with the tip of my dick. "Inside, David, put it in," she urged. She turned to look at me, breathing through her open mouth, her face red. "Oh, Christ, let me help you. Where's the lube?" Rolling over, Carol took the bottle off the nightstand, squeezed out some white gel, rubbed her hands together, and grabbed my cock. The lube felt ice cold. At her first touch, I exploded with a force that covered her hand and wrist with semen. The muscles in my groin contracted again and again. I closed my eyes and felt the fluid coming out of me. I wanted to stop it, but it was too late, I couldn't. I stood panting, my legs trembling and looked down at her slender hand dripping with my semen.

"Oh, you baby!" she cried. "This is supposed to be on the inside, not on my hand. Damn it, couldn't you wait?" Her face twisted with anger. Semen dripped onto the rug. "You child!" she yelled. Her eyes flashed. She slapped me on the face.

I knew how my father would have treated Carol. I slapped her back with my open hand. Surprised, she fell on the bed. When I hit her again, she gave out a tiny cry and her head jerked sideways from the impact. I slapped her once more, hard. Her mouth began to bleed and she rolled into the fetal position, covering her face with both hands. She didn't cry, but rocked back and forth on the bed, whimpering. I put my foot against her bare back and shoved her off the other side of the bed onto the floor. "You bitch," I shouted.

I don't remember leaving room six or walking down the stairs, but I was outside the Centennial Hotel and it was 10:45 p.m. You couldn't see Willie's bright lights of Denver now, because it was pouring rain. I was wearing my dirty clothes again and water ran down my face. I had to get away from the hotel. A white Denver Police car passed. Did Carol call them? She could have dressed and gone downstairs to show her bleeding face to the man at the front desk.

That bitch—she deserved it.

I walked back toward the bus terminal, the duffel slung across my shoulder. Crossing Larimer Street, I saw a sign against the side of the adult video building not visible from the opposite direction. It was a billboard for the Denver and Rio Grande Western Railroad, *The Royal Gorge Line*. Floodlights illuminated it through the rain. I covered the last two blocks on the run as the rain came down with more force. The Bus Center was empty. The sole occupants were two old men playing cards on a bench. If the police were looking for me, they would come here and arrest me. I had to get on a bus, wherever it was going, but the departure area was empty, everything was closed. I walked across the deserted terminal and out to the street where three taxis stood with their lights off. I opened the door to the first taxi and climbed in the back seat. "Take me to the train station," I told the man in front.

He flipped on the meter, which registered $5 and turned to me. "That's on 17th and Wynkoop, six blocks from here."

"Never mind, I'll walk." I reached for my duffel.

"Too late, the meter is on. Besides, it's pouring."

The taxi took me back down 20th. I slumped in the back seat. Carol deserved what she got. *"That'll teach you a lesson."* That's what my father always said to my mother after he hit her.

NINETEEN
Malibu, California

DRIVING DOWN THE DIRT ROAD to the parking lot, I saw a man wearing jeans, a denim shirt and cowboy boots come out of Deb's trailer. I stopped and watched him dash behind the barn. He was in a hurry. Moments later, a black Dodge Ram pickup truck, the type with the snarling grille, came barreling out and flew toward me. As he passed my Jeep, I got a quick look at the driver. His face was tanned, his hair cut short. I guessed he was in his early 30s. He was just the kind of guy who would appeal to Deb—a handsome, rugged cowboy type. He had parked behind the barn so no one would see him. It was a truck people would recognize and Deb must have told him to keep it out of sight. She was having an afternoon with one of her other boyfriends.

I gripped the steering wheel of the Jeep and pulled as hard as I could. The bitch. I thought she was joking when she said she had other boyfriends. I wondered how long he had been in the trailer with her. How long did it take to get his cowboy boots off? Did she help him? What did she say when she came? "Hi–ho, Silver!" I drove into the parking lot and stopped near the steps to the trailer. Deb opened the door as I got out of the Jeep.

"Hi, Greg, what a surprise?"

"I'll bet it's a surprise."

"What?"

"I said, 'I'll bet it's a surprise.' "

"What's the matter?"

I climbed the three steps and brushed past her into the trailer. "Is the bed still warm?"

"What are you talking about?"

"Do you want to do it twice in one afternoon with two different guys?"

"Are you out of your mind?"

"Don't lie to me. I just saw that guy come out of here. The cowboy. Did he do you with his boots on?" The bitch was cheating on me.

The smile disappeared from Deb's face. She looked at me, her mouth open. "You think that guy was in here screwing me? Is that what you think?" Her voice was shrill. "You jerk," she shouted. "That's our vet. He's here every week. He takes care of the horses, you idiot." Her mouth began to tremble.

"Here in your trailer?"

"This is also my office." She pointed to the small dining table. It was covered with papers, a calculator and a notebook. "We were fucking? That's Doctor Barringer, for Christ' sake. How could you think that, Greg? Do you think I screw every guy who comes around? How could you?" She sank down at the table. Tears welled up in her eyes and began to run down her cheeks onto the papers. I looked at her, unsure I believed what she was saying. She began to cry harder, hands over her face. She rubbed her eyes with her fingers. "I'm not sure I even know you."

"Deb, I—"

"I don't need this grief, and I don't need you." Still crying, she opened a drawer in the small kitchen. "Here's the Kings tickets." She ripped them in half, ripped them in half again and threw the pieces at me. "Get out—get out, I don't want to see you again. Get out!" she screamed.

As I drove back to camp, my hands were shaking and my stomach began to churn. The thoughts I'd had of spending time with Deb, going places with her, sharing my life with her, all vanished. I felt abandoned.

TWENTY
Sacramento, California

"Hey, it don't open till five thirty."

"What?"

"The station's locked up at midnight."

I looked around, but didn't see anyone.

"You gonna stand out there all night in the rain? C'mon under here, this way." Denver Union Station had a metal awning covering most of the sidewalk. It was supported by thick steel cables anchored to the building halfway up the three-story walls. "If you have money, you can stay over there, at the Oxford Hotel. It's $165 for the night." Out of the shadows in the corner of the building, next to a cement bench, a dirty hand extended from a green Army jacket and pointed across the street. I stepped under the metal awning, wiped away the water running into my eyes and saw a man sitting on a blanket, wedged between the wall and the side of the bench. His hair and beard were one tangled mess. "I have a friend over at the hotel. He cleans up at night, brings me stuff that's left in the kitchen. He comes around one o'clock." He leaned toward me.

"What's up, kid?"

"I have to get a train to California."

"Not until morning. The station's locked until five thirty. Sit down—take a load off. Roger McKlusky." The dirty hand extended again. "I'm a physics professor at DU"

"DU?"

"University of Denver. Right now I'm on sabbatical."

"You're a physics professor?"

"Yeah. String theory's the thing, and quantum mechanics. You can be here and there at the same time. Understand?"

"What?"

"That's quantum mechanics. You have to know where your electrons are. You're a nanoparticle on the face of the universe. Why're you going to California?"

"I'm going to—"

"Know why California is like a granola bar? Because it's full of fruits and nuts and flakes. Heh. C'mon, sit over here."

After my evening with the bitch Carol, I wasn't about to listen to this weirdo. I'd probably have to punch him to get him to shut up. I started down the sidewalk.

"Hey, where you going?"

The other end of Union Station had the same metal awning, the same cement bench, but no raving lunatic. I stretched out, my legs hanging over one end, used my duffel for a pillow and watched the red light from the "Travel by Train" sign reflected in the puddles on the street. It was a long night. I must have looked at my watch 20 times before it was 5:30 a.m.

"You wanna go to Sacramento, California? Right? Today?"

"How much is the cheapest fare?"

"Are you making a reservation, or just asking?"

"I don't know. How much is it?"

"Adult, right?"

"Yes."

"No, wait, there's a student discount. Are you a student?"

"Yes."

"You wanna ticket?"

"How much is it?"

"Seventy-five dollars. That gives you a reserved coach seat. Not up above in the Vista Dome, down below. The *California Zephyr.* Thirty-one hours to Sacramento, arrival tomorrow afternoon at three forty-five. Moffat Tunnel; Rockies; Salt Lake City; Reno; Sacramento. Do you want a ticket?"

"*Let's go, David, you're on.*"

"Yes."

"Is this credit card or cash?"

"Cash."

"Seat twenty-eight, a window. Track Eight. Eight fifteen a.m. Do you wanna make a dining car reservation?"

"No."

"Here's some info about the *Zephyr*."

Union Station was deserted. The morning light was beginning to shine through the cathedral windows.

I waited.

"Welcome to Amtrak. *The California Zephyr*. The most beautiful train trip in all of North America. Lower-level coach seats."

"Let's go. David, you're on."

"Trails and Rails, fostering appreciation of America's natural heritage, the Moffat Tunnel; Glenwood Canyon; the heart of the Rockies."

"Whoa, not yet, not yet."

"Breakfast selections include a variety of hot and cold entrees; a breakfast omelet is $9."

"We've got to follow a procedure."

"Lunch is available in the dining car between 11:30 a.m. and 3 p.m. Reservations are suggested. Dinner choices include braised beef, pork chop, lamb shank, seared catfish, herbed cod fillets or tri-color tortellini, starting at $12.50."

"Bite, I said, not suck."

"Glenwood Springs, Colorado; Green River, Utah; Salt Lake City, Utah."

"Harder."

"Dessert choices include Mississippi Mud Cake or cut fruit. Coffee, tea, milk or juice is included."

"Slap me on the ass."

"Lounge and café cars also provide comfortable, casual seating for playing cards or other games."

"Now, stick it in."

"Elko, Nevada; Reno Nevada."

"No, no, you baby."

"Truckee River; Donner Lake; Sacramento, California."

"*You child.*"

The bitch, she deserved it.

"Will you accept a collect call from Greg Kowalski in Sacramento, California?"

"A collect call?"

"Vicky, it's me. Accept the call."

"I'm not supposed to—"

"Vicky! Accept the call."

"Yes, OK, I accept the call."

"Hi, Vicky."

"Where are you?"

"Sacramento."

"Dad's been on a rampage since you left. He said if you called collect, not to accept the call."

"I just—"

"I'm not supposed to be talking to you. Why are you calling? You've only been gone three days."

"It seems longer. I want to talk to Mom."

"She's not here."

"How are you?"

"I'm trying to stay out of the house, away from Dad."

"Is he home now?"

"No. Listen Greg, don't call back. He'll be pissed, and you know what that means for us. I'm going to hang up now."

"I'm doing great—thanks for asking, Vicky."

"Bye, Greg."

"California Department of Forestry and Fire Prevention."

"Could I speak to Valerie in the Fire Training Office?"

"Just a moment…"

"…This is Valerie."

"Hello, my name is Greg Kowalski. I'm here from Michigan for a seasonal firefighter job. I'm supposed to call you when I get to Sacramento."

"What's your last name again?"

"Kowalski."

"Just a moment…Yeah, I've got it. Gregory, where are you?"

"It's Greg. I'm at the train station. Here in Sacramento."

"You're supposed to be in Auburn."

"Auburn?"

"Fifty miles east on Highway Eighty."

"How am I supposed to get there? I just got off the train. No one told me I had to be in Auburn."

"Just a minute Gregory, hold on."

"It's Greg—"

"…Gregory you're in luck. Someone's going out to Auburn in about an hour. Wait in front of the station, under the entrance that has the Amtrak sign over it. Look for a white station wagon with a red stripe and Cal Fire on the side. Welcome to California, Gregory."

TWENTY-ONE
Pozo, California

WHEN THE NATIONAL WILDLAND FIRE OUTLOOK was posted in the Camp 8 office in May, Dozer predicted there would be a colossal fire. Drought conditions were intensifying in much of the West and the fire potential in California was rated "extreme" due to low humidity, elevated temperatures and limited precipitation. Fuel conditions were "significantly drier than normal" throughout the state. Reading between the lines, Dozer said it meant trouble.

It came in July.

We had just returned from assisting with the first course of the Malibu summer training program for the Community Emergency Response Team, run by the county to teach civilians basic disaster and fire response skills. The P.A. erupted and TB called us into the meeting room. "The Pozo Fire up near Santa Margarita is getting nasty," he said. "This is the ninth day. It's burned almost sixty-eight thousand acres and only fifteen percent contained."

I glanced at Luis.

"We got the call from SoCal Dispatch," TB continued. "There's eighteen hundred firefighters on the lines and Nifsee's calling for seven hundred and fifty more."

The guys leaned forward in their chairs. The testosterone was starting to flow. The hair on the back of my neck stood up. Finally, we had a major wildfire.

"How long will we be up there?" Luis asked.

"I don't know," TB said. "It could be two or three weeks. I'm heading up late this afternoon and I'll meet you for a briefing at eight o'clock sharp tomorrow morning. Dozer's got directions. It's a four-hour drive. Everyone stays here tonight."

"Hey guys," Art said. "Here's your chance to head out to the Big One. The fun's just starting. You'll get to sleep on the side of a mountain and drink crappy coffee."

"Yeah, bullshit," Jerry Dunham said. "The big fires aren't nearly as great as they're made out to be, especially in the Los Padres. It's steep and the vegetation's thick. It's a bitch."

"I know, but don't tell them," Art said, winking at us. "They just wanna have fun and be interviewed on the six o'clock news."

We left Los Angeles in the crew truck Saturday at 4 a.m., heading up Highway 101 to the Central Coast. Driving along the ocean as the summer sun rose, we saw tiny profiles of offshore drilling rigs in the Santa Barbara Channel. We listened to KZLA and Clint Black kept us company.

Raphael checked messages on his cell phone. "Can you believe it—I'm on my way to fight a wildfire and my wife wants me to go to divorce mediation this afternoon."

"I didn't know you were getting a divorce," Luis said.

"Yeah, I'm moving out. Sandra's keeping David."

"Have you tried counseling?" Luis asked.

"I don't think it'll help and neither does Sandra."

"You should do it for your son," Luis said. "He needs to grow up with a mother and a father."

"That's a crock," said Red Eye, resting his head back against the seat with his eyes closed. "Half the marriages in the U.S. end in divorce—higher in California, and even higher for cops and firefighters. The kids grow up just fine." With a year of college, Red Eye often quoted statistics and facts and spoke with more authority than the rest of us.

"Bullshit, " Luis said. "Divorce is the reason there are so many fucked-up people in the world. "

"Just because people stay married," I said, "doesn't mean the kids won't be fucked up."

"And you're living proof," Jake said, jamming his elbow into my ribs.

This was our crew. We knew each other's hang-ups and personal problems. We shared our lives and joked about all the sensitive stuff. No one got angry.

It reminded me of playing hockey. We were a team, in it all together. We took care of each other and it felt reassuring to be surrounded by this group of guys. This was where I belonged. TB was right. It was like a family—a good family.

As we drove north, our anticipation of the Pozo fire increased. Everyone in the truck was jazzed; we couldn't wait to get there. The sky ahead of us began to show a brown haze and, as the highway turned inland at Pismo Beach, we saw the gray plume of smoke from the fire rising thousands of feet in the air. Pushed by the wind, it drifted east.

"Look at the size of that," Raphael said. "There's your convection effect."

"What exactly is that?" Luis asked.

"You get a vortex," Raphael said. "Hot air spinning upward, heavier cold air moving down to replace it. Some of these updrafts are twenty thousand feet high."

We turned off the 101 and headed for Santa Margarita, five miles east. Trucks and SUVs were parked in front of the solitary convenience store in the small town. People were stocking up on food and bottled water in case of an evacuation. We continued east on Pozo Road, a two-lane country road bordered by forest and grassland. A mile off to the side we saw the coastal mountains of the northern end of the Los Padres National Forest, covered with dense brush and trees. San Luis Obispo County—the locals called it "SLO"—was known to have one of the worst wildfire environments in California. Eight fires in 15 years had each burned between 50,000 and 100,000 acres.

Along Pozo Road, dilapidated homes, many with horses in pipe corrals and others with goats and cattle behind wooden fences, dotted the landscape. We passed a weathered sign for the "Flying LB Ranch," hanging in front of a rotting farmhouse. We were trained to be aggressive, to protect property and to attack in the face of flames, but would anyone risk his life to save a worthless building like the Flying LB?

We stopped at the Rinconada General Store, another weathered wooden building with an ancient Esso sign hanging above what was once a gas station. At 8 a.m., it was already warm. The relative humidity was in single digits and the temperature was rising. The county sheriff had established a checkpoint and closed Pozo Road to all but emergency vehicles. The cut-off to the incident command post at Lake Santa Margarita was just beyond the line of sheriff's cars. Fire equipment from Los Angeles, Santa Barbara, Ventura, Kern and SLO Counties filled the dirt lot in front of the store. Forest Service and BLM engines, Highway Patrol and SLO sheriff's cars idled in one lane on Pozo Road. A Cal Fire D-6 bulldozer rested on a flatbed at the side of the road. Every vehicle blazed with red and orange flashing lights. Federal, state and local organizations had come together to fight a major burn. Art squeezed the crew truck in behind a Forest Service engine and we found TB standing in a dirt lot, wearing his Nomex pants and a blue T-shirt, talking to a group of firefighters.

We stepped out into the smoky air and stretched our legs while TB spread a map of the Los Padres Forest on the ground. "Morning, guys. We've got a monster fire and they've called in a Type I incident command team." He bent over the map. "It started at a place called Turkey Flat, probably from a campfire, and moved into the forest. There's a lot of dead pine from pitch canker and the whole forest is full of dry brush and vegetation."

"Let's get at it," Raphael said. "The sooner I'm on the fireline, the harder it'll be for my wife to call me."

"The F-ban says it's severe fire weather up here," TB said. "Low moisture levels and plenty of heat. Forty miles of direct and indirect line has already been cut, a lot of it in difficult terrain." TB ran his finger across the map. "The problem is, the fire's moving north and east during the day, but it's not lying down in the evening. Sundowner Winds are taking it west during the night, so the flank of the fire during the day is becoming the head during the night and playing havoc with containment." Bits of ash settled on us as we stood listening to TB. "There's major air support. A lot of crews and equipment are being shuttled in by helicopter." He smiled, shook his head. "Yesterday one of the P-3s dropped a load of retardant on a Forest Service handcrew."

I had heard stories of men suffering broken bones when they were hit with retardant, which was nothing but fertilizer mixed with red dye and water. Sometimes the fertilizer didn't dissolve and it came down in chunks. In Auburn, they told us to hit the ground if there was incoming retardant, face in the dirt, head covered with your helmet.

"Hector, what color do you get when you mix retardant red with Forest Service green?" Jake said.

"I give up Jake, what color?" Hector said.

"Retardant red," replied Jake. "It covers everything."

"Is that supposed to be funny?" Hector said.

"Of course it's funny." Jake never missed an opportunity to make fun of Hector, who had no sense of humor.

"We're meeting a Forest Service crew in Pozo," TB said. We're going into the base of the hills to do backfiring. A D-6 will be in there to help us."

"How big's Pozo?" Art said.

"It's not a town anymore," TB said, "just the Pozo Saloon."

"I'll stay and protect it," said Jake.

"C'mon Jake, cut the crap," TB said, his eyes flashing brief anger.

Art handed out the King radios and we got back in the truck.

TWENTY-TWO

Pozo, California

GINA WAS THE CAPTAIN of the U.S. Forest Service station in Pozo. Short and muscular, she looked too young to be the captain of anything. Standing in a shop filled with tools, fire hose and supplies, we studied a 3-by-6-foot sandbox resting on metal sawhorses. Someone had drawn out roads, molded some of the local mountains and placed small sticks and plastic spoons in the sand to indicate places of importance. Gina spent 10 minutes showing us the area and the contour of the land. "We're on the Southwestern perimeter of the fire," she said. "We're working on finishing a direct line that'll tie into a Jeepway that runs along here." She turned to point to a thin blue line on a Forest Service map that covered the entire wall of the shop. "We'll backfire when the wind holds. There's regular weather updates."

"If you have the feeling the brush is growing back as fast as you cut it, you're probably right," one of the Forest Service crew added. "It's thick out there."

Gina picked up her daypack and started out the side door. "Follow us down Pozo Road," she said. "The pavement ends in a mile and it turns into dirt. It gets steep and there's a lot of washboard, but the traction's alright. There's a Cal Fire inmate crew already in there with eighteen men. Two Forest Service Hotshot crews will join us this afternoon. They were on their way to New Mexico, but got called back. We have extra water on the truck, but if you need to fill up, now's the time to do it."

We trailed Gina and her four-man crew in a new mint green Forest Service engine onto Pozo Road and past the saloon, which stood alone in the middle of a field. It was one more dilapidated, rotted wood building. I wondered why people didn't use paint out here. No one in Michigan would let a building go unpainted like that. Pozo Road ran another quarter of a mile, made a sharp right turn and the pavement ended. As we started to climb into the La Panza Mountains, the four-wheel drive Forest Service truck threw up a cloud of dust that covered our windshield. Art let them pull ahead.

As the day progressed, the humidity dropped, giving the fire more momentum. We heard the growl of the D-6 working somewhere ahead of us and we tied our line into the area the dozer had scraped clear. Behind us, an inmate crew widened what we had cut. A crew behind them started backfires. If everything worked, the wind created by the oncoming main fire would suck the backfire toward it, burning out the fuel in between.

We took short breaks to drink water and Gatorade. "I remember spending five hours cutting line at the Old Topanga Fire in '93," Art said, during one of our breathers. "We really busted our asses. Then the wind changed and we had to clear out. The freaking fire burned through that line like it wasn't even there. We moved a mile back and started over. That sucker burned ten thousand acres in the first twenty-four hours, and we thought Malibu was a goner."

We stopped once for half an hour to eat MREs. The radios kept everyone connected to the fire. Conversations between crews working the lines filled the tactical frequencies. Water and retardant drops were directed from ground frequency to the air. Periodically, we received weather updates and status reports from the command channel. In some places the fire was burning on the ground, feeding on dry brush and dead trees. In other places, the flames had moved up to the crowns of trees, where the wind carried the blaze through the treetops and burning embers sailed through the air, starting spot fires miles away. Smoke and heat rose into the sky everywhere.

Back on the line, we worked for five or 10 minutes at a time in silence, punctuated by Art or Dozer calling "bump." The hard work felt good. Swing the Pulaski, pull the brush and plants away, bump up, swing the Pulaski, wipe away the sweat. TB was right—the foliage was thick and tenacious.

Hector, with years of experience on handcrews, related incidents from the Northwest. "In Montana," Hector said, "one morning we had to hike in eight miles over rough terrain. We were headed for a place called Rat Creek. When we got there, we couldn't find the fire and—"

"And you realized you were on the wrong mountain," Red Eye interrupted.

"Hell, they were in the wrong state. The fire was in Idaho," Jake said.

Hector paused. He was relating the oral history of his life and he never let the ribbing deter him from finishing. "…we sent one guy up to the top of a Lodgepole Pine and found out the fire was in the next canyon. There was a road on the far side, which was within a mile of the actual fire. A Hotshot crew drove in had it contained before we even got there."

Luis was the anxious one in our crew. He tried to keep a mental image of the entire situation, which was impossible at an incident this size. Luis wanted to hear every briefing and every radio report. He was concerned about the weather and wanted to know what the fire had done and what it was about to do. Luis didn't care about himself. He worried about entrapment and burnover because he feared what might happen to his wife and son without him.

Over the years, wildland firefighting had made significant advances with the application of technology. Fire behavior was studied in laboratories and now commanders could model fire conditions on laptops in the field. Weather forecasts were accessed in real time and plugged into the equation. Satellite mapping was available. Air support and the use of retardants had been improved. But even with all these bells and whistles, in many ways nothing had changed. Cutting line down to the soil and clearing shallow trenches across fields and mountainsides was still the backbone of any suppression effort. Hardworking crews like ours still cleared firelines using basic hand tools—saws, shovels, Pulaskis and McLeods. Muscle, sweat and persistence were still the most important components of fighting a wildfire. It wasn't a scientific process. Every fire was unpredictable at certain times and under certain conditions, and crews regularly made tactical decisions on the fireline. Luis understood that, and that's what made him edgy. The outcome of a fire could not be foreseen. To find out how it ended, you had to be there at containment, alive and in one piece.

For 11 exhausting hours, under a burning midday sun, an afternoon sun, and a setting sun, we sawed, hacked and scraped brush. As a quarter moon rose in the evening sky, we had cleared almost 2,000 feet of line to use as control for burning back to the main fire higher in the mountains.

As night approached, the Sundowner Winds made conditions more dangerous. The backfiring stopped at dusk but we continued to cut and clear. In the dark, with headlamps, we worked and moved more slowly. At 10 p.m., fresh crews replaced us and we were ordered off the line.

We were fortunate; we returned to the Forest Service station and didn't have to spend the night in sleeping bags in the forest. For the first time in 14 hours, we took off our Nomex. We ate canned chili and eggs heated on the gas stove in the kitchen, drank water and juice until our stomachs felt bloated and collapsed after midnight on foam rubber mats placed on the floor of the office and in the workshop. We slept in our clothes. A shower was available, but no one had the energy to wash up. At a fire, life consists of working, eating and sleeping, in that order. Everything else is secondary. After five hours' sleep, we got up and prepared to go back to the line. We drank coffee, which tasted terrible but was hot, and we ate a mixture of fried eggs and potatoes, which tasted better than it looked.

That morning we traveled farther up the dirt road into the hills and worked one foot in the black, cutting a 3-foot wide fireline. It was tough, slow work. The hillside was steep and the D-6 couldn't get in to help us. Everything had to be done by hand. In some places, the ground was dirt and loose shale and the footing was treacherous. Jake led with the saw, followed by Red Eye and Hector with their Pulaskis, chopping at the vegetation, hacking at brush and roots.

"Bump down."

"Careful Red Eye, watch it."

"Man down, man down."

"Watch it."

"Bring a Pulaski back, take out these stumps. Break those fuckers, widen it, widen it."

"Hold and improve here. Widen this dog-leg."

"This looks good. Bump down."

"Looking good guys, bump down."

"Go three-feet high, three feet on that brush."

"Swinging."

"Branches coming down, watch it."

"Have you got it? Knock that down."

"Rocks coming down. Watch it, rocks."

"Hey, Hector, who was the third president of the U.S.?"

"I give up."

"Crazy Horse."

"Heads up, branches coming down."

"Watch the embers. Greg, hit that."

"Clean that out. McLeod! McLeod!"

"Bump. Bump."

In addition to the physical effort, we felt the radiant heat from nearby walls of fire and were soaked with sweat. Black flies buzzed around our faces.

By 7 p.m., the down slope winds were picking up again and Command radioed to take us off the line. We were exhausted and headed to Lake Santa Margarita for showers and some decent food, leaving the glow of the fire behind us in the hills.

The largest, most complex and environmentally most sensitive fires are classified as Type I. The Pozo Fire had been designated a Type I incident on its third day and an interagency command team took control 24 hours later. The team, with approximately 120 personnel, one of many on standby, was drawn from federal, state and local fire agencies. It operated like a small army and its headquarters for the Pozo Fire was at Lake Santa Margarita.

The incident command post was housed in the SLO Rowing Club building near the entrance to the parking lot. The number of trucks, vans, and logistics trailers exceeded the open space around the lake and the access road was jammed with parked vehicles. Part of the area was lit with floodlights. At the far end of the parking lot, fire-fighting supplies and equipment were being unloaded from semitrailers. Twelve packs of shovels, McLeods and Pulaskis, cases of fusees, hardhats, goggles and other personal protective equipment were piled on the ground. A crew using grinders powered by portable generators sharpened hand tools brought in from the field, spraying sparks onto the dirt. Rolls of orange plastic flagging spilled from a container. Boxes of AA batteries for radios and flashlights, Army canteens and USFS plastic water containers were available to anyone who needed them.

Two dozen ragged army tents with cots had been set up in an area outside the floodlights. Some men slept on their engines or in other vehicles. Shower trucks were available and a mobile kitchen up against the marina bait building served food and drink under a large open tent. Cases of bottled water were stacked outside. Wooden picnic tables surrounded the tent. Trash containers overflowed with paper plates, cups and plastic utensils.

Tired and filthy, covered with two days' sweat, dirt and ash, we headed to the tents while TB checked in at the incident command post.

TWENTY-THREE
Santa Margarita, California

I FOLLOWED JAKE INTO ONE OF THE ARMY TENTS and wandered through a maze of cots with my fire pack hanging off one shoulder. The air was heavy with the odor of stale sweat. Weary firefighters tossed in various stages of sleep. Most slept with T-shirts or caps covering their faces. A few sat on their cots, palms pressed against their eyes. Clothing, packs, tools, canteens and hardhats littered the dirt floor. Chainsaws and drip torches were left outside.

We found empty cots at the far side of the tent. They were uncomfortable and too short, but tonight it didn't matter, I could sleep on a bed of nails. I pulled off my boots and was about to head to the showers when TB stuck his head into the tent.

"Hey, Kowalski?" he called. "You in here?"

"Yeah, over here."

"There's a message for you." He walked over to my cot and lowered his voice. "You should call your mother in Michigan right away."

"My mother?"

"She's been calling all over the state. County Fire finally plugged her in to Boise. There's…uh…been a death in your family."

"A death?"

"I'm sorry." He put his hand on my shoulder. "Your father died at a fire. You need to head home."

I looked at him. I was stunned. I felt as though TB had hit me in the stomach. A firefighter in the tent began to cough. Others around him stirred. I glanced over at Jake. He was already asleep. "My father's dead?"

"I can have someone help you if you need a plane reservation," TB said.

"I'm not going anywhere."

"You need to go home."

"When the crew goes home, I go home. Not before."

"Greg, your father's had an accident. Your mother needs you. You should be with your family."

"I am with my family. I'm not leaving."

TB ran his hand over the stubble on his cheek. His hand was filthy; his nails were black with dirt. "It's your decision, Greg. The message is to call your mother ASAP. You can use a phone over at the command post." He took a step closer to me and said, "I'm too tired to get into this tonight, but if you're staying around, I have to be sure you can function out there on the line. Let's talk about it in the morning."

I pulled my boots back on. Exhaustion made it hard to think. Leaving the tent, I saw black sky. The smoke and soot hanging in the air obliterated any light from the stars. I walked past a row of outdoor toilets, their sweet chemical odor mixing with the smell of the fire. All the lights were on in the SLO Rowing Club.

By the time I reached my mother, it was after 2 a.m. in Saginaw. A full complement of fire managers in the command post pored over maps and weather reports under the bleak light of bare bulbs. A fire meteorologist down-loaded weather data from a satellite link. A small group looked at a map spread on a table. "It established itself at the bottom of the Logan drainage and it's making runs up the Potrero Ridge," one of the men said. "We made progress today burning out…"

I turned toward the wall, trying to get some privacy. "Hey, Mom, it's me, Greg. Did I wake you up?"

"Yes," she said. "You got the message? I called everywhere."

"I'm working a fire, Mom."

"You have to come home. Dad had an accident." She was silent for a moment and I heard a faint hissing on the long-distance line. "Greg, he's dead. A warehouse on Swan Creek Road burned down. Part of the roof collapsed and a water tank crushed him."

I smiled. Wait until the guys hear this. Of all the ways a firefighter could die, this was special. The prick was killed by a falling water tank. Christ.

"The Mayor's coming and a bunch of other officials. You have to be here."

Her voice was faint.

"Mom, I'm at a fire in Central California, my first major incident. I've got a job to do. I'm here with my crew and I can't leave right now. When's the funeral?"

"The day after tomorrow."

"Well, I won't be there. How's Vicky?"

"Vicky's living in Ann Arbor. She's not coming, either. I'll have to go by myself."

"I guess she got out of the house," I said.

"What?"

"What's Vicky doing in Ann Arbor?"

"She's living with a guy."

"Living with a guy? She's only seventeen."

"Well, that's what she's doing. I guess neither of you care enough about your father to come to his funeral."

"Mom, I'm not getting into a long-distance discussion about Dad, but you're right, I don't care. Why should I?"

"Because he was your father."

"He didn't act like my father. He couldn't stand me."

"That's not true, Greg."

"You know it is. He wouldn't even let you talk to me on the phone."

"It's over now, Greg. Let it go, it's finished."

"How are you doing, Mom?"

"I guess I'm alright. Just a little stunned."

"I'll call you as soon as I get back to L.A., OK? I don't know how long I'll be up here. It's a major fire."

"I wish you would come home, Greg."

Outside, I picked up a rock the size of my fist and threw it into the darkness toward the lake. I heard it plunge into the water. I felt anger, not grief. The prick was dead.

Back in the tent, I lay on the cot with my eyes open, staring into the darkness, listening to the other firefighters breathing, snoring or mumbling. My body needed the restoration of sleep, but it wouldn't come. My father had died before I could show him anything. He wouldn't be around to see what I had accomplished. He would never see how I had learned to handle the challenges of firefighting. None of the conversations we might have had—sharing experiences at fires and talking about common dangers—would ever happen now. He would never tell me how proud he was even if he hadn't wanted to admit it. Did it matter now that I was a firefighter? I might as well be a garbage collector. Who cared? My thoughts went in circles. Finally, exhaustion prevailed and I fell asleep.

I stood outside our house. My father rode his Harley up and down Janes Road and I ran after him, crying, trying to catch him. Each time I came close, he laughed and sped away from me.

"Rise and shine," Jake said, shaking my cot so hard I almost fell off. "Pull on your boots and let's go eat."

It was early morning, the sun was coming up and gusts of heat were already blowing through the tent. I sat up, feeling groggy, as if I had not slept at all. My feet hurt. I had blisters on my toes. The fog in my head began to clear and I remembered—*my father.* I said nothing to Jake.

Jake dug through his pack. "Do you have any sunscreen I can use?"

"Help yourself." I reached into my pack and handed him the spray bottle. "What's the weather forecast?"

"Same as yesterday. Hot, Eighty-plus, RH around nine percent, moderate winds, gusty." Jake took off his T-shirt and sprayed his arms and neck with sunscreen.

"Where's your pullover?" I asked. Regulations required every firefighter to wear a long-sleeve cotton pullover for burn protection under his Nomex regardless of the temperature. Polyester or synthetics were out; they could melt against the skin in the heat of a fire.

"Don't be my mother—I've already got one," Jake said. He pulled on his shirt. "C'mon, I'm hungry."

We walked out of the tent into chaos. Fire equipment filled the marina. Ambulances, Red Cross vehicles, FEMA, BLM and California Office of Emergency Services cars and trucks jammed the entrance to the lot. Yellow and black Atascadero school buses pressed into service to transport firefighters, sat with doors open, engines idling, spewing diesel exhaust into the already polluted air. Men and equipment were everywhere. The smell of smoke was overpowering.

Seven or eight hundred firefighters passed through the mess line each day, coming in after 36 or 48 hours on the lines, trying to pack in enough calories for the next effort. Five hundred gallons of coffee were consumed. During the academy, someone told us a fire like this could cost a million dollars a day. I was beginning to understand.

I didn't care much for the green chilies, which often appeared at breakfast. I asked for "eggs straight," but I got eggs with chilies anyway. Loading my breakfast tray, I remembered how one of the Cal Fire instructors joked about preparing for a major fire. "Spread dirt and pine needles on your sheets," he said. "Turn on a radio and all the lights before you go to sleep. In the morning, make an omelet, but sprinkle dirt on it before you eat. Refrigerate your coffee for 15 minutes before drinking it. Cheer up, it'll be worse when you get out there." What he didn't tell us was how to prepare for a morning's work when you heard the night before that your father had died. At the end of the food line, I grabbed two bottles of water, a banana, and several MREs, stuffing them into my daypack. Jake and I filled our canteens from a stack of cubies.

Outside, a group of pilots stood eating and talking. Next to the top command, the pilots were the best informed about fire conditions. "Thermo-Gel's offering custom colors," one pilot told the others. "We dropped blue on a grass fire in New Mexico earlier this summer. You can pick a retardant color to match your mood."

Dave Fortune, the least friendly helicopter pilot in L.A. County, was with them. "Who hit the forest crew yesterday?" he asked.

"We just followed the spotter," said another pilot, and shot a stream of tobacco juice into the dirt. "You know how thick the smoke was."

Dave looked at him without smiling. Dave was one of the best. Before he came to County, he flew fixed-wing aircraft in the Air Force and was a test pilot for Hughes Helicopters. He was also an expert at dropping water using night vision glasses and he was always the last pilot to put his helo down. Dave had 36 years of flying experience and was an old, old man by firefighter standards.

Luis stood next to him, pack slung over one shoulder, and listened to the pilots shoot the shit. The rest of our crew materialized out of the hundreds of men in the mess area. We were drawn together like magnets. "We're flying today," Luis said.

"What's it like out there?" Art asked Dave.

"Aside from all the metal in the sky?" Dave said. "Extreme conditions, dry as a bone. We're dropping crews in the mountains on the eastern flank. If the fire burns up over those ridges, we'll be fighting it in the next county."

TB joined us after the morning briefing. He pointed to the far end of the parking lot and said, "Next to those buses is a green and white half-ton Park Service stake truck. That's our ride out to the helibase." We picked up our packs and walked through the crowded lot. TB put his hand on my shoulder. "How're you doing, Greg?" he asked.

"Fine. A little tired." My thoughts about my father were my business.

"Did you speak to your mother?"

"Yes."

"And?"

"And I told you, I'm staying here with the guys."

"You sure you can function today? Not lose your concentration?"

"I'm good"

"One person's mistake can put the whole crew in danger. You certain?"

"I said I'm alright, TB. No big deal."

"No big deal? If I thought you believed that, Greg, I wouldn't even let you on the Bird."

Raphael stopped at the information board, scanning hundreds of messages to see if his wife was still pursuing him.

The truck threw up a small cloud of dust as it swung out to pass a line of buses loaded with firefighters headed back to the lines, fresh from a decent night's sleep and a real breakfast. We stood in the back of the truck, holding on to the gates. Smoke and ash blew in our faces. Haze filled the sky.

My father was dead.

TWENTY-FOUR
Black Mountain

FROM THE AIR WE LOOKED DOWN on a landscape of charred trees and earth. The mountainsides were scorched. Fires dotted the canyons where snags still burned after the flames had passed. A few remaining pockets of green and brown showed life in deep creases of the land.

The skids of the Bird barely touched ground and dropped nine of us on a rocky plateau near the ridge on Black Mountain. We unloaded our daypacks, tools, food, water and the chainsaw. The area was just big enough for a staging point for our limited supplies. We stood at the top of a rugged canyon and watched the underside of the helo lift away. Looking down, we saw pine, oak, sumac, manzanita, chaparral and scrub brush growing together in a dense maze. Rocky outcrops interrupted the steep slope into the valley.

It was still morning. A light breeze blew ash across the side of the mountain and a plume of gray smoke reached thousands of feet into the Central California sky. From our vantage point the massive Pozo Fire was a sobering sight, burning across mountains and through canyons. It moved in our direction along the floor of the valley below, consuming everything in its path. Fish were poached in their streams as the flames passed over. Bears, coyotes, deer, squirrels, lizards, snakes and all manner of wildlife in the Las Padres were fighting for life, fleeing the fire and smoke. Across the valley, crews were cutting line with a D-6. It would be easier work down there, on flat ground with a bulldozer to scrape out a wide firebreak.

We stood around TB as he briefed us on strategy and organized our effort. Our job was to cut a line to prevent the Pozo Fire from running up the canyon and over into the next valley. "This spot is our safe zone and anchor point," he said. "We'll cut an indirect line across and down and fire it out. Three feet wide, no slopover." Putting the toe of his boot on the Stihl, he said, "Jake, you take the chainsaw and start cutting trees and stumps. Red Eye, you be his bucker. I'll work the head of the line and do some scouting as we go. Greg, you're behind me. Luis, Raphael, Hector and Art in that order. Dozer, you be the lookout. There's a Forest Service spotter over there," he said, pointing across the valley. "Stay in touch with him. Blue channel. Everyone understand what we're doing? Any questions?"

We hacked and scraped, clearing a three-foot wide fireline down to the soil. Everyone else was energetic after a night's sleep and a warm breakfast, but I felt tired and was having difficulty concentrating. The roar of the chainsaw nearby discouraged conversation and I tried to focus on cutting brush. It didn't work. All I could think about was my father's death. Now I wouldn't have to worry about what he thought. There would be no more abuse. There would be nothing. He was gone. I tried to understand my feelings. Was I happy or sad? I looked into a black void—no light, no reflections and no revelations. I thought of the incident on Yankee Jim Road when someone was alive, then suddenly wiped from the face of the earth. I swung my Pulaski.

The head of the fire continued to burn on the valley floor, hot spots and fingers of flame were now visible on the lower edges of the canyon below us. The brush was thick, in places 10 feet high and we were making limited progress. We continued to cut our way across and down the side of the canyon and as we worked, the footing became more difficult. From time to time, we checked in with Dozer on the squirrel channel. He moved around near the top of the ridge, trying to get the best view of what was happening on the mountainside below.

TB sent me back to the safe zone to get a cubie of water and climbed part way up with me to get a better view. I heard him radio to Dozer and the Forest Service spotter. "We're not going anywhere. At this rate it'll take forever. I'm going to scout a route to side-hill in at a sharper angle and anchor into the rock in the middle of the canyon. "

"You're OK to do that," the spotter replied, "but watch the terrain, it's very steep farther down."

I brought one of the five-gallon water containers back down the line and we stopped for a break, put down our packs, opened our brush jackets and drank water. Jake silenced the chainsaw below us. Despite the low humidity, the cotton under our fire suits collected sweat and I was soaking wet. Maybe Jake had the right idea, it would be nice to have short sleeves today. I ate the banana I had stuffed into my webbing. The heat had already turned it brown and mushy.

TB put his shovel down and said, "I'm gonna take a closer look farther down." He set off through the brush and minutes later, he radioed back, "It's getting steep down here. I don't know if we can pull this off."

We drank more water and waited for TB to come back. Raphael, standing next to me, turned his face toward the sky and said, "Did we just get a wind shift?"

"I don't know," I said. Turning my head, I thought maybe I felt a difference, a slight breeze blowing in my face. "Yeah, I think we did." I sensed a change, but wasn't sure what was happening.

We stood in the thick brush, trying to see what was going on below us. Without warning, the difference in the wind became obvious as it began to blow up toward us. A spot fire below us appeared out of nowhere and erupted into a blaze. In seconds, we saw fire below us begin a run up the side of the canyon. A cloud of black smoke rose from the flames and I heard the injured fire chief in the Forest Service video warning, "Never forget to watch for weather changes and be aware of your situation at all times. If there's a blowup, you'll have thirty, maybe sixty seconds to get out."

Our radios began to crackle. The lookout across the canyon told us, "The fire has turned up slope. Move out, move up to the safe zone!" Up the line, Dozer and Art began calling on the squirrel channel, "Get out!"

Puffs of smoke and fingers of fire were now clearly visible. A rush of fear washed away my lethargy. I realized the entire side of the mountain had preheated and was about to explode into flames. Trying to regain my composure, I shouted to TB, Jake and Red Eye below me, "Move out! Safe zone! Safe zone!" Where were they? I couldn't see them. My first thought was to go down to them, but they had radios, they would know what they had to do. I felt a spike of adrenaline start in my stomach and spread through my body. It seemed like forever until I caught sight of Jake and Red Eye emerging from the brush. Jake was carrying the Stihl. Why did he still have it? "Drop the fucking saw," I shouted. Where was TB?

I knew I had to get up to the safe zone as fast as possible. I started to move back up the line we had cleared. It looked insignificant, a 3-foot-wide cut through acres of thick brush. I dropped my daypack and it took my fire shelter and radio with it when it fell to the ground, but I couldn't stop. The footing going uphill was treacherous and running was impossible. The side of the canyon was steeper than had I realized working on the way down. The ground was covered with small rocks, shale, and bits of granite that slipped away. In places I was on my hands and knees as I tried to climb.

I looked below again and saw a wall of flames 80 or 90 feet high. Black smoke, the result of incomplete combustion and a sure sign of a fast moving fire, billowed up. Jake must have realized how close the flames were, because he finally dropped the saw and was trying to move faster. Red Eye struggled behind him. Below Red Eye, I saw TB's yellow Nomex in the brush. "Safe zone," I screamed, but I knew they couldn't hear me. The oncoming fire roared around us like a freight train as it consumed trees, brush and our oxygen.

A finger of flame made a run uphill on one side and was now above us. A fire whirl, 50 feet high, came out of the flames and spun around, spewing burning branches and smoke before it was sucked back into the firestorm. The superheated air, carbon monoxide and thick smoke hit me. I tried to control my breathing and take shallow breaths as I moved, but the exertion was too great. I needed air and I couldn't get it. My chest was tight, my eyes began to burn. My legs felt like rubber. In the panic, I left my shroud tucked up under my helmet and my goggles on top of it.

Glancing back again, I thought I saw TB's helmet and yellow brush jacket for a moment before he disappeared into the wall of advancing flames. I struggled up the hillside as fast as I could, slipping again and again. Through the smoke, I saw other yellow figures above me, moving in the same direction, each clawing his way to the plateau. The back of my neck, my ears and my bare wrists were stinging from the heat. Gasping, my eyes were slits as tears streamed down my cheeks. My leg muscles screamed with pain from the climb. I knew if I fell or slid back, I would die.

Sparks showered around me and I felt the suck of the air being drawn away as the flames consumed the last of the oxygen. I thought I had just a few seconds to live. Survival instinct took over and I concentrated on getting to the ridge. I forgot about the rest of the crew—my own life was all that mattered. Each second became a minute. I was in a place between life and death. As I pushed my body and struggled to breathe, thoughts and images flashed through my mind. I lay exhausted, face down on the hockey rink after a practice, the cold ice smooth against my cheek. My father stood in the kitchen saying, "You're not tough enough." Carol taunted me, "You child." Chief West said, "It could happen to you." My mother said, "I married your father because I was pregnant."

Jake was now just a few feet behind me. I heard voices from his radio, but couldn't understand anything. Stumbling in the smoke, I reached the safe zone. The fire was at our heels. Jake swore as he slipped back. Without thinking, I turned and grasped his arm and dragged him up onto the rock. We both collapsed. On the plateau, I dimly saw deployed fire shelters and a couple of bodies lying face down, gloved hands holding helmets over their heads. I pressed my body against the rock and felt the unbearable heat of the fire. My lungs fought for the small quantity of oxygen that remained near the ground. I was certain I would die from inhaling superheated air. I smelled burnt hair. It was mine.

The firestorm reached the top of the ridge where it paused for a few seconds in the cross winds, then blew past us down the other side of the mountain. I heard hissing and popping— rocks exploding from the intense heat.

Silence.

I sat up, coughed and vomited the banana and my breakfast onto my shirt. I struggled to clear my lungs. My chest hurt and my eyes burned. Everyone was black with ash. Hector was on his hands and knees. Saliva dripped from his mouth, black snot and soot ran from his nose. Luis sat, legs crossed, staring straight ahead. Blood ran down Red Eye's forehead. Art was the first to stand up.

I knew I had radiant heat burns on my ears, the back of my neck and the exposed flesh on each wrist between my gloves and brush jacket. The hair on the back of my head was singed. Next to me, Jake cursed and groaned and I remembered he wasn't wearing a cotton undershirt. "Thanks, Greg," he said. "I think my arms are burnt."

Dozer's radio lay on the rock. The lookout's voice from across the canyon screamed for information. "What's happened? Is everyone out? Give me a headcount!" Dozer seized the radio.

"Where's TB?" I asked. He wasn't with us. "Where's TB?" I shrieked. The pain in my chest and on my skin disappeared and my mind emptied of everything but the image of our captain as he disappeared into the flames. Tears streamed down my cheeks, but not from the smoke.

We left TB to die in the brush.

Dozer yelled into the radio, "We have entrapment. We've got burns and a possible fatality. Get a Medivac in here. Send a Medivac!"

We regained our senses. A headcount confirmed only TB was missing. Shocked and physically drained, we stood on the plateau for a moment, heads down. We were stunned by what had happened. We knew TB could not have survived.

"I'll go see about him," Art said. "He's still down there."

"Let's go," I said.

"I'm coming with you," Luis said.

"Me too," Hector said. "Watch it, the ground is super hot."

"Not everyone needs to see this," Art said in a low voice, "I'll go alone."

Art didn't go alone. We sensed we were about to see something horrific, something no one wanted to see, something we wouldn't forget, but no one wanted to remain behind. We all followed Art back down what had been our pathetic fireline. Snags and spot fires still burned. The entire side of the canyon, which minutes earlier had been covered with thick growth, was charred. We approached the spot where we thought we had stopped work and looked for TB.

Nothing.

We edged further down and traversed the side of the mountain, fearful of what we would find.

We saw him. TB had no chance to deploy his fire shelter. His stiff body lay 20 feet below us on his stomach. He must have lost his footing and slid down the slope. His arms were stretched out as though he were still trying to climb up the steep incline. Charred edges of his yellow Nomex fire suit stuck out from beneath what remained of his body. Below him, the melted remains of his helmet and goggles lay in the dirt. Along with the smell of the fire, there was something else—the odor of burnt flesh. I wanted to look away, but I couldn't.

Tears dripped onto the vomit on the front of my shirt. Dozer came up behind me and put his hand on my shoulder. "There's nothing we can do now," he said, and uttered something in Spanish.

I heard a helicopter. Looking back up toward the ridge, I saw Cal Fire paramedics hover jump onto the plateau with their equipment.

TWENTY-FIVE
Malibu, California

TWO PARAMEDICS FLEW BACK from Black Mountain with us. Dozer and Raphael, closest to the safe-zone, had missed the worst of the heat. The rest of us had suffered radiant burns. All of us coughed, still clearing our lungs. Jake had more serious burns on his arms and back. They weren't life threatening, but he was starting to feel the pain. My ears and the back of my neck were stinging. Blood trickled from Red Eye's forehead. One of the medics passed around an oxygen tank and kept asking us if we could breathe. Another gave us eyewash.

We landed at the helispot and were delivered to the medical tent at the lake. A doctor pulled Jake aside and went to work on him while the rest of us showered and changed into clean clothes. A nurse put salve on the tender parts of our skin, washed out our eyes again and patched Red Eye's forehead. She gave us grape Gatorade. "You need to rehydrate—drink," she ordered.

The doctor returned. "Firefighter Mangan has some second-degree burns," he said. "It's not serious, but we should get him to Grossman today." He examined our skin and checked for other injuries. "All I see are minor burns, all first degree." He stood with his hands in the pockets of his clean white coat, a stranger in our world of ash and soot. "I'm sorry about your captain." He examined Red Eye's forehead. "All you can do now is try to let the pain go."

We slumped on the cots in the medical tent, but I was still fighting my way up the side of the mountain. TB's charred body in the dirt replaced the image of my father on a Saginaw sidewalk. The first part of my body to react was my stomach.

A van from County Fire arrived to take us back to Los Angeles. It was a quiet ride. The radio stayed silent. From time to time, someone said a few words, half-aloud, but no one wanted to talk. We stopped in Sherman Oaks and left Jake at the Grossman Burn Center.

By the time we arrived at the camp it was dark. Jerry Dunham, now acting superintendent, met us, his face a mask of sadness. "C'mon guys, there's chow if you want it." No one wanted it. "There's a stress debriefing tomorrow after lunch," he said. "It starts at one p.m., Station 70. You'll meet with Dr. Stern. Greg, make sure Jake knows what's going on."

Each of us wanted to be alone. Group support would come later. I went into the room Jake and I shared and lay on my bed. My ears and neck hurt The images returned. I tossed and turned and was sick to my stomach.

When I awoke, it was 2:30 a.m. I decided to go to the apartment in Canoga Park.

Malibu Canyon was quiet as a grave. The moon had set and the dark mountainsides melted into a black sky. My high beams bounced off rock walls, sometimes illuminating the eyes of creatures looking back at me from the brush. It felt good to be driving, just to be doing something. The 101 was empty. I pushed the Wrangler to its top speed and the wind whistled through the holes in the top. It was no use, I couldn't outrun my thoughts. Maybe a Porsche would have done the trick. I exited on Topanga Canyon Boulevard and passed through a world of orange sodium streetlights. When I got to the Topanga Villa, the first hint of sun was already in the sky.

Later we learned that while the Pozo Fire still burned, a five-man investigation team went to Turkey Flat. Based on burn indicators on rocks and vegetation, they placed the origin of the fire at the back of the campground. They were unable to determine whether the blaze was the result of a campfire started too close to the vegetation or whether it was arson, which would have made TB's death a homicide.

TWENTY-SIX
Canoga Park, California

JAKE SPENT THE NIGHT at Grossman and came home in the morning. Most of his burns were first degree with red painful skin, but he had spots on his shoulders, neck and arms where second-degree burns had created blisters. By the time I woke up, it was mid-morning. He stuck his head in my room. His shirt was off, his upper body covered with Neosporin and part of one arm covered with gauze. "I thought you were spending the night at the camp," he said.

"I came home around 4 a.m. I couldn't sleep."

"Jesus, it smells in here, you sick?" Jake said.

"Yeah, I've got an upset stomach."

"Well, open the window—let some fresh air in. I brought some stuff for your skin."

"Thanks, how do you feel?"

"I'm hurting, but I'll survive. They're on my ass because I wasn't wearing long sleeves."

"We've got a stress debriefing at 1 p.m. We're meeting at Station 70."

"I made some coffee, if you want it. How're you doing?"

"Part of me is still up there on the mountain," I said. "I can't stop thinking about it." I got up, put salve on my neck, ears, and wrists, and slipped on a pair of jeans.

I joined Jake to drink coffee on our small second-story patio overlooking Topanga Canyon Boulevard. We called it a patio, but it was only wide enough to accommodate a tiny round table and two chairs. Jake and I made small talk, not ready to get into yesterday's nightmare.

"Nicole's coming over later," he said. "They wouldn't let her come to Grossman at night."

"Jake, I need to be alone today." Nicole was friendly and good-looking. I liked her, but sometimes she talked too much. Today I didn't want her around.

"This isn't the time to sit here by yourself," Jake said. "Don't be the goddamn Lone Ranger. I wish you had a girlfriend to take care of you."

"I don't need anyone to take care of me."

"Yeah you do. You ought to call Deb and tell her you'd like to see her again."

"Don't start up about Deb. I can't just call her and run over there. I haven't seen her in four months. Can't you go over to Nicole's?"

Jake scowled. "I suppose so. After the debriefing, I'll head over there and spend the night. But we'll come by in the morning and go out for breakfast, OK? You can't sit here and do nothing."

"Fine," I said, anxious to have the place to myself. "Don't worry. I'm fine."

"Maybe you should call your mother, or your sister. When's the last time you talked to them?" Jake still didn't know what had happened to my father.

The last thing I needed now was to get into my family issues. I had a fierce headache, my stomach was in an uproar and I couldn't think straight. I was tired and drained. I ignored Jake's question and went into the living room, turned on the television and watched part of The Godfather. Jake called Nicole.

I sat on the couch and thought about my mother, but I didn't seem able to pick up the telephone. I considered calling Vicky to find out who she was living with, but couldn't do that either. I didn't have her number anyway. I went back into the kitchen and asked Jake, "Don't you think we should have tried to pull TB out of the brush?"

"We couldn't have gotten to him."

"How do you know? Shouldn't we have tried?"

"Red Eye and I were the closest to him and we figured he was coming out behind us."

"I can't stop thinking about it."

"Hey, you saved me from third-degree burns."

"You were right behind me. All I did was grab your arm and yank. It's not the same thing. We should have gone back down after TB."

"You couldn't have saved him," Jake repeated. "You've got a short memory. Remember how fast those flames were coming at us? It was a thousand degrees.

You wouldn't have made it."

Jake went out to get food and came back in 15 minutes with a small bag of groceries. When he returned, it was time to go to the debriefing. We took separate cars. I was glad to drive alone; I didn't have to talk.

Station 70 was on Pacific Coast Highway, six miles from the camp. The guys on duty would normally come out to greet us. We would joke around and slap each other on the back and someone would have a girlfriend story. Dr. Stern must have told everyone to leave us alone, because no one appeared.

The main office was empty except for Long Board, the station mascot. As a pup, he had learned to respond to the firehouse tone and ran out to the garage whenever he heard the loudspeaker. The story was that Long Board learned to discern the different orders, choosing to ignore calls involving just the paramedics. Now he only ran into the garage when all the station's equipment and the entire crew was rolling. The dog was either very smart or very lazy.

Luis, Jake and I were the only ones who didn't spend the night at the camp. Luis, always early, was outside waiting for us. The rest of the crew arrived moments later. Other than Dozer, no officers joined us. The debriefings excluded brass to allow those who were part of the incident to speak freely and share their emotions without concern for appearances around superiors.

Dr. Stern waved us inside to the meeting room. "Gentlemen, come in and sit down. You can call me Victoria," she said. She wore black jeans and a black pullover. I wondered if the color was intentional. A small woman in her 50s, she didn't look like a shrink. She moved around arranging chairs in as much of a circle as the room would allow. Long Board came in to join us and collapsed on his foam mat.

"My sister's name is Vicky," I said.

"And you are?" Dr. Stern asked.

"Greg Kowalski."

"Hello, Greg." She turned to the others and said, "The purpose of today's meeting is to give you a chance to share your thoughts about what happened." She closed the door to the office. "You've gone through a horrendous experience. You're in what we call the 'post-crisis phase.' I don't know if any of you have been through this before, but it's going to affect you in surprising ways and it will take a while to get over it."

I looked around the room at the crew. Everyone sat quietly, listening to Dr. Stern, but looking off in various directions. Most of the guys were still on Black Mountain. Only Dozer looked directly at her.

"It's tough when you see anyone hurt or killed," she continued. "When it's another firefighter—someone you know—it's even worse. In the next few weeks, you may have some frightening thoughts." She paused and scanned the group. "I need a picture of what happened. Who can tell me what you saw?"

We looked at each other. There was a moment of silence. Red Eye spoke up first. "Jake and I were the closest to TB. We were working the Stihl, cutting trees and bush. TB went ahead, to scout out where he wanted us to cut line."

The station intercom cut in. Lunch was ready.

"You were all on the side of a mountain, right?" Dr. Stern asked.

"We were dropped in by helicopter," Luis said in a low voice. "It was mid-morning. We were cutting line for about an hour and it was going slow. TB wanted to see if we could change the angle to make more progress. He went down into the lower brush—"

"We had a spotter and radios," Raphael blurted out. "We did everything we were supposed to do. It was terrible, it happened so fast. It was over before we knew what was happening."

"I was down with Red Eye," Jake said. "The brush was so high we couldn't see anything until the spotter told us the fire was making a run up the mountain. He told us to get out. We didn't realize how steep it was until we started coming back up."

"Where was Captain Bratton at this point?" Dr. Stern asked.

"He was below us," said Art. "We couldn't see him. I was higher up, with Dozer. There was no way we could have gotten down to him."

"We didn't know he needed help until it was too late," Jake said, looking at Art. "We couldn't see anything either. The spotter said clear out and that's what we did. We thought he was coming up behind us."

"No one said you were supposed to pull TB out, Jake," Art said.

"Well, Jake and I would have, if we had known he was in trouble," Red Eye said. "We wouldn't have just left him there…we wouldn't have left him if we had known."

"Gentlemen," Dr. Stern said, "feeling a sense of guilt is natural. Firefighters don't like to think they've let someone down, particularly a comrade. We're not here to assign blame."

"No one could've gotten to him," Dozer said. "I've been through this once before. Don't blame yourself."

I couldn't sit still. I stood, stretched and wandered over to the board with the shift calendar. The days of the month alternated in red, blue and green, the duty days for each shift. Today was a green day, C-shift. My stomach was getting worse. The skin on the back of my neck and ears hurt.

"Greg, what do you think?" Dr. Stern asked.

I turned to face the group, but my eyes didn't seem to focus on anyone. "We should have saved him…I should have gone after him. This didn't have to happen."

"Greg," Art said. "Anyone who went back would have died with him. You followed your instincts to get out. That's what you're trained to do, that's what you did."

I looked at the shift calendar again. Red days, blue days, green days. TB died on a red day.

"You know how fast these things happen," Raphael said. "I was near the top. We had about sixty seconds to get out of the way. These guys," he pointed to Jake and Red Eye, "had to move a lot faster, they had more ground to cover."

"It did happen fast," added Luis. "I thought about TB for a second and after that, all I could think about was getting up the hill and getting away from the flames and the heat. Jesus, it was hot. I was terrified."

"I looked back at one point," Red Eye said, "and I saw TB coming out of the brush. The flames were all around him. That's the picture I can't forget. It was too late to do anything but run."

"From higher up we couldn't see anything—the smoke was too thick," Art added.

Red Eye blinked back tears. Luis shrank down in his seat. Jake was in physical pain, but met everyone's gaze and kept control of himself. Dozer had been through this before. He seemed calm but sad. His eyes were damp. Raphael and Art had been the closest to the top—they didn't live through the terror of the desperate scramble up the side of the mountain. Hector was Hector, going with the flow, silent, not revealing much. I looked out the window at the cars passing on PCH.

"The worst part was after the fire passed," Luis said. "When we went back down to look for him. He was face down." Luis started to come unglued. "I'll never forget what that looked like." Tears rolled down his cheeks. "His helmet melted; it was on the ground. His helmet melted."

"Who 'went down?' " asked Dr. Stern.

"The whole crew," Luis said. He wiped his face with his hands

"Then what?" Dr. Stern said.

"We climbed back up to the ridge." Hector said. Those were his first words about the tragedy.

"Everyone was coughing and choking," Jake said. "We could barely see, and we had burns." Jake held up his arm. "The Medivac came and pulled us out."

I was still in the part of the discussion where we saw TB's body.

"What am I supposed to tell my wife?" Luis said.

"What do you want to tell her?" Dr. Stern asked him.

"I couldn't sleep, but I didn't want her to see how upset I was. I sat in the kitchen half the night."

"Would you feel better if you shared this with her?"

"She worries about me all the time. I don't think she needs to know about something like this, but I feel like I'm shutting her out."

"Some wives and girlfriends want to know and share," Dr. Stern said. "Some don't. Don't drag someone in who would rather not hear about it, but don't shut someone out who is strong enough to share it with you. There's no right answer."

"I'll leave her out," Luis said.

"It's going to be difficult for a while," Dr. Stern said. "Understand that this is natural. Each of you has suffered a major trauma, and you can expect your body to react emotionally and physically. Don't let it overwhelm you."

Overwhelm? The events of the last few days had hit me like a rogue wave at the beach, pounding me into the sand, breaking me apart, dragging me under. I was drowning. I fought for air.

"Try not to make important decisions that affect your life," Dr. Stern went on. "Make little decisions. Decide what to have for dinner, decide to go to the movies, get through each day. Keep busy, try not to drift. Talk about it among yourselves. I don't know how many of you are married, but let your wife or your girlfriend hug you. Let someone love you."

I couldn't imagine who that would be. I thought about Jake's insistence that I call Deb. Maybe he was right.

"No alcohol—it's a depressant," Dr. Stern said. "Eventually, you'll start to feel stronger and be finished with this experience. At some point when you're ready, imagine a picture of what happened up there and tear it up into little pieces you can throw in the trash. When that picture's gone, it's over." She looked at each of us. "Does anyone want to say anything else?"

No one spoke. Even Jake, who always had the wicked smile on his face and a sarcastic comment ready, seemed at a loss. His face was blank.

"That's it," Dr. Stern said. She opened the office door and Long Board jumped up, wagging his tail. "All of you are on stress leave for a week. Spend some time with the people you care for, have some fun if you can and try to relax. Thank you."

Almost two hours had passed. The afternoon breeze off the ocean blew through Malibu as we walked out of the station. Jake and Dr. Stern followed me outside. "So, Greg, you mentioned you have a sister named Vicky?" Dr. Stern said. "Are you close to her?"

"No, not now. We were close when we were kids."

"Have you told her what happened?" Dr. Stern said.

"She already knew, and I think she hated him as much as I did."

"What?" Dr. Stern asked. She and Jake stopped to look at me.

"No, my father, she knew before I did." As soon as I realized what I had said, I bit my lip.

"Greg, what the fuck are you talking about?" Jake said. "You're not making any sense."

"My father died in a fire last week in Saginaw."

"Your father died last week?" Dr. Stern said. "What're you doing here? Why aren't you with your family?"

"I am with my family."

"Two deaths within a week, that's enough to bring down the strongest person." She put her hand on my arm. "You've got to talk to someone about what's happened, Greg. Share your grief. Don't keep it bottled up inside, it'll consume you."

"Thanks, Dr. Stern." I tried to control my tears, as I did around my father when I was a child. It didn't work.

"Your old man died?" Jake said. "Why didn't you tell me? When did it happen?"

"Two days before the burnover. My mother called me in Pozo."

Jake put his bandaged arm around my shoulder. Everyone was touching me. "No wonder you're such a wreck. Jesus, I'm sorry, Greg."

"Just leave me alone for now. I'll be alright. I just need to be by myself."

"If you need someone to talk to," Dr. Stern said, "Call me." She gave me her card.

I went for the Wrangler.

"Nicole and I will come by tomorrow," Jake called after me.

In 45 minutes, I was back at the Topanga Villa. I made the trip barely aware that I was driving. I wanted to go back to Station 70, walk out again and get in my Jeep without telling anyone that my father had died.

Our apartment was never a bright place. Today it was gloomy, full of shadows moving across the floor, climbing the walls, strangling the weak sunlight. I stood in the kitchen, scrambled some eggs and drank one of Jake's beers. I took a shower, put salve on my neck and ears and drank another beer. I went into my bedroom and pulled the Detroit Piston's cap out of a drawer. It still looked new. I'd had it 13 years but never wore it because I was always afraid I would ruin it or lose it. It seemed the right time to wear it now. I put it on and went into the living room. My head started to spin and I hoped I was getting drunk. The feeling lasted 10 minutes and then my stomach began to churn and I threw up. So much for getting drunk.

I watched the late afternoon sun drop below Walgreens. I sat in the kitchen, stood on the patio, watched television on the couch and lay on my bed. I finally dozed off for a few hours, still wearing the cap.

When I woke at 3 a.m., my body was covered with sweat. The pillow and sheets were soaked. This was the hour when my fears took over. The safety and clarity of daylight were gone and the darkness seemed infinite. This was the hour when life seemed hopeless. As a child, I laid awake at night, afraid that I had done something so terrible that my father would desert me. Tonight I was a frightened little boy again and it had finally happened—my father had abandoned me.

At 5 p.m., I turned on the early news and watched a dozen weather and traffic summaries, reports of the latest drive-by-shootings and coverage of a home which had burned in Pomona. The clock inched forward.

I showered, reapplied the salve, and called Jill Bratton a 8:10 a.m. She answered on the second ring. "Mrs. Bratton, it's Greg Kowalski."

"Hello, Greg." She said in a flat voice.

"I hope I'm not calling too early."

"It doesn't matter, no one was sleeping."

"I wanted to tell you how terrible this is…I feel so bad about it. How are you getting along?" I had no idea what to say.

"Thank you for calling, Greg. My mother is here. Tom's brother and his wife came in from Fort Irwin last night. They're helping me and the girls get through this. It's all so unreal."

"Could I come by?" I surprised myself by asking. I had no experience at comforting anyone.

"Give us another day. Come tomorrow. We aren't ready to see the whole camp, so come alone."

"When's the funeral?"

"We're having a service Sunday for the family. The county's planning a public memorial at the Santa Barbara Bowl later."

"I'll see you tomorrow, Mrs. Bratton."

Another day disintegrated. Jake called. He had to go back to Grossman. The burn on his arm was causing him a lot of pain. He started to talk about my father and I told him I was fine, that I didn't need any counseling. I hung up. The television stayed on. I finished the all the eggs. I heated up a frozen pizza for lunch, which tasted like cardboard. For dinner, I made canned corn. I wasn't hungry but I ate it anyway. The images wouldn't stop. TB and my father dissolved into one person surrounded by flames, screaming for help.

Luis had a wife and a son. Everyone in the crew had a family or a girlfriend or someone. Hector had an entire Native American tribe to embrace him. Even Raphael, whose wife was leaving him, had a son who cared about him. Everyone else had one foot in the black. I had no escape route, no safe zone. I had no one.

I should have saved Tom Bratton or died trying.

TWENTY-SEVEN
Simi Valley, California

J ILL BRATTON LOOKED FRAIL when she answered the door. Her eyes were red, her face streaked and puffy and her brown hair was tangled. She wore jeans, a County Fire Department sweatshirt and sandals. She clutched a wad of tissues. "Hello, Greg," she said and held out her arms for an embrace. "Thanks for coming over."

She felt tiny—all bones. "Hi, Mrs. Bratton, I'm so sorry...."

"Jerry Dunham told me you lost your father just days ago. How terrible for you."

"It happened at a warehouse fire in Saginaw."

"Why are you here? You should be home in Michigan." She stood against the screen door holding it open. A large fly sailed in.

"I want to be here for TB."

"You poor guy." She held my hand.

"Your husband treated me better than my father ever did. He cared more about me. He should have been my father." I wanted to be strong and I had come to comfort TB's wife. Instead, I was starting to cry again, I couldn't control my own sorrow.

"Come in, Greg." Jill managed a weak smile.

I followed her into the living room with the glass case full of china and porcelain figures. The little boys still sat on stones and mushrooms, holding flowers for the little girls. Figures still stood under trees filled with delicate butterflies and birds. Glass shelves held the same animals and elves I had seen the night Luis and I came for dinner. The collection of pictures on the coffee table was gone.

Several women—wives of fire officials and other friends of the Brattons—sat in the living room. Tom's young daughters, Jenna and Jean, sat on the couch, their hands pressed between their knees. Between them was an indentation on the cushion where Jill had been sitting. Half-filled coffee cups, glasses and plates were spread about the room. Zeus rested on the carpet next to the couch. Today he seemed different and lay still, his head between his paws, ears up, brown eyes looking at the people around him. A few of the women nodded to me.

The only man in the living room had to be TB's younger brother, Ted. TB spoke often about Ted, an armored unit commander in Desert Storm. He was bigger than Tom and had more hair, but it was obvious they were brothers. He stood and grasped my hand with both of his. "Hey, Greg, I'm Ted."

"Hello, Ted."

"You're from the camp, right?"

I nodded. "This is a hard loss. No one had time to do anything. It was over in less than a minute. We all—"

"I know." Ted said. "A death in the field is hard to accept and hard to forget." He turned back to the others in the living room. "Tom and I always argued about whose job was more dangerous. I said it was his. Tom said, 'No way, you're the one dodging bullets; all I have to do is tend fires.' He insisted that he was the older brother and that he would do the worrying for both of us. I always worried about him." Ted rubbed his eyes. "But not enough."

Jill returned to the couch, put her arms around her two daughters and pulled them toward her. Jill's mother came in from the dining room. "Is that Gregory? How are you doing?" she said.

"Hello, Mrs. Irons."

"There's a lot of food," she said. "Please have something to eat. Do you want some coffee?"

I went into the familiar dining room. The table offered a platter of pastries, a bowl of fruit, bottled water and a pitcher of orange juice. An enormous coffee urn cast a blinking red eye at me. I thought of Red Eye and for the first time remembered seeing him slip and strike his forehead as he tried to scramble up the hill. More images from Black Mountain flashed through my head, ending with TB's charred body outlined by the yellow Nomex. I remembered the evening Luis and I sat at this table, enjoying the wonderful dinner, talking to TB, Jill and Mrs. Irons. The thought of food now was disgusting. I felt nauseous.

I retreated into the living room and mopped sweat from my face with a paper napkin. Porcelain figurines stared at me in accusation.

"Jill, there's something we should talk about," the wife of a camp superintendent said. She glanced at Jenna and Jean.

Jill got the signal. "Mom, can you take the girls out for some fresh air?" Mrs. Irons came in and took the girls through the kitchen and out into the yard.

"Do you know anything about Tom's death benefits?" the woman asked.

"I have a rough idea."

"You can expect financial support from the Wildland Firefighter Foundation and the California Fire Fund. They're a godsend in times like these."

"I can't even think about that right now."

"I know, but you have to know something about it when you start dealing with your future. At some point, you have to plan your finances. Let me know if I can help." She had been through this before.

The conversation turned to the pursuits of the living. One of the wives spoke of her activities in the Fire Explorer Academy, helping youths from broken and troubled families. "Next week," she said, "we have twenty-six boys graduating. I'm always so proud of them. It gives them a focus."

"Is that one of the county outreach programs?" asked another woman.

"We call it a youth rescue program." The first woman said. "Some of the kids even go on to train as firefighters. We have one whose parents moved out of state while he was in class. He stayed in Los Angeles with a cousin in order to graduate."

Jill was lucky to have all these people around her. I tried to imagine a support group coming to comfort my mother. Did any wives of Saginaw firefighters come to our house on 29th Street to share her grief and dispense knowledge about death benefits? How many even knew her? My poor mother was left alone to arrange my father's funeral. I felt a moment of panic and thought I should call her. My stomach rumbled. The discussion turned to teachers and homework assignments and Jill wandered into the kitchen. I followed her.

"Greg," she said, "the funeral on Sunday is for our family and a few fire officials." She ran her hand through her hair. "You should come. I think Tom would have wanted you to be there."

"I'd be honored. Where is it?"

"Ten o'clock at the United Methodist Church," she said. "Up on Erringer Road, right off the 118."

I watched Mrs. Irons walking around in the backyard with Jenna and Jean.

"Tom's been cremated," Jill murmured. "There's no casket." Was she talking to me? She clenched her teeth trying to control herself. "He left detailed instructions in case anything happened."

I pictured TB sitting in his office at the camp, door closed, sipping a cup of coffee and writing out his funeral instructions. He would have shoved them into a drawer, thinking how unnecessary they were and then walked outside to watch us working out on the Grinder.

"He wanted his ashes dropped into the ocean below the camp," Jill said. "One of the county helicopters is going to take us up after the funeral service." She paused. "Do you want to come with us for that, too?"

"Yes, thank you."

Jill stood by the sink, watching her daughters outside. I wanted to tell her I was sorry I had failed, that I should have tried to save her husband. I had let them both down. He should be alive now, standing here in his kitchen with his wife. In the silence I walked out the back door. Jill was in another world—she wasn't even aware I had left.

Tom Bratton returned to Los Angeles in a gray body bag. His death certificate made no mention of his frantic effort to climb to the safe zone in a firestorm. "Thermal injury" was the official cause of death, "resulting from extensive third-degree burns and inhalation of superheated air." Tom's body was almost annihilated in a wildfire and a cremation had completed the process. Was it his sense of order that specified cremation, not wanting his wife to deal with a half-burnt corpse? What if he had been crushed by a falling water tank?

Simi Valley was hot, dry and windy. Driving home, I thought about Deborah. I turned off the freeway and headed across Kanan Dume Road toward Highland Farm. I had no idea whether she still worked there and if she did, whether she was around today. I didn't know if she would even speak to me. Four months had passed since she threw the Kings tickets in my face. I should have gone to see her sooner and apologized.

Twice I decided not to go to the barn, slowed, then changed my mind again and kept driving. I tried to understand how I felt about Deb, but nothing made sense. I couldn't finish a thought before it was interrupted by another. Just before the turn-off to the barn on Mulholland, I decided it was a bad idea to try to see her. It wasn't the right time. I made a U-turn and drove back to the apartment.

TWENTY-EIGHT
Simi Valley, California

THE UNITED METHODIST CHURCH in Simi Valley shared the intersection of Saticoy and Erringer with a Chevron station, a Von's supermarket and a Carl's Jr. fast-food restaurant. It was a strange-looking star-shaped building, built with tan brick and covered with the orange roof tiles common in Southern California. A cross on the roof, anchored with wires, stood against the strong winds. The wall near the entry had two small, square stained glass windows.

The only funeral I had ever attended took place in Saginaw when I was 13. The wife of one of the firefighters at the Hess Avenue Station was killed in an automobile accident and my father took us to the memorial service. The woman was a stranger to me and the ceremony meant nothing. TB's funeral was a different matter. I didn't own a dark suit, but I wore my dress uniform. I left my beat-up Wrangler on the far side of the parking lot so it wouldn't insult anyone and waited in the parking lot under the hot sun. Cars and trucks sped down Erringer Road and the rest of the world went on about its business, unaware that one family was mourning the loss of a son, husband and father. I wanted to run out into the middle of the street, put my hands up, stop the traffic and order everyone out of their cars. "Stop!" I would shout. "For just a minute, stop whatever you're doing. Tom Bratton has died."

A stretch limousine with tinted windows arrived at the entrance of the Church. Jill, her two daughters, Ted, Jill's mother and an older couple who must have been Tom's parents, emerged and walked inside. Minutes later, our battalion chief, Don Hardy appeared with Jerry Dunham and a small collection of people I didn't recognize. I followed them inside.

The interior of the church was unadorned and had a a vaulted ceiling supported by exposed steel beams. One small window, matching the two in the entry, cast a faint red light. I felt as though I was back in the auditorium at Zilwaukee Middle School. Our modest group filled the first two rows of pews. Jill had been adamant about a small service, leaving the memorial ceremony as the official event marking TB's death. Flowers covered the altar. Below the pulpit was a table with a picture of TB and a pale green urn containing his ashes. A woman wearing a black dress played a harp.

Jenna, Jean and Jill all wore black. Ted stood in his Army jacket and trousers, combat medals on his chest, holding his black beret in his hand. Battalion Chief Hardy, in uniform as well, had three gold stripes on his sleeve, each signifying five years of service with Los Angeles County Fire. Tom's parents sat next to Ted. His mother clutched Ted's hand. In a gesture of intimacy, the Reverend Eugene Hoyt stepped from the pulpit and stood in front of the mourners, next to the table with Tom's picture and ashes.

As we read Psalms 23 and 121, Jill and Jean dabbed their eyes with handkerchiefs and Jenna wiped her nose with the back of her hand. I looked at TB's picture. He looked back at me. I wanted to tell him I was sorry I had failed him. I focused on the green urn. It was hard to believe TB had been reduced to something the size of a quart milk container. The woman in the black dress continued to play the harp.

Don Hardy, a tall handsome man with gray hair and a full gray firefighter's mustache, stood up to speak. He inspired confidence. A woman would easily drop her baby from the third-story window of a burning building into his strong arms. "This is a difficult time," Chief Hardy began. "Each of us deals with loss in our own way." He looked at Jill and the two young girls and said, "I know you have suffered a tremendous loss. Tom Bratton was a good man, a good father and a good husband. He spent his life as a firefighter. He was respected and loved."

I thought of the first evening when I met TB, standing outside in the camp parking lot under the flagpole.

"Firefighting is a noble and heroic profession," Chief Hardy went on. "Every day Tom risked his own life to protect other people's lives and property. We will never forget his sacrifice. We can never forget him. We will always remember the superintendent of Camp 8 with great pride." Chief Hardy looked at the group seated in front of him and was silent. When he finished, Jill stood and hugged him. He towered over her. The girls remained seated, looking up at the chief and their mother.

Ted rose and looked at his brother's picture. "Tom," he said, "my brother, I love you. There is so much I still wanted to say to you. I hope you can hear my prayers. We won't forget you. Godspeed."

Jill stood and tried to speak. She began to weep, struggled to control herself and then lapsed into silence. Ted stood up to steady her and she rested her head against his shoulder. After a moment she was still crying, shook her head and sat down.

Reverend Hoyt walked closer to the group in the first row. "Do not let your hearts be troubled...."

My father knocks me down on our gravel driveway. The garage door is open and my bicycle has been stolen. He shouts at me, "Haven't I told you to take care of your things?" I feel the sting of his hand on my face.

My mother comes running out of the house, screaming, "Joe, leave him alone! You're hurting him—he's bleeding."

My father stands over me, hand raised, glaring.

I know he's going to hit me again.

"...For thine is the kingdom and the power and the glory, for ever and ever. Amen."

My mouth was dry and my stomach was churning. Jerry Dunham stepped forward and took the pale green ceramic container with TB's ashes. We walked out of the church with the music of the harp trailing after us. For a moment, the sunlight blinded me. "Greg, hold on to this," Jerry Dunham said, passing the urn to me. "You ride in the limo to Pacoima. Chief Hardy and I will meet you there. Dave Fortune's taking us up."

I walked to the open door of the limo and stood clutching the urn. It was heavier than I expected. I was afraid I might tip or drop it and I imagined Tom's ashes spilling out and blowing into the street.

Ted came to the limo with his arm around his mother. As I held the urn, she touched it with her fingertips and pressed her lips against it. His father stood behind her and wiped his eyes. "She's not strong enough for the helicopter trip," he said. "We'll say goodbye to Tom here." They retreated a step, their gaze fixed on the green container.

Ted took the urn from me and cradled it in his arms. He waited until Jill, her mother and the girls got into the limousine and then joined them. I followed, closing the door behind me.

On the 118 heading east, Jill said to the girls, "The three of us are going to have to be strong and help each other now, right?" The girls looked at their mother and nodded. Jill was tiny and looked frail, but I realized how tough and determined she was. In the midst of her grief, she had taken control of the events following her husband's death. I knew she would make it through this difficult time. I wondered about myself.

The limo moved quickly. Deep in the black leather seats, each of us was absorbed in our own thoughts. The air conditioning was ice cold. I was freezing, but didn't say anything. Jenna tapped her toe. After 20 minutes, we turned onto Osborne Road and entered the County Fire Heliport on the back side of Whiteman Airport. Eddie waved us in without moving from his booth at the entrance. Eddie's job was useless, but it gave a firefighter on disability something to do. Two black and white sheriff's cars drove past us and stopped at the gas pumps. We moved down the cement drive passing fire, rescue and emergency trucks. At the end of the drive, several D-8 bulldozers, each the size of a small house, were lined up, blades facing incoming traffic. As we made a right turn and headed toward the helipad, I could see Number 16, washed and gleaming in the midday sun.

We waited in the limo with the door open and the air conditioner blasting until Jerry Dunham and Chief Hardy arrived. Dave Fortune must have seen them and he emerged from the Ops Building in his blue flight suit. A man I had never seen before followed him. Dave approached the limo. "Mrs. Bratton, I'm Dave Fortune." He bent down to extend his hand. "Please accept my sincerest sympathy. It's an honor to take you up today. This is Captain Martinez, he's our crew chief." It was the warmest tone of voice I had ever heard from Dave.

I was the first one out of the limo. Ted handed me the urn, got out and helped Jill, her mother and the girls. Jenna and Jean looked at the black and yellow helicopter with awe. As we approached the Bird, we realized the women would need something to stand on in order to get on board. To accommodate the 1,100-gallon water tank on her underside, the Bird had extended wheel struts, which raised her several feet off the ground. Captain Martinez ran back to Ops and returned with an aluminum stepladder. Standing on the water tank, he helped everyone aboard.

It was the first time I had been in a helo since the flight from the ridge on Black Mountain. A wave of anxiety washed through me and I began to sweat. The scene seemed unreal. Accustomed to seeing a fire crew with full gear in the rag and tube seats, today's group looked out of place. Jill and the girls sat together. Jill was closest to the door. Ted and Jerry Dunham sat facing them. Mrs. Irons, already frightened, chose a seat behind Jerry Dunham, against the bulkhead. Chief Hardy sat with her. I slid the door closed and helped Jill and the girls with their safety harnesses.

Dave spoke into the mike on his helmet, "Whiteman tower, this is Fire Sixteen at Barton Heliport for southwest departure." He turned to look back at us and gestured with a thumb's up. As we lifted off, I watched Jill's mother hold the metal frame of her seat in a death grip. Jenna and Jean sat with mouths open and wide eyes looking straight ahead, the oversize harnesses snug against their small bodies. Jill stared out the window in the side door. Ted held the urn.

The flight to Malibu lasted 15 minutes. As we flew over the Santa Monica Mountains, I struggled to block the memories of Black Mountain. I looked down at the chaparral and coastal sage scrub. The whole area was a fire waiting to happen. Some days the sky was hazy and some days it was brown with pollution. Today the air was clear and as we approached the coastline, the horizon was as sharp as a knife's edge. To our left, the Palos Verdes Peninsula surrounded the South Bay of Los Angeles. Ahead of us, Catalina Island rose up out of the Pacific Ocean. To our right, we could see the distant Channel Islands near Santa Barbara. The ocean reflected the sunlight in glistening patches of silver.

Tilting to one side, the Bird made a wide arc a quarter mile offshore then descended and hovered at 500 feet. I released my harness and moved to slide the door open. A rush of cooler air filled the cabin along with the odor of hydraulic oil and exhaust. The roar of the rotors was deafening. I motioned to Ted, indicating that he should take my place by the door, near Jill. He shook his head and held up the urn. I knelt on the floor in front of the open door and loosened Jill's safety harness to allow her to lean forward. Ted handed me the urn and I took off the top. Inside, I saw gray and white ashes and bits of what looked like sand. I was looking at Tom Bratton.

I passed the urn to Jill. She clasped it, looked at her daughters and with tears streaming down her face, leaned toward the open door. Her lips moved but I couldn't hear what she was saying. She bent as far as the harness would allow and spilled the contents of the urn into the air. The rotor downdraft pushed most of the small cloud of dust and ashes toward the water, but as I crouched by the corner of the open door, bits of TB's remains blew back into my face. Grit flew into my eyes and mouth.

I ran my tongue over my lips.

TWENTY-NINE
Malibu, California

IT WAS MONDAY EVENING. Jake and I drove over to the Malibu Inn on PCH to meet the rest of the crew and the lawyer from the 1014, the firefighters' union. The Inn offered live music after 10 p.m. and was a late-night hangout for bikers, electricians with ponytails and off-duty firefighters. Tonight Sicky Dicky was featured. A few men were at the bar when we walked in, but otherwise the place was empty. Monday was a slow night and we were early. Marilyn Monroe, Alan Ladd, Robert Mitchum and other movie stars from the '50s and '60s looked down at us from the walls and thick rafters. Art had pulled two tables together next to the windows and we joined the rest of the crew looking out across PCH at the Surfrider Board Shop and the Malibu Pier. The evening traffic from Los Angeles was heavy.

"Hey, Luis," Jake said, taking a seat, "does your wife know you're out boozing?"

"Right," Luis answered, drinking from a can of Diet Coke.

"I can't believe there's an investigation," I said.

"The Forest Service had a bad accident in the late '40s," Hector said. "A bunch of smokejumpers were caught in a blowup and died. That's when the investigations started."

"Mann Gulch?" Red Eye asked.

"Yeah," Hector said, "Washington or Idaho."

"You were there, I suppose?" Jake said.

"No, but it's part of Forest Service history," Hector said.

"There's always an investigation," Dozer said. "Anybody here remember Glen Allen? In '93, two guys from a Helitack crew were killed in Altadena."

"I remember it," Art said.

"The county conducted a major inquiry," Dozer said. "And you know Scott Turan?" Dozer continued. "He suffered full thickness burns, but lived through it. His elbows were sewn into his stomach for three months to regenerate the skin. He was—"

Jerry Dunham and the lawyer walked through the side entrance and came to our table. "Sorry to use your time off guys," Jerry Dunham said, "but this is important. This is Tim Penworthy. He's a lawyer with the 1014."

"Hi, Tim," Dozer said. "Good to see you."

Penworthy was no more than 5 feet 7 inches tall. He had pouches under his eyes and a fringe of short, gray hair. He wore a baggy blue suit, a white shirt open at the collar and a necktie at half-mast. Without saying hello or offering to shake hands, he asked, "This is everyone, the whole crew, right?"

"Those who are still alive," Raphael said.

"We lawyering up?" asked Red Eye.

"Well, not exactly," Penworthy said. He took off his suit jacket and hung it over the back of his chair and sat down. "This is an information meeting, off the record. I'm not representing you and technically I'm not supposed to talk to you, but it's important you understand what's going on. Anytime there's a death, there's an investigation. Anyone been through one of these?"

"I know how it works in the Forest Service," Hector said. "Is this the OIG?"

"What's the OIG?" Luis asked.

"Office of Inspector General, Department of Agriculture," Penworthy said. "No, it's not the OIG."

"Hey Hector, for a dumb ass, you're pretty smart," Jake said.

Hector gave Jake the finger.

The world's oldest waitress, Dori, came to our table. "Hi, Jerry," she said. "This looks like a serious discussion. You guys want anything to eat?"

"I think we're all set," Jerry Dunham said, waving her off.

"After a burnover in the '60s," Penworthy continued, "Congress passed a law requiring the OIG investigate Forest Service fire deaths. This is different. It happened in a National Forest, but Tom was County, so we have an inter-agency investigation. They're looking for the same thing though— negligence and violations of fire safety rules. It can get nasty."

"Who's in charge?" Raphael asked.

"The San Luis Obispo County Fire Chief, Gary Eaton," Penworthy said, "and the managing fire officer from the Los Padres National Forest, Buck Johnson. I don't know Eaton, but Johnson's a good man."

"There's always a bunch of guys, right—a whole team working on it?" Hector asked.

"Right," Penworthy said. "Usually there's a fire safety officer, a fire behavior analyst, an equipment specialist, somebody from Cal-OSHA and a representative from the 1014. He's…."

I tried to remember the warehouse on Swan Creek Road. It was an old three- or four-story brick building with windows made out of small panes that tilted outward. It covered most of a block down near the tracks. Where was my father when it happened? Running up the inside stairs wearing his breathing apparatus? On the roof, cutting a ventilation hole? What was Mike Bentak doing? How many engines were there, casting a red glow on the warehouse walls? Where was the water tank? Did my father say anything before he died? I should have asked my mother.

"Earth to Greg, are you listening?" Dozer said.

"Yeah," I said.

"No you're not," Jerry Dunham said. "Pay attention, Greg, this is important."

Penworthy droned on. "One or both of the chiefs will interview each of you under oath. They're going to want to know if you understood your instructions and if you knew where your escape routes and safe zones were."

"We had one escape route," Luis said. "It was up the fire line, and one safe zone."

"That's fine," Penworthy said, putting his hands up in a defensive gesture, "as long as you knew. They'll also want to know if you had a chance to ask questions and if anyone felt the assignment was too dangerous. Did you get a weather report? Who had the radios?"

"Most of us had radios," said Art.

"Were you on the right frequencies?" Penworthy asked. "Was there any interference from taxi dispatchers in Mexico? Did the spotter warn you?"

"Yeah, he warned us," Jake said. "But I stopped listening when I started running for my life."

"Is this about trying to save TB?" I asked.

"I don't know," said Penworthy. "I wasn't there."

"Don't start with that again, Greg," Jake said.

"We should have gone back to save him?" I said to Penworthy. "Is that what you think?"

"I told you," Penworthy said, "I wasn't there. Besides, my opinion doesn't matter."

"Do they want to find out what went wrong, or just blame someone?" Red Eye asked.

"Guys, the whole idea is to understand what happened and prevent it from occurring again," Jerry Dunham said.

"So some asshole is going to ask us what went wrong at Black Mountain?" I said. "We were out there risking our lives and now we have to explain what we were doing? This is a fucking joke."

"No, this is serious and you need to treat it that way," Penworthy said. "Everybody gets interviewed, from the incident commander on down. They'll be looking for anyone who didn't operate by the rules or who exceeded his authority. The golden rule is 'firefighter safety comes first.' Don't forget that."

A group of bikers clad in black leather came in and marched across the wood floor in their heavy boots. Laughing, they shouted out beer orders to Dori.

"If they ask a question you think is a trick," Penworthy continued, "or if you don't know the answer, you can always say you don't know or you don't remember. If you have something to say, answer in a few words and that's it. Don't talk too much. Give them facts. Keep your opinions to yourself."

Hector leaned forward, took the menu from the middle of the table and looked through it. "Do they still have the chili dogs?" he asked.

"We've lost our captain," I said, "and we have to go through an interrogation? I'll tell them what I think—"

"No, you won't," Dozer said. "Christ, Greg, chill out here. Don't fuck with these people. You'll regret it."

Penworthy slid a saltshaker across the table from hand to hand and looked at me. "I don't think anyone is going to be charged with anything. But you were above a fire on a mountain that was steeper than you thought and there was a blowup. Who knows, maybe more thorough scouting ahead of time would have led to a different tactic." He stopped sliding the saltshaker and added, "Or, maybe there would have been a different outcome."

We were silent for a moment, and then Art said, "That's what was happening. Tom was down the hill scouting it out."

"I know," Penworthy said, "but Tom's not here to tell them what he was thinking and you guys are on the spot. You might want to review the Watch Out Rules before you go in. Situations 9 and 11 were definitely violated. You're gonna hear about that."

"Fuck this," I said. "I forgot to stop in the middle of a fire to review the Watch Out Rules."

Penworthy pushed his chair back from the table and looked at me. "I'm sorry if you don't want to hear this," he said. "I'm just the messenger." He shrugged his shoulders. Hector fiddled with the menu. Luis rubbed the side of his nose. Jake seemed to be looking at his tattoo. The bartender scooped ice into a glass. The sound of boots echoed on the hardwood floor as more bikers arrived.

"I think we've about covered it," Dozer said, standing up and glaring at me. "Thanks, Tim." He extended his hand.

"Give short answers to the questions," Penworthy repeated.

As we walked out, Dozer pulled me aside. He paused for a moment while the others went to their cars. "Greg, you're way out of line," he said. "Are you feeling any better?"

"Any better than what?"

"You know what I mean. All this anger. I know you've had a couple of bad jolts. I'm thinking you need some help."

"I'm fine, I don't need any help."

"No, you're not OK. Call Dr. Stern and make an appointment to see her."

"I saw her at the debriefing."

"Make an appointment to see her one on one, and make sure you go. This is an order. You remain on stress leave until you talk to her."

"That's great, Dozer, thanks. That's just what I need, more time off."

THIRTY
Los Angeles, California

D R. STERN'S OFFICE was in a West Los Angeles highrise on Wilshire Boulevard. I expected a clinic with pathetic people sitting around staring at the ceiling and nurses in white uniforms leading them into examination rooms where they strapped them onto tables. When I arrived, the waiting room was empty. To my surprise, it had a fancy rug, two large, colorful pictures on the wall and several plants.

My stomach was in its usual upheaval and I had to ask the receptionist for directions to the men's room. She handed me a key attached to a large metal ring and said, "Down the hall, just past the elevators."

When I came back, I waited 10 minutes until Dr. Stern came out to greet me. "Hi, Greg, I'm glad to see you. Come in."

"It wasn't voluntary, but I'm here." I tried to smile.

She escorted me into her office. Her desk was clean, with only a telephone, a laptop and a stack of files. Diplomas and pictures of firefighters and cops filled one wall. Another wall had a bookcase with medical books and more pictures. The walls and carpets were pale blue. Two couches faced each other near floor to ceiling windows. A box of tissues was available on a coffee table.

"Sit down, Greg. How are you feeling?" Dr. Stern moved to one of the couches.

"I guess I'm not thinking too clearly."

"I'm not surprised—you've been through a lot."

"With everything else, there's an investigation into the burnover. We have to testify under oath."

"That's standard, whenever there's a death," she said.

"I guess so."

"So tell me, Greg, how are you dealing with the death of your father?"

I shrugged my shoulders. "What can I say?"

"What are you thinking about? How do you feel?"

I felt trapped sitting in the couch facing Dr. Stern. I stood up and walked over to the windows. I could see part of the UCLA campus and white steam came from the tops of some of the buildings.

How did I feel? My father had been crushed in a building collapse. My captain had burned to death. How the hell did she think I felt? "I guess I'm not too happy right now," I said.

"Tell me about your family."

"There's not much to say. I have a mother and you know I have a sister named Vicky. My father was a city firefighter in Saginaw."

"Greg, sit down please. I can't talk to you while you're looking out the window." She motioned toward the empty couch. "What was your family life like?"

I sat down. "Do you really want to hear this? "

"Yes."

"My father screamed at us all the time. He beat my mother and sometimes he punched me. When I got big enough, he stopped hitting me, but he was always on my case. He hated me. After all the physical workouts up at the camp, I'm finally strong enough to beat the crap out of him and it's too late, he's dead."

"What brought on the abuse?" Dr. Stern asked.

I thought of all the unexplained bruises my mother had.

"Did he drink, or use drugs?"

"Yeah."

"Yes what, Greg?"

"Yes he drank. I don't think he used drugs."

"How did your mother react?"

"She tried to stay out of his way. When I was little, she sometimes stood up to him. As time passed, she became quieter. I think she finally gave up. He just beat her into submission."

Dr. Stern sat on her couch without moving. She kept staring at me. How many questions did this woman have to ask me? Didn't she need to take notes or something?

217

"Was she able to protect you?" Dr. Stern asked.

"Not really. My father could get very angry and then all hell broke loose. I was always afraid of doing something wrong."

"How old are you, Greg?"

"I'm twenty." I felt pressure in my lower gut. I wondered if Dr. Stern could hear my stomach rumbling. "I can still remember every rotten thing my father did to me when I was a little kid. It's like yesterday, it's so clear."

"Those memories may never go away, Greg."

"I can still hear him shouting. I still remember how it felt when he hit me."

"Have you ever talked to anyone about this?"

"No."

"I didn't think so. Tell me, Greg, how did you get out to California?"

"The bus."

"That's not what I mean."

"I applied to Cal Fire for a seasonal firefighting job and they hired me. I thought my dad would be proud of me, but he got pissed and told me to get out of the house and never come back. So that's what I did."

"And now he's gone."

"Yeah, now he's gone. He'll never see me as a firefighter."

"Are you disappointed about that?"

"Sure."

"How about Captain Bratton? Do you spend a lot of time thinking about what happened to him?"

"Everyone in the camp does."

"I'm asking specifically about you. How do you feel about his accident?"

"I keep seeing his body on the side of the mountain. I think about it all the time. I know I should have gone down to save him." I wanted to ask Dr. Stern if she thought it would be worse to be crushed by a water tank or burned on the side of a mountain. Maybe that would keep her quiet.

"Don't blame yourself for his death—that's a natural response."

"Why are we talking about all this?" I couldn't sit still. I stood up and walked over to the windows again. It was becoming hazy and the UCLA campus was disappearing.

"Are you eating and sleeping?"

"Not much of either. I want to get back to work."

"I can give you something, an antidepressant. It would help you sleep and clear your mind while you're trying to get through this."

"You mean Prozac or something?"

"There are better medications."

I sat down. "No way, I'm not taking Prozac. Firefighters don't take Prozac." What I needed was something for an upset stomach.

"You'd be surprised what firefighters take. It's not a disgrace. It would help you get some rest and let you start thinking clearly."

"No, I'm not taking anything."

"Firefighters are reluctant to admit to psychological or emotional problems. But I can tell you from experience, Greg, if you don't get over the macho attitude and find some help, your job performance will suffer and eventually your life will become dysfunctional."

"I'm not taking any pills."

"Do you have a girlfriend?"

"Off and on. Not right now."

"What's the longest relationship you've had?"

"When I was in high school, I had a girlfriend my senior year."

"That's it?"

"That's it."

"How do you feel about me counseling you?"

I smiled, and the doctor must have been reading my mind.

"Do you feel a woman could ever be a close friend?" she asked.

"Hasn't happened yet."

"Sports?"

"I was a good hockey player, almost a great hockey player. One year, we were second in the state. I was co-captain of the team. No one plays hockey out here. I was going to learn to ride a horse."

Dr. Stern leaned toward me. She had small hands and didn't wear a wedding ring. "Greg, let me level with you. The county pays me to help firefighters and police officers get over traumatic stress—when someone is shot or burned or hurt in some way. If I do my job, people get past the event and get back to work. It's not my job to give long-term counseling."

"That's what I need?"

"Yes, I think so. You're very resilient. You've had some success in your young life. You say you were a good hockey player, a team leader. You came to California on your own and made it as a firefighter. How many people could do that?"

"And?"

"And, you can have good things in your future. However, I think you've got to see someone to work through your family issues. You had an abusive father. You have to understand your feelings about him and what he did to you. You have to work through your opinions about women. Do you have outbursts of anger?"

"Sometimes."

"I'm sure you're very angry about the way your father treated you and upset that your mother didn't help you or protect you."

"My father was an SOB."

"This is an inflection point in your life. It's a chance to deal with your problems and move on. But you need someone to help you do this."

"What's an inflection point?"

"A crossroads, a turning point. If you understand your feelings about your father and your mother, your relationships with people, especially women, might be better. You'll be happier."

"A shrink is going to help me with all this?" I wanted to go out to use the men's room again.

"A psychiatrist or a psychologist."

"I don't think so. I'm not crazy."

"No one said you were crazy, Greg. People have bad family history and sometimes they need help to get over it. It's nothing to be ashamed of. No one chooses his family."

"Thanks, but no thanks, Dr. Stern."

"It's your decision. You have my card. If you change your mind, call me. I can refer you to several good therapists who could help you."

"I'd have to pay to do that, right? Or does the county cover it?"

"No, the county doesn't cover it."

"Right now I have a six-year-old Jeep that isn't going to last much longer. I've got to save for a new car."

"Some counseling would be money well spent, Greg." She stood up and I realized the session was over. I followed her out to the lobby. She stuck out her tiny hand for a handshake.

I waited for the elevator and didn't ask for the key to the men's room. I wondered where Dr. Stern grew up. She probably grew up in the same place as all the college kids. Where the road was straight and flat, like it was in Kansas. Somewhere where you could see exactly where you were going and knew exactly where you had been. No bumps, no curves. I lived on Yankee Jim Road. It was steep and it had sharp, blind curves. It had no guardrails and if you made a mistake, you sailed off, crashed, burned and were wiped off the face of the earth. I wasn't at a crossroad, I was lurching down Yankee Jim.

The elevator doors opened.

THIRTY-ONE
Santa Barbara, California

THREE WEEKS AFTER TOM BRATTON DIED on the side of Black Mountain, a memorial service was held at the Santa Barbara Bowl, a peaceful open-air venue surrounded by trees, nestled in the hills overlooking the ocean. A LODD—line-of-duty death notice—advising of a memorial for a fallen firefighter was sent nationwide by Los Angeles County and the California Professional Firefighters Association. More than 4,000 first responders attended.

By the time our crew arrived on Sunday morning, the CHP had closed the upper part of Milpas Street to all traffic except vehicles coming to the memorial. The parking lot and access road leading up to the amphitheater were filled to capacity with engines, crew trucks and other emergency vehicles from towns, cities, counties and federal agencies throughout the West. The parking lot was a rainbow of red, white, yellow, blue and green vehicles.

"I must be getting old," Hector said, as we got out of the truck. "I've been to too many of these services."

"Wait until you see the brass," Art said to me. "A lot of stars and stripes."

Camp 8 personnel had been asked to take VIP seats in the second row behind TB's family and we walked up the broad flagstone steps together. At the entrance to the amphitheater, programs were distributed with TB's picture and the County Fire insignia on the cover. The Firefighter's Prayer was printed on the back.

The stage was draped in black and a row of chairs for dignitaries sat empty. The Santa Barbara City College Choir sat to one side, next to a piano. A large picture of Tom gazed out at the mourners from a table covered in black. His badge lay in a box lined with purple velvet next to a yellow fire helmet and a brass fire bell. Flowers were everywhere.

Men and women sat quietly or stood talking in small groups, waiting for the service to begin. The usual firefighter jokes and backslapping was replaced with solemn handshakes and embraces. Chiefs, assistant chiefs and battalion chiefs with stars and braid on their shoulders and gold and silver stripes on their sleeves were everywhere. Captains, superintendents, engineers and ordinary firefighters arrived in dark-blue dress uniforms. Forest Service personnel in green, wore their distinctive hats with gold braid. Many of the mourners brought their children, introducing them to the reality of firefighting.

I had never seen so many fire personnel at once. Most didn't know TB personally, yet had come long distances to attend his memorial. Today wasn't only about grief for him, it was a show of brotherhood and an acknowledgment of the threat we all lived with. Every firefighter in the Santa Barbara Bowl knew he could easily suffer the same fate. This awareness drew us together. After all the jokes and gallows humor, after all the testosterone spent proving nothing bad could happen, the Beast had shown its claws and we accepted the truth.

The rest of the crew made their way to the VIP seats, but I climbed the steep stairs to the top of the amphitheater and looked down on the sea of people. A group of bikers from the Central California Motorcycle Club— brawny, paunchy men with thick tattooed arms, long hair, gray beards and leather vests with their club insignia stitched on the back, sat by themselves two rows below me. One turned, looked up at me, nodded and said, "We're here to pay our respects."

It was peaceful at the top of the amphitheater and I felt disconnected from the events below. I thought about my father and wondered what kind of ceremony had marked his death—who had spoken for him and what was said? I wondered if years from now I would regret not attending. I thought about the fact that I would never see him again. I loved him and I detested him. Mom was wrong, it was not over and it never would be, not for me. I sat alone in the last row.

The crowd rose as Jill, Jenna, Jean, Ted and Tom's parents walked into the amphitheater. The seats on the stage filled with dignitaries and fire brass. The County Fire honor guard posted the colors while the choir sang "Ave Maria." The crowd then sang the national anthem, hats pressed over their hearts and the fire chaplain read an opening prayer.

I watched two hawks soar in the air above our seats. I could see the individual feathers at the ends of their outstretched wings. They made lazy circles, riding the air currents without effort.

Fire Chief Doyle stepped forward to address the mourners. "Today it doesn't matter what uniform you wear or what color truck you came in," he said. "All our thoughts are for Captain Tom Bratton and his family. As firefighters, we know how capricious nature can be. In the face of danger, we cannot do justice to the heroism and strength of spirit of firefighters who place themselves in harm's way. Tom Bratton exemplified these characteristics. He was a beloved son, husband, father, friend, mentor and fire professional." Chief Doyle went on to describe firefighting as a noble and heroic profession and concluded by saying, "We will never forget Tom Bratton's sacrifice."

A light wind blew through the tall eucalyptus and pine trees surrounding the amphitheater.

The Chief of the U.S. Forest Service addressed the crowd. "How moving it is to see so many people here. Tom's family is embraced by this enormous circle of friends. Tom was a man who loved his job and a man who loved going home. This time he cannot go home...."

I looked out toward the water. A cloud of fog moved toward shore.

A U.S. senator from California praised "the seamless interagency cooperation in fighting complex fires in California" and thanked FEMA for its assistance in funding most of the cost of the state's large conflagrations.

The mourners sat with moist eyes as each speaker praised TB, recognized his sacrifice and acknowledged the bravery of all firefighters.

The director of the Governor's Office of Emergency Services reminded everyone that forest fires are an essential part of the wildland ecosystem. Knowing that the press was present and a larger audience was listening, he told California residents, "The urban-wildland interface is a wonderful place to live, but in the last ten years, over eight million homes were built there. As urban areas expand into the wildland, these places become more dangerous. Everyone expects fire protection wherever they are and at whatever cost. Millions of dollars are spent each year in California alone for that purpose."

The fog reached the shore. The ocean was obscured and mist began to wrap itself around the palm trees lining the walk at the edge of the water.

Jerry Dunham, the last speaker, spoke on behalf of Tom's family and Camp

8. "I hope we can celebrate Tom's life as well as mourn him. Each day, when Tom laced up his boots and reported for duty, he led by example. Tom worked the hardest and assumed the greatest risk. He was a true firefighter. In addition to his commitment and bravery, we'll miss his positive attitude. In the most difficult of times, Tom could always be counted on to bring cheer to his comrades, share their burden and make them laugh." Jerry Dunham stopped. I could see his smile from the last row. "No member of Camp 8 will ever forget the Tom Bratton annual 'Rookie Rock Run.' " Jerry looked at Jill and the rest of Tom's family. "Bump up Tom, bump up," he said, and returned to his seat.

After weeks of sadness, the memory of the Rock Run made me laugh. "*How many rocks did you put in their packs?*" Jill asked TB in their living room. My vision blurred. I was laughing and crying.

The fog continued inland, now white, now gray, preparing an assault on the Bowl and the hills surrounding the region. The reflected light was incandescent. I had no religious beliefs and scoffed at supernatural explanations, but that cloud had to mean something. I was just on the wrong radio channel to get the message.

The chaplain came forward and asked everyone to stand and recite the Firefighter's Prayer:

When I am called to duty, God
Wherever flames may rage
Give me strength to save a life
Whatever be its age

Let me embrace a little child
Before it is too late
Or save an older person
From the horror of that fate

Enable me to be alert
And hear the weakest shout
And quickly and efficiently
Put the fire out

I want to fill my calling
To give the best in me
To guard my friend and neighbor
And protect their property

And if…according to your will
While on duty, I must answer death's call
Bless with your protecting hand
My family, one and all.

Jerry Dunham went to the table with Tom's picture. Jill, Jenna, Jean and Ted came forward. Jerry handed the helmet and Tom's badge to Jill. He embraced her, bent down and held each of the girls. He shook hands and embraced Ted. In a moment of absolute silence in the amphitheater, Jerry Dunham rang the fire bell once. Its clear sound echoed into the surrounding hills and disappeared. As the sound of the bell died, it was replaced by the unmistakable noise of helicopters. Four thousand people looked up to see four L.A. County Firebirds and two Cal Fire Super Hueys come over the mountain ridge behind the amphitheater and fly across the sky into the fog in the Missing Man Formation.

The Honor Guard entered while bagpipes played "Amazing Grace." Flags were removed and the guard exited to the beat of a single drum. The Bratton family followed them out.

THIRTY-TWO
La Cañada, California

IN LATE SEPTEMBER, each man in our crew was interviewed in connection with the burnover at Camp 2, the headquarters for the Los Angeles County wildland camps. I walked into a cramped, stuffy office with a drawn shade. San Luis Obispo County Fire Chief Gary Eaton, a fire safety officer from the Forest Service whose name I immediately forgot and a stenographer whose name I never heard, sat around a square table.

"Come in, Greg," Chief Eaton said. He stood and shook my hand and gestured to the empty chair. "This is a formal hearing and what you say will be recorded, but try to relax and just answer my questions. It's important for us to learn what each person saw." He smiled, a man with white hair, someone's grandfather.

Chief Eaton wasted no time and began with the moment I jumped off the helicopter. "Did you understand where your safety zone was…?"

I looked at the clock behind him. It was 10:45 a.m.

"Did you understand what your assignment was…?…Did you have an opportunity to ask questions…?"

10:55 a.m.

"As your crew started to cut line, where were you…?…Where was Captain Bratton…?…Who had the radios…?"

11:05 a.m.

"How long had you been cutting line when Captain Bratton went down to scout the terrain…?…Did he talk to the spotter…?"

11:10 a.m.

"Did you feel a wind change…?…Did you see spot fires on the floor of the canyon…?…When did you see the flames making a run up the canyon…?… which side were the flames on…?…what happened next?...where was each man on your crew?where were you?what did you do?whogavethefirst warning?whathappenednext…?"

11:30 a.m.

I was another person in the room, sitting beside Chief Eaton, listening to the Kowalski kid going through each moment on Black Mountain, recounting the moment Captain Bratton was lost in the advancing wall of flames. The separate scenes and images I had remembered for weeks came together in my mind during the inquiry as one full-length IMAX movie.

I shook hands with Chief Eaton and walked out of the BC's office into the hallway. It was 11:50 a.m. Jake and Luis were in the hall waiting for me. Jake had been interviewed in an adjacent office. Luis had gone before me. It wasn't as tough as Penworthy had predicted, but each of us relived every minute on Black Mountain one more time.

The investigation, all the people asking questions and all those interviewed confirmed it—Captain Tom Bratton had died in a burnover in the Los Padres National Forest. A line-of-duty death had occurred. For the first time since the firestorm, I accepted the fact that TB wasn't coming back and there was nothing I could do about it. I could remember him, care about him—maybe love him—but he wasn't coming back. I would carry the pain and the loss forever, but it was over.

I stood in the hallway and thought about what Dr. Stern had said. I decided it was time to destroy the movie of Black Mountain. In my mind, I yanked yards and yards of film out of the cassette and let it fall to the ground. I crushed the plastic case with the heel of my boot. I lit a box full of matches, dropping them one by one on the tangle of film at my feet. It ignited and the flame burned as high as my knees, a small firestorm, a fire I didn't have to try to put out. I just let it go on. When it was over, there was nothing left, no burn marks, no ashes, nothing. It was over.

I stood in front of a glass case on the wall that held parchment paper on a black background. It was a list of the Los Angeles County firefighters who had lost their lives in the line-of-duty. It began with 1929. *Clyde Lockhart, Peter Carter, Stanley Sherrill.* Each of these men once had a life, a family and a history, but their names were now meaningless. *Salvador Ruezga, Joseph Hughes, Jr., Philip Rockey.* Tom Bratton's name would soon be up there and one day some dick-head like me would be reading this list and would have no idea who Tom Bratton was or what he meant to those who knew him. By that time, Tom's file would be buried somewhere in the basement of County Fire headquarters. It was all so unfair. For an instant, I felt a flash of anger and thought of putting my fist through the glass, but I didn't. TB wouldn't have liked that—it would have been a dumb thing to do.

I wondered if there was a similar list somewhere in Michigan with my father's name on it. Someday someone might stand in front of it and see the name Joe Kowalski—another brave firefighter who had lost his life in the line of duty. They wouldn't know anything about his personal life, he would just be a brave firefighter. I wondered if I could ever just think of him in those terms.

"I guess that about does it," Luis said.

I had a few more names to read, I wasn't quite ready to come back to the living.

Jake looked at another case with the names of those who had left the camps to work for other fire departments. "You guys know what happens when you leave to work for another fire department?" Jake asked.

"No, what?" I said.

Jake was all smiles. "You get 'pied,'" he said.

"'Pied?' What's that?" I asked. Jake's humor was our shield against dark thoughts.

"They save all the leftovers from the Camp 8 kitchen in a pot outside in the heat for a couple of weeks. It turns into one stinking mess. Then they tie you up in the Stokes basket and dump all that slop on you."

I could see myself bound up, smelling the rancid food running down my face and dripping onto the wire of the Stokes. "That's disgusting," I said.

"I'm hungry," Luis said. "You wanna get some lunch? I know a place where we can get some great ribs."

I glanced back at the black case. *Kenneth Miller, William Torres, Richard Grady.* "Yeah," I said, "let's go."

We walked outside. It was noon. The Southern California sun was up there, hot and unforgiving.

Jerry Dunham was acting superintendent of Camp 8, but we knew a new "super" would arrive soon. Art qualified for a swift water rescue team and went up to Santa Clarita. Two FSAs from Camp 9 were transferred to our camp. We did the same workouts on the Grinder. Sometimes I looked up and expected see TB coming out of his office to watch us. We spent three days at a grass fire in San Bernardino, the "Inland Empire." Luis' son got an ear infection and had to take antibiotics. Fifty acres burned at Tapia Park near Calabasas. I was just a few months away from the legal drinking age and the bartender at Duke's at the bottom of Las Flores Canyon started serving me beer. We polished the trucks on Sunday mornings. Life at Camp 8 went on.

Six weeks passed. *The Black Mountain Entrapment Investigation*, the inquiry into Captain Tom Bratton's death, was released and the camp received the official 38-page document. Jerry Dunham had copies made for all of us at his own expense.

Jake and I sat in our luxurious living room in Topanga Villa one evening drinking beer and talking about the report. Nicole, wearing cut-offs and showing nice legs, was with us.

The investigation didn't overlook a single fact, no matter how insignificant. Seventy people were interviewed, starting with the incident commander and concluding with the Medivac crew. A bunch of experts visited the ridge and surveyed and measured the hillside where the burnover occurred.

"Can you believe they constructed a fuel model?" I said.

"What's a fuel model?" Nicole asked.

"It's a fire behavior burn sequence," Jake said. "They use wind, humidity, topography and flame length."

"Thanks Jake, that explains everything," Nicole said.

The report went on for pages. More measuring, more reconstructing, more information. They reviewed radio frequencies and the flow of communications. They confirmed the location of the safety spotter. They evaluated the orders that sent the handcrews onto the ridges.

"You'd think they were reconstructing the Battle of Gettysburg or something," I said.

They reviewed the procedures for downhill fire line construction. Penworthy was right, Watch Out Rules 9 and 11, relating to fire and fuel below a downhill line, were ignored. In addition, they concluded Rule 17, escape on difficult terrain was also violated.

"That's old news," Jake said. "We're always on a hillside cutting line above a fire. That's the way a wildland fire's fought. Something happens, there's an investigation, and they tell us not to do it again. Then they issue some new rules, talk about 'lessons learned,' and we go out and do it again."

"You know the only question they never asked me?" I said to Jake.

"What?"

"If I thought I should have gone down and tried to rescue him," I said.

"They didn't ask you that because they knew you couldn't," Jake said.

"I don't know, Jake...."

"Greg," Jake said, putting down his beer bottle, "it says right here that TB had no time to deploy his fire shelter. The heat exceeded one thousand three hundred degrees. There was nothing you could do."

In the end, the report didn't find fault with the strategy used to fight the Pozo Fire and no one was held responsible for TB's death. It concluded that more thorough scouting could have led to a different tactic or withdrawal from the side of the mountain. It said TB lost situational awareness.

"Situational awareness and more thorough scouting, what a crock," I said to Jake. It was plain to me that the investigators thought TB's death was his own fault and could have been avoided. "He was checking the hillside to keep us out of trouble. That's what he was supposed to do, right? He was protecting his crew," I told Jake. It wast hard to understand what else TB should have done. I threw the report on the coffee table and went for another beer.

"Did Captain Bratton's wife see this report?" Nicole asked.

"She insisted on having a copy," Jake said. He pulled Nicole to him on the couch and began tickling her. Nicole squealed. "Little darling," he said, "I'm gonna start a fire behavior burn sequence for you."

THIRTY-THREE
Saginaw, Michigan

MY STOMACH WAS DOING BACK FLIPS. Why was I so nervous? I was only going to visit my mother. Dad wouldn't be there to yell at me. The kitchen would just be the kitchen—a place to eat—not a torture chamber. There will be no screaming, no criticism, no confrontation, no pain. I had no reason to be afraid.

Heading north up I-75 to Saginaw from the Detroit Airport, I was a kid again. I thought about school—the classes I hated, the miserable food in the lunchroom and the hockey games with my friends. I turned on the radio and found the country music station I listened to growing up. The heat was on high in the car. The hot weather in California had thinned my blood and I shivered.

Trucks with three rear axles carrying metal automobile parts filled the right-hand lane. Eight-foot-high cement sound barriers ran for miles along the highway adding to the barren landscape. The triangular gold and blue Michigan highway markers had icicles on their steel supports. As I neared home, the familiar sign appeared before the off-ramp: "SAGINAW MICHIGAN, HOME OF SAGINAW STEERING GEAR, A GENERAL MOTORS COMPANY."

South 29th Street wasn't far from I-75. It was an old neighborhood filled with small brick houses. There were no secrets among neighbors here; the homes were too close to each other. Coming up the street, I saw Bobby Eccles' old house and then my own. Neither had changed much, but they looked smaller than I remembered. The trim on our house needed paint and the roof still had two kinds of shingles where a tree had fallen and my father had repaired it himself. Overgrown bushes were covered with snow. The dented aluminum trashcans were gone, replaced by blue plastic containers on wheels standing in the same place.

I pulled onto the driveway and heard my tires crunch on the gravel under the snow. My mother opened the door and I got out of the car and walked up the porch steps.

"You been fighting that fire for five months?" she asked. "It's December. Your father's funeral was last July."

"I got here as soon as I could, Mom."

The real fire was the one here at home. It had gone on for 20 years.

"It's good to see you, hon. I missed you." She stood and looked at me as cold air rushed into the house. "I swear, you look just like your father. You coming in?"

I hadn't seen her since I left on the bus for California a year and a half ago. In that time, my entire life had changed. Whoever I was now, I wasn't the kid who left with the olive-colored duffel and the Pistons cap. I stepped into the hallway and we hugged each other. I remembered clinging to my mother as a child, arms around her legs, burying my face in her dress. She was heavier now, and her hair was gray not black, but it was cut short, more stylish. "It's good to see you, too, Mom. I worried a lot about you."

"Come in," she repeated. "Do you want coffee or some lunch?"

I remained in the hall with my coat on, still shivering. I wasn't ready to go through the house.

"He's not here," she said. "He's gone, you can come inside."

"I know Mom. Let's head over to the cemetery and get that out of the way."

"I'll get my coat," she said.

When she came downstairs, she wore a gray coat with black buttons that I had never seen before. It was the first time I could remember my mother wearing anything new. "I like your coat," I said, opening the car door for her. "When did you get it?" She didn't answer. We drove across the city to the cemetery. Mom sat with her hands folded in her lap. "Looks like Saginaw's had a lot of snow already," I said.

"We're having an early winter."

It was tough to start a conversation. After all the years when my father shouted at her and bullied her, for the first time I saw my mother as a person apart from him. I didn't know what to expect. I wasn't sure I knew her.

The Mount Olive Cemetery was desolate. Piles of snow had been plowed to the sides of the road and the trees were bare. The cloudy light of a winter day left no shadows; everything was indistinct. Inside the cemetery, we parked and walked to an area reserved for fallen firefighters and police heroes. Most of the headstones had crosses, though a few had the Star of David. Some stones had "MPFFU," Michigan Professional Fire Fighters Union, engraved in small letters beneath the deceased's name. Others said "Beloved Son…" or "Father of…" Faded plastic flowers left at tombstones in better weather stuck out of the snow. Two workers in heavy parkas stood near a backhoe. One cupped a cigarette in his hand.

I followed my mother along an icy path spread with sand to the spot where my father was buried. She pushed some of the snow aside with her boot. "Five months have passed and the headstone still isn't ready," she said. She bent to brush the remaining snow away with her hand. I saw a piece of square white tile with "Joe Kowalski" written in block letters with a black magic marker.

Joe Kowalski.

I tried to picture him in the frozen ground, under this simple piece of tile. Were his hands folded on his chest? Did he still have that angry glare? He was probably pissed because his tombstone hadn't arrived. I wanted to tell him how much I hated him, how much I loved him, but he wouldn't hear me.

"It was an impressive ceremony," my mother said. "The mayor was here, the fire chief and Dad's entire company of twenty men. We even had two battalion chiefs from Detroit."

"Was Mike Bentak here?" I asked.

"Yes, and the Michigan Troopers sent motorcycles to lead the hearse from the church. The monsignor came, and a fire chaplain. The department took care of the entire funeral and made all the arrangements. They bought this plot and ordered the stone." She looked down at the white tile.

"I talked to Mike once," I said. "I told him I joined L.A. County." I gazed out over the cemetery, moving my feet to stay warm. My breath came out in small white clouds. "I was going to stop by to see him today, but he's away on a training program."

"The people he worked with were his real family," my mother continued, as though she didn't hear me. "They were here for him at the end."

"Mom, I have to ask you something."

"What, hon?"

"Did Dad ever tell you he loved you?"

"Well, sure, in the beginning-"

"Because I don't remember him ever saying it to me," I said. My mother looked at the ground, she had no reply. The backhoe started up. "It must be hard to dig graves when the ground is frozen," I said.

"Let's go, Greg," my mother said. "There's nothing else to see. You're not going to understand your father any better standing out here freezing." We started to walk to the car. She looked back at the tile with my father's name written on it and said, "I hope you have some peace, wherever you are, you son of a bitch." She wiped a tear from her eye with the cuff of her coat, turned to me and said, "It's finished now. I hope he gets his tombstone because I'm not coming back to see it." My mother had found a new voice. She leaned against me as we walked along the icy path. "I've got his uniform, the flag and the medal at home. You're his son and the firefighter now, you should have them."

Driving back home she said, "You know I got a death benefit from the state. I'm selling the house and using the money to move to Chicago. I'm going to live with a friend."

"Are you going to marry him?" I asked.

"He's a she, Greg. Just a friend." She pulled a small mirror from her purse, looked at herself and straightened her hair. "When we get home, I want you to come in and take a last look around. If there's anything you want to take with you, now's the time."

"I don't think I want to come in," I said. "I have enough memories to take with me."

"Hon, let me give you some advice," my mother said. "Don't live your life like your father did. Don't be hard and angry. When you go back to California, find a nice girl and marry her. Have some children and take good care of them. Be happy. Do things with your family and stay together. Try to be the father he could never be."

I kept my eyes on the road. "There are more good-looking girls in California than you can shake a stick at."

"That's not what I mean. I'm talking about loving someone." We pulled into the driveway. "Are you sure you don't want to come in?" she asked. "Last chance."

"No, I'll wait out here." Twenty-two thirty-two South 29th Street wasn't my home anymore. My home was at the top of Las Flores Canyon in Malibu in Southern California. My home was the Bay of Pigs and the Grinder. My home had a rattlesnake coiled in the shape of an 8 on its walls.

"Just a minute, let me get your father's things."

I stood by the car, looked at the old wooden garage door and remembered how many times I had heard it opening, fearful about what would happen when my father walked into the house. All my life I had worked at overcoming physical challenges. I had been strong, but stupid. The real battles had been emotional and I had lost every one.

My mother returned with a plastic bag containing the mementoes from the funeral. I tossed it in the back seat.

"When was the last time you spoke to Vicky?" she asked.

"It's been a long time, Mom—more than a year."

"Here's her new number." She handed me a slip of paper. "Call her. The man she's living with isn't treating her right."

"Isn't she a little young to be living with a guy?"

"Yes, and he's fifteen years older than she is."

"So what am I supposed to do?"

"Talk to her. She's your sister. When you were kids, you were close. She might listen to you. Tell her to get out of there. She won't listen to me. If she stays with that guy, he'll destroy her. I know."

"I'll call her when I get back. I've got some money saved, maybe I can get her to come out to California."

My mother put her arms around me. "I did the best I could for you and Vicky. I did. It wasn't easy for me to live with your father. I had to protect myself, too. I know we didn't have a happy home life, but try to remember that I love you and I want the best for you." Her eyes filled with tears. "Your father was the first man I went out with. I didn't know anything. I thought I loved him. Years ago, I thought of a hundred reasons to stay married to him. Now I can't remember a single one."

"I'm sure you tried your best, Mom. I love you too," I said. I hugged her and got into the car.

Before I started the engine, she tapped on the window and I lowered it. "Take care of yourself—don't get hurt," she said. "I'll call you and give you my address in Chicago."

"I promise I'll keep in touch," I said. I raised the window and backed out of the driveway.

I tried to see the "Saginaw Steering Gear" sign again in the mirror, but missed it. I drove south; each minute left South 29th Street a mile behind. I thought about getting back to California, the warm weather, the camp and the crew. I wanted to see Jake, Luis, Hector and the others. I wanted to listen to them complain about the food and bitch about the long hours, knowing they loved every minute. I wanted to get to the next fire and work myself to exhaustion on a fireline, my sweat dripping onto the arid California ground. I was a firefighter, it was my life.

Heading to the airport, my gut was still churning, but the closer I got to Detroit, the better I felt. I didn't have to stop along the way.

I dropped the car at the rental return and hurried to catch the shuttle to the terminal. Before the bus doors closed, the agent came running after me. "Sir, you left this in the car." He held up the plastic bag with my father's mementoes.

"It's trash. Just toss it."

THIRTY-FOUR
Malibu, California

"TOO BAD ABOUT YOU AND DEB," Luis says, standing up on the Pepperdine lawn and interrupting my gaze at the brown crap in the sky. "It sounded like she really liked you. Flames out for good?"

"She said she didn't know me, whatever that means."

"You have to work at it, Greg. Go back and see her. The worst that can happen is she says she doesn't want to talk to you."

"I may do that." I can't even understand why I was so angry. "Yeah, I might call her."

"Do it, because..."

Luis is about to launch into his family-values speech, but the Bird's engines come alive and the blades start to turn. Hector loads the last of the gear in the tail as we join the others and climb aboard, heads bent against the downdraft. Jake is in front of me. "MAGAN—LOS ANGELES COUNTY FIRE" visible in large black letters on the back of his brush jacket. Captain Walton, the new superintendent of Camp 8, is the last to board. By the time he slides the door shut, we're already off the ground.

Inside, it's too noisy to talk, but no one has much to say. Each of us is thinking of the blaze north of the 101. We sit packed together in the jump seats. I'm by the door. Jake is on my right, Red Eye and Luis are facing me. Extra equipment and one of our large pumps is strapped into the remaining seats. As many times as I have flown on the Bird, there is always the split second at lift-off when my stomach feels as if it wants to stay on the ground. Today we're flying, so we're Crew 8-1 and I am thankful to be part of it. I plug my headset into communications. Someone is talking about a union problem: "...and the guy was promoted too fast and…" followed by a change of channels and then a report from the incident command post in Calabasas: "…if the south end of the fire isn't contained by eighteen hundred, Sheriff's Department is going to start a mandatory evacuation of the Bell Canyon area."

We climb up over the steep ocean hillside, skimming over houses and I look down and see people standing outside shading their eyes from the sun and looking back at us. I see a man standing out on his deck with a young girl and a boy. He has an arm around each of them. We gain speed and altitude and their faces grow indistinct. Clearing the ridge, an expanding cloud of gray and black smoke looms before us.

I lean across to tell Luis that I've decided to call Deb when we get back. He points to his ear and shakes his head. He can't hear anything I'm saying.

ACKNOWLEDGMENTS

DURING MY RESEARCH, I met firefighters of all ranks and kinds. I spent time with wildland crews and inmate crews and met heavy equipment operators, helicopter pilots, paramedics, arson investigators and retardant experts. The firefighting community is a group of close-knit, positive-thinking, selfless individuals who regularly risk their lives to keep others safe. Thank you all.

Special thanks to: **Bob Martin,** fire captain and superintendent (retired), Fire Suppression Camp 13, whose good humor and patience helped launch me on this project; **Larry Tucker,** fire captain and superintendent, Fire Suppression Camp 13, who took me to fires and talked about testosterone.

County of Los Angeles Fire Department, Fire Suppression Camp 8: Ernie Varela, fire captain and superintendent; Chris Hansen, engineer; Oscar Perez, FSA and crew leader; Nick Ling, an FSA and recent graduate of the Camp 8 Academy; the entire crew at Air Attack Camp 8 who welcomed me, fed me, and taught me about wildland fire fighting.

State of California, Cal Fire: Ronny J Coleman, chief deputy and state fire marshal (retired); David Hillman, chief, fire prevention and law enforcement; Paul Sans, battalion chief.

Culver City Fire Department: Fire Captain Brian Savage and EMT Anthony Barbi, a former FSA at Camp 8.

Mel Hokanson, deputy fire chief (retired), Los Angeles County Fire Department. **Dr. Victoria Havassy,** PhD, clinical and consulting psychologist.

Dr. Anne Coscarelli, PhD, UCLA. **George Kasparek,** reserve officer, L.A.P.D. (retired). **Mark Basore, Jack Grapes, Brandon Cesmat, SanDee Sans and Karen Terrill.**

Thank you, **Denise Middlebrooks,** my editor, for you continued support.

Last, but certainly not least, thanks to my wife, **Connie,** for her encouragement and eagle eye.

STANDARD FIREFIGHTING ORDERS*

1. Keep informed on fire weather conditions and forecasts.
2. Know what your fire is doing at all times.
3. Base all actions on current and expected behavior of the fire.
4. Identify escape routes and safety zones, and make them known.
5. Post lookouts when there is possible danger.
6. Be alert. Keep calm. Think clearly. Act decisively.
7. Maintain prompt communications with your forces, your supervisor, and adjoining force.
8. Give clear instructions and ensure they are understood.
9. Maintain control of your forces at all times.
10. Fight fire aggressively, having provided for safety first.

* The **Standard Firefighting Orders** were prepared by the U.S. Forest Service in 1956 after the Inaja Forest Fire Disaster in the Cleveland National Forest, near San Diego, California. Eleven men lost their lives in that fire blowup.

WATCH OUT
SITUATIONS

1. Fire not scouted and sized up.
2. In country not seen in daylight.
3. Safety zones and escape routes not identified.
4. Unfamiliar with weather and local factors influencing fire behavior.
5. Uninformed on strategy, tactics, and hazards.
6. Instructions and assignments not clear.
7. No communication link with crew members or supervisor.
8. Constructing line without safe anchor point.
9. Building fireline downhill with fire below.
10. Attempting frontal assault on fire.
11. Unburned fuel between you and fire.
12. Cannot see main fire; not in contact with someone who can.
13. On a hillside where rolling material can ignite fuel below.
14. Weather becoming hotter and drier.
15. Wind increases and/or changes direction.
16. Getting frequent spot fires across line.
17. Terrain and fuels make escape to safety zones difficult.
18. Taking a nap near fireline.

GLOSSARY OF FIRE AND RELATED TERMS

Anchor Point: A location from which to start building a fire line. Used to reduce the chance of firefighters being flanked by fire.

Backfire: A fire set along the inner edge of a fireline or control line to consume the fuel in the path of a wildfire and change the direction of the fire.

BC: Battalion chief.

BIA: Bureau of Indian Affairs.

BLM: Bureau of Land Management.

Banjo: Round, flat 1 1/2 gallon water container. Resembles the lower part of a banjo.

Bird: Helicopter. See Firehawk.

Blowup: A sudden increase in the fire intensity or rate of spread strong enough to prevent direct control or to upset control plans. Blowups are often accompanied by violent convection and may have other characteristics of a firestorm.

Boise (Idaho): The National Interagency Coordination Center (NIFC) in Boise, Idaho is the focal point for overseeing all interagency coordination activities throughout the United States. See NIFC.

Bucker: A firefighter who assists others using chainsaws to clear brush. Carries fuel, tools.

Bump/ Bump Up/ Bump Down: When each worker on a fire line has completed clearing his space with his particular type of tool, the crew boss will call out "Bump," at which time all workers move ahead one space and resume work. Depending on whether the crew is moving uphill or downhill, the call may be "Bump Up," or "Bump Down."

Burn Out: Setting a fire inside a fireline or control line to widen it or consume fuel between the edge of the fire and the control line.

Burn Over/Burnover: Firefighter death caused by entrapment.

CDC: California Department of Corrections.

CDF: California Department of Forestry and Fire Protection or CDF. In 2007 the name was changed to Cal Fire.

Chaparral: A dense thicket of shrubs and small trees, including sage, yucca, prickly pear, and scrub oak.

Cold Trailing: Controlling a partly dead fire edge by inspecting for heat and digging out live spots.

Contain a Fire: Completing a fuel break around a fire.

Control a Fire: The complete extinguishment of a fire, including spot fires.

Crew Boss: A person in charge of a group of firefighters, responsible for their performance and safety.

Cubie: A square five-gallon water container.

D-6, D-8: Size designations for large bulldozers used to cut firelines.

Dozer: Any tracked vehicle (bulldozer) with a front-mounted blade used for exposing soil, creating a firebreak.

Drip Torch: Hand-held device for igniting backfires by dripping flaming liquid fuel.

Engine: Fire vehicle capable of pumping water; carries hose, water, equipment, and a crew of two or more.

Entrapment: A situation in which personnel are caught in a fire in a life-threatening position when planned escape routes or safety zones are absent or compromised.

Escape Route: A planned route firefighters take to move to a safety zone or low-risk area.

FSA: Fire suppression aide. Entry-level job at Los Angeles County Fire Department wildland fire camps.

F-ban: Fire behavior analyst.

Fire Shelter: An aluminized tent offering protection by reflecting radiant heat and providing a volume of breathable air in a fire entrapment situation. Also referred to as a "Shake and Bake."

Firestorm: Wind drives flames into the fuel in front of the advancing line of fire. Spot fires are started by radiant heat in advance of the main fire. The spot fires become so numerous and the preheating of the fuel so intense that the area seems to ignite all at once, creating a firestorm. A wildfire can burn with such intensity that most of the oxygen is burned out of the air around it. If the wind suddenly changes and brings fresh air and oxygen, a ground fire may explode into the branches and crowns of the trees around it. A crown fire may then create its own weather. As hot, lighter air rises, cold, heavier air moves down to replace it in what is known as a convection effect, which causes tornado-like winds, which may reach 80-90 miles per hour. These winds may become a rotating vortex, known as a fire whirl, which throws off burning twigs, branches, even logs. The center of the vortex is a downdraft full of deadly gas, primarily carbon monoxide, with a temperature as high as 2,000 degrees. The outer ring of the vortex is an updraft, which may reach 20,000 feet into the air. The explosive effects of such fire conditions create the roaring sound often described as that of an approaching train.

Firehawk: Sikorsky UH60L Blackhawk Attack Helicopter converted to fire fighting use. Rated as a Type 1 helicopter, it carries 16 people including pilot, has a payload of 5,000 pounds, and a retardant tank holding 1,100 gallons. In use by Los Angeles County. Referred to by firefighters as the "Bird."

Fireline: (Control line) A fire barrier scraped or dug down to the soil. A fireline is usually located some distance from the main fire and the intervening vegetation and fuels are burned out to make a much wider strip devoid of fuel. This is called backfiring or burning out.

Full Thickness Burn: Third-degree burn to the subcutaneous layer below the epidermis and dermis skin layers.

Fusee: A colored flare used to ignite backfires. Also used in an emergency to burn out an area for a safe zone.

Helitack: The use of helicopters to transport crews, equipment and fire retardants to the fire line.

Hotshot Crew: A trained fire crew used to build fire lines by hand. Generally regarded as the most highly skilled among fire crews.

Incident: A human-caused or natural occurrence, such as a wildland fire, that requires emergency action to prevent loss of life or damage to property.
Incident Commander: Individual responsible for the management of all operations at a fire.

McLeod: A double-sided rake-like tool with large teeth on one side and smaller teeth on the other side. Used for cutting firelines, removing vegetation and ground litter.

NIFC: National Interagency Fire Center, the national wildland fire-management center in Boise, Idaho. Wildfire suppression is built on a three-tiered system of support, including the local area, one of 11 geographic areas, and finally, the national level. When a fire is reported, the local agency and its firefighting partners respond. If the fire continues to grow, the agency can ask for help from its geographic area. When a geographic area has exhausted all its resources, it can turn to the NIFC for help in locating what is needed, from air tankers and radios to firefighting crews and incident management teams.

Nomex®: Trade name for a yellow fire-resistant synthetic material used in the manufacture of pants and shirts used by firefighters. Provides fire resistance, but must be worn over long-sleeve cotton T-shirt and cotton pants, which provide insulation from heat and burns.

OIG: Office of the Inspector General of the Department of Agriculture charged with investigating fire casualties among USFS firefighters.

P-3: Lockheed Orion four-engine naval patrol bomber converted to use as a fire retardant tanker.

Personal Protective Equipment/PPE: Firefighting equipment and clothing used to protect wildland firefighters from exposure to hazardous conditions. PPE includes 8-inch high-laced leather boots with lug soles, fire shelter, hardhat with chinstrap and shroud, goggles, earplugs, Nomex shirts and trousers, leather gloves and first-aid kits.

Pulaski: A chopping and trenching tool, which is half ax and half hoe. Named after Edward Pulaski, a USFS firefighter.

RH: Relative humidity.

Radiant Burn: A burn received from the radiant heat of a fire.

Safety Zone: An area cleared of flammable materials used for escape if a fireline is outflanked by fire or in the event of a blowup.

Spot Fire: A fire ignited outside the perimeter of the main fire by flying sparks of embers.

Stokes Basket: Wire basket used to immobilize and lift bodies during rescue operations.

Squirrel Channel: Radio frequency often used by fire crews to communicate among them.

Swamper: a) Inmate crew leader at prison fire camps, b) see Bucker.

Type – Fire: Fires are classified according to severity and acreage burned. A **Type IV Fire** is the lowest designation, a fire in its initial stages. **Types III** and **II** are more complex and severe, and **Type I** is the most severe.

ALSO BY KURT KAMM

"Full body tattoos and Goth fetishists—an exciting trip
through the Los Angeles underworld. Great Story."
—Justice Howard, Internationally Renowned Tattoo and Fetish Photographer

CODE
BLOOD

KURT KAMM

Body Parts, Blood, Fetishism . . . and Death

Colt Lewis, a rookie fire paramedic, is obsessed with finding the severed foot of his first victim after he fails to save her. His search pulls him into the connected lives of a graduate research student with the rarest blood in the world and the vampire fetishist who is stalking her. Within the pressured corridors of a university research laboratory, the shadow world of body parts dealers, and the underground Goth clubs of Los Angeles, Lewis uncovers a tangled maze of needles, drugs, and maniacal ritual, all of which lead to death—but whose death? An unusual and fast-paced LA Noir thriller.

Code Blood won a Public Safety Writer's Association Award in 2011.

Code Blood is the winner in the Fiction: Cross Genre category of the 2012 International Book Awards.

Praise for
CODE BLOOD

"From blood work to blood play, this thriller takes the reader
from the high-tech world of academic medical research
to the subculture of body parts dealers."
—Weijie Huang, PhD, Senior Research Scientist

"Kurt Kamm grabs readers by the gut and takes
them on a wild but credible ride in this complex but
wholly satisfying novel of real meets surreal."
—Grady Harp, Top 4 Amazon Reviewer

ALSO BY KURT KAMM

RED FLAG WARNING

THE WRITTEN ART AWARDS 2011

Purple Dragonfly Book Award
FIRST PLACE

A SERIAL ARSON MYSTERY

by KURT KAMM

RED FLAG WARNING: A Serial Arson Mystery

Los Angeles County is burning! A serial arsonist is setting the parched hills on fire. Plunge into infernos and face the smoke, heat and danger with the men on the fire lines. While NiteHeat prowls in the darkness, setting fires and taunting investigators, the Los Angeles County Fire Department's Arson Unit struggles to find the fire setter and stop the devastation.

Royal Dragonfly/Five Star Book Awards
First Place – Mystery 2010

The Infinite Writer
First Place – Mystery 2010

The Written Art Awards
First Place – Mystery/Thriller 2010

Public Safety Writer's Association 2010
Honorable Mention – Published Novel

Praise for
RED FLAG WARNING

"NiteHeat is memorable—another lunatic out setting fires."
—Mike Cole, CalFire battalion chief, law enforcement

"Enough suspects and false leads to keep even a cop guessing."
—George Kasparek, Los Angeles Police Department, retired

ABOUT THE AUTHOR

 Kamm lives in Malibu with his wife and has sur-
vived several devastating local wildfires. The
Canyon Fire in 2008, driven by 60 MPH winds,
destroyed neighbors' homes and burned to his
doorstep. Kurt has attended fire training at CalFire
and El Camino Fire Academy. He spends much
of his time at the wildland firefighter camps, inmate camps and fire stations of Los Angeles
County Fire Department. He has attended Arson
Investigation and Hazardous Materials academies
and has used his experience and access to CalFire and Los Angeles County
firefighters to write novels involving the lives of firefighters and paramedics.

Kurt was previously a businessman and semi-professional bicycle racer. He
is a graduate of Brown University and Columbia Law School. He was Chairman
of the UCLA/Jonsson Comprehensive Cancer Center Foundation and is an
avid supporter of the Wildland Firefighter Foundation.

Visit Kurt's Author/Firefighter website to view some spectacular fire pictures
and pages on aerial firefighting and smoke jumpers: www.kurtkamm.com.

Kurt also writes a blog called FIREFIGHTER'S WORDS.